Critical praise for

RIDE A PAINTED PONY

"Vivid descriptions, superbly depicted characters
at all levels, a touch of violence, and a beautifully
developed romantic relationship add credence to
this story of two wary, badly damaged people—
a loner with a guilt-ridden past and a mother
who will do anything to retrieve her son—
who eventually find healing, peace, and love.
A poignant, heartfelt story."
—*Library Journal*, top 5 romance of 2006

"Exceptional—a deeply romantic and wholly
entertaining novel… Eagle's smooth, sweet
storytelling works magic on the emotions of the
reader who expects slightly larger-than-life fantasy
along with her romance reading."
—*wnbc.com*

"Eagle…delivers her signature energy."
—*Publishers Weekly*

"An excellent choice for book clubs looking for
a thoughtful, yet uplifting read."
—*BookPage.com*

"Eagle's an expert at creating characters that seem
ready to step off the page, a skill in evidence here."
—*Romantic Times BOOKreviews*

Also by KATHLEEN EAGLE
A VIEW OF THE RIVER

KATHLEEN EAGLE

RIDE A PAINTED PONY

MIRA®

MIRA®

ISBN-13: 978-0-7783-2508-6
ISBN-10:   0-7783-2508-3

RIDE A PAINTED PONY

www.MIRABooks.com

Printed in U.S.A.

First printing: December 2006

ACKNOWLEDGMENTS

Finding the key to a plot problem isn't always a *Eureka!* moment. Keys must be ground to fit the lock, and that can be a grueling part of the writing process. But those keys are invaluable. Two important sources of inspiration for this book were the wonderful group who attended Midwest Fiction Writers' "Big Retreat to Little Falls" at Linden Hill in Little Falls, Minnesota, and a series of articles concerning Indian gaming and casino race books in one of my favorite sources for real news, *Indian Country Today,* both the newspaper and its wonderful Web site.

For the Prairie Writers Guild—
Pam, Sandy, Mary, Judy and Kathy. *Vive* PWG!

And
to honor the memory of
Little Ted

1

Twenty-seven miles of dark road and driving rain were all that stood between Nick and the bed he'd reserved for what was left of the night. He might have pulled over and waited for the downpour to pass, but he was set on having himself some pleasure this night. Real, rock-solid pleasure. He was *this close* to laying himself down flat, stretching out his whole long, bone-tired body over fresh white sheets and soft pillows. If he had just pulled over, he might have spared himself the one thing he always took care to avoid. Nicholas Red Shield hated surprises.

But more than the surprise of a pair of wild eyes staring back at him in his high beams, he hated making roadkill.

Eyes left. Wheel right.

It was a tricky maneuver. His empty horse trailer fishtailed as he shifted into Neutral, kicked the brake and arced the steering wheel to the left. Getting the trailer in line was only half the battle now that the rubber no longer met the road. Every scrape against the pickup's precious chassis felt like a bloody gouge in Nick's own leathery hide. His beautiful blue two-ton dually—as near to new as any vehicle he'd ever had—mowed down a mile-marker post, jolted, shuddered and went still.

Rain pelted the roof of the cab.

Nick took a deep breath and slowly loosened his grip on the steering wheel. He glanced in the rearview mirror, searching for familiar eyes.

"You okay back there, Alice?"

His passenger popped her head up to assure him that she was only slightly less bored with him than usual.

Nick was okay, too, *thanks for asking.* A little shook up, but he wasn't going to let it show, even when nobody but the cat was looking. Bad form was bad form.

And stuck was stuck. He couldn't tell whether the main cause was mud or the mile marker, but his efforts to get loose soon had six tires spinning in all gears.

Nick was not a man to curse his luck. He wasted nothing, including breath. Ever equipped to handle his own problems, he practiced taking care of business to perfection. If the mile marker was the hang-up, he hoped the business of jacking his baby off the damn

thing wouldn't take all night. He chuckled and started humming as he reached under his seat for the flashlight. "Jackin' my sweet baby off," he sang softly. Times like this, a little humor couldn't hurt. He exchanged cowboy hat for yellow rubberized poncho and climbed out of the truck with an unconscious smile. He could really be funny when nobody was listening.

But the sight of his truck's skewered underbelly was nothing to laugh at. It would take more than a flashlight beam to assess the damage, especially with the cold spring rain rolling off the hood of his poncho. He could have sworn he heard her groaning softly, just like a real woman.

"What do you expect me to do in this rain, girl? Beam you up?"

Something behind him snapped. Nick pivoted and swept the light over the roadside slope until it hit on a clump of bushes and a clutch of bobbing branches. Damn, had he clipped that deer after all? He grabbed his pistol and a loaded clip from the glove box and then sidled down the steep, wet slope. He'd been lucky. Better his precious pickup had impaled herself on a post than gone tumbling trailer over teakettle down the hill.

The bushes weren't much taller than he was, but they were dense and filled out with new foliage. And they weren't moving on their own. There was definitely something in there. Nick parted the branches with his gun hand, flashed the light into the tangled thicket and found two more of the night's thousand eyes.

They weren't doe eyes, but they were almost as big.

"Don't," a soft voice pleaded as the eyes took refuge from the light behind a small, colorless, quivering palm. "Please don't."

A woman? A child? Nick's heart wedged itself in his throat. He flashed the light away from her face.

"It's okay. I won't..." He shouldered branches aside and dropped down on one knee to discover a woman who wasn't much bigger than a child. "That wasn't..." He could barely get the words out. She was curled up, soggy and shaking to beat hell. "Jesus, that couldn't have been *you* in the road. Could it?"

"Wh-who are you? Who sent you?"

"No one sent me. Listen, did I...did I hit you?"

"Who are you?" she demanded, pumping up the volume.

"Name's Nick Red Shield. I could've sworn I missed the, uh..." He gestured toward the scene of the crime with the barrel of his pistol. "Sorry. I was expecting a deer." He tucked the gun in his belt and then pulled the poncho over his head. She needed it worse than he did. "How bad are you hurt?"

"I don't know."

"Anything broken? Can you move your..."

Move what? The arms she'd knotted around her knees? He felt like some idiot hunter who'd awkwardly wedged himself into a rabbit's hole. They were nearly nose to nose, but he didn't dare touch her, and she didn't dare move. She couldn't draw back any

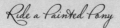

farther without becoming part of the undergrowth. Her violent quivering made his bones vibrate.

"Let me help you." He offered his hand, palm up, as though she might want to sniff it first. "I'll be real careful."

"What kind of a name is Red Shield?"

It seemed like a crazy question, under the circumstances. *Check out my hand, sure, but my name?*

"I'm an Indian." He couldn't help bristling. Squaring up, he braced the rebuffed hand on his upraised knee. "Sioux. South Dakota. Look, I didn't see you until you were right in front of me, and I did everything I could to avoid hitting you. If you want me to try to flag someone else down, I will, but there isn't much traffic tonight, and I don't have any way to call anyone. Do you?"

"C-call who?"

"A cop or an ambulance."

"You...you'd call the police?"

"I would, but I don't have a phone. And if I leave you here and go for help, I'll damn sure get charged with hit and run. So make up your mine. What'll it be?"

"What are my choices?"

"Trust me or don't. Can you walk?"

She stared at him, sizing him up while she drew several breaths, miserably shaky on the uptake. Finally she loosened her grip on her folded legs and felt around for something besides him to hang on to. She didn't seem to care what the bushes were doing to her hands, and he could barely hear her answer.

"I think so."

But it was tricky. She was such a little thing, he could have carried her like a baby if the rain hadn't made the hill slicker than a cat's ass. He put the flashlight in her hand, covered her with his poncho and hauled her up against his side, which left him one hand for grabbing whatever solid ground he could find. And, like a cat, she hung on. He could feel her trembling, feel her fighting for control against chills, pain, fear—probably all three—and he gave her credit for holding back on the noise she could have been making, tears she should have been crying, curses she must have been saving up for a time when the man who'd done this to her wasn't the only help around.

He put her on the backseat of his crew cab, took the wet poncho and started backing out the door.

She grabbed his arm. Shivering and scared, she was little more than the huge pair of eyes that questioned his every move.

"I've got blankets in the trailer, and maybe something to…" What he could see of her face now gave him pause. Mean dark patches spattered over frail and pale skin added up to battered flesh and flowing blood. "Listen, lady, I've gotta get you some help."

"Can you…please…get me away from here?" She had him by both arms now, had him with her eyes and surprisingly strong hands. "Can you, Nick?"

"Yeah." He nodded, swallowed hard, tried to ignore the goose bumps crawling over his shoulders and down the back of his neck. He slid into the seat beside her and felt her relax her grip. "Sure. I can do that." He reached over the front seat and felt around for his denim jacket. Locating the jacket also meant he found the cat, but he was able to claim the jacket without trading a strip of skin. Alice wasn't totally pitiless after all.

"What's your name?" He didn't mean to pry, but he'd told her who he was, and he needed to say something while he was wrapping her in his jacket.

But the question set her off on a sobbing jag.

Damn. Now what? He drew the jacket tight around her, his fists coming together beneath her chin, whispering, "Try to keep it together. You've been doing so good. Do you live around here?"

"No. Oh no." Head bowed, she slumped toward him, shuddering and sobbing and saying, "Oh no, oh no, oh no."

"Shh. Just tell me your name."

"Ohh…" She was like a wet rag, starch draining away, drooping, dripping, sagging against his chest. "Joe-eeey, Joey, Joey…"

"Joey what?"

But she was all out of answers. And he'd never been one to ask too many questions. Part of a name was enough for now. She could give the rest of it at the next stop, where somebody with a form and a uniform would be writing it all down.

"You want some dry clothes?"

Still leaning on him, she shook her head against his chest, forming his chilled nipple into a glass bead.

"You'll have pneumonia on top of—"

She shook her head again and whispered blubbery words that made no sense but sounded as desperate as he was beginning to feel.

"Okay, Joey." He patted her hair clumsily. "Okay, we'll get movin'."

With a hydraulic jack and a heavy dose of cowboy ingenuity, he was able to lift the pickup off the hook he'd accidentally made of the steel post, then twist the thing out of the way without ripping the guts from his sweet ride. He'd unhooked the gooseneck trailer in the hope of getting the truck back on the road. But nobody ever expected great traction from a dually, and his four back tires were only spinning themselves deeper into the Missouri mud. Without a push, his baby would soon be up to her axles in moonshit. He threw her into Neutral, braced his chin on his left arm and glowered at the road untraveled.

"Joey?"

A glance in the rearview mirror revealed nothing. He hadn't heard a peep out of her since he'd turned the heater on full blast and she'd thanked him before he'd gone back out into the rain. He turned now and found her huddled up in the corner with the cat. The two pair of eyes peered expectantly toward the front seat.

"Joey, I need you to help me. Do you think you can take the wheel? I need a driver."

"Drive…the truck?"

"I need a hand to rock the cradle, so to speak. You know how to do that?"

She made a funny sound, like laughing through tears. "Rock the baby?"

"Yeah. Rock my baby. With a little rockin', a little pushin', I know she can get us out of here. You rock; I'll push. Can you help me?"

"I think so."

"Only you gotta be careful not to run me over," he said as he opened the back door. Hovering over her with his back catching the rain, he helped her out of the backseat and around the door toward the front.

"Not run you over," she repeated as she mounted the running board and pulled herself up by the door handle.

"Yeah, 'cause then we'd be in big trouble." He lifted a lever and pulled the front seat from one extreme adjustment to the other. "Can you reach the pedals?"

"Of course." She demonstrated. Brake was good, gas was only just.

"You drive a stick?"

She nodded.

"Can you see over the dash? I'm gonna be right there." He pointed to the front corner on the right. "As long as you can see me, we're fine. If I disappear, then you stop the music. Okay?"

"Stop the music." She almost smiled. "Like hold the presses?"

"Yeah, like that. How many fingers?"

"One," she answered. He doubled his digits. "Two."

"Good. You pass. One back, two forward. One finger, you put it in reverse and I push. Two, you put it in low, and I get out of the way. Timing is everything. You think you can handle it?"

"If you can push this thing, I can steer."

Nick's brawn harmonized with Joey's timing on the gear changes. Soon the pickup was free from the mud and Nick was covered with it. He threw his tools into the box, used the water in the portable tank to wash off some of the mud, and grabbed a blanket from the trailer.

He found her slumped over the steering wheel.

"You okay?"

She responded simply by sitting up.

"Can you slide over?"

She did, but not easily. She was hurting.

He took her place, making every effort to reassure her while he tucked the blanket around her. "We're in business now, Joey. I'm gonna find you some help." He reached across her. "Here, let's buckle you in."

"I feel sick. I need to lie down." She leaned toward him as she pushed the seat belt away. "No, no, this thing hurts. If I don't lie down, I'll probably...get..."

"Please don't." He gave up on the seat belt and took charge of the wheel while she toppled over beside him, head at his hip. "But try not to fall asleep, okay?"

"How about if I just pass out?"

"Don't do that, either."

"Talk to me, then," she muttered as they finally hit the highway.

"It's better if you talk," he told her. He felt a little sick himself, watching his precious gooseneck trailer shrink in the side mirror. He hoped to hell it would be there when he came back for it. "Where do you hurt?"

"Inside. I'm aching in ways you can't understand, Nick. You're a man."

"Oh, Jesus," he groaned. Females and their mysterious inside parts. It was a wonder there wasn't blood everywhere. "You're not, like, pregnant or anything, are you?"

"No."

"That's good." At least the hit wasn't a twofer. "I'm not from around here. Maybe you could tell me—"

"I'm not, either."

"Oh, yeah," he said, remembering. He glanced at the mop of wet hair that had become a fixture on his wet hip. "I'll find you a hospital just as quick as I can. I'm having trouble makin' out the road signs in this damn rain, but don't worry. I'll find you some help."

"All I need is a bed. I need to be still for a while, so my head stops spinning."

"Lady, what were you doing on the road like that?" he demanded, more heated than he'd intended. "In the night," he added softly. "In the rain."

"Fell out of a car."

"*Fell?*"

"No more questions, Nick. Please."

"I'm sorry. I swear to God, I didn't—"

"It was my fault. My own fault."

"Like hell," he muttered, craning his neck, squinting. Like squinting would do any good. "Is that a hospital sign?"

"No, please. No hospital." Her hand found his thigh. "No more trouble, Nick, please."

"Shit. 'Falling Rocks.'" He sniggered. "Hell, how about one for 'Falling Women'?"

"*Fallen* woman." She gave a sad, soft groan as her hand slid away. "What a joke. Here's your sign. Wear it in good health."

"Sorry. This is no time for smart-ass remarks."

"No, it was funny, Nick. And true. I just can't laugh right now." She paused, then added quietly, "Keep talking to me, Nick."

"'Deer crossing,'" he read aloud as they passed another sign. It wasn't much, but it was what he could do to keep himself talking. If she wanted a talker, she'd thrown herself in front of the wrong truck. He chuckled. "Now they tell me. I thought you were a deer, Joey. I thought I'd swerved to miss a deer. Are you a Deer Woman?"

"I'm dear to somebody," she said. "I hope so, anyway."

"Somebody who drove off and…" *Shut up, Red Shield.* She didn't need him rubbing it in. "Forget I said that."

"No. Someone else. I have someone else."

"Somebody we can call when we get to a phone?"

"No. He can't help me." She raised her head, pushed herself up for better effect. "But you can, Nick. You seem like a good man."

He spared her a glance. The wounds on her face made the wounded look in her eyes that much harder for him to bear, knowing he'd caused it all. "I'm not about to put you out on the road, if that's the measure of a good man."

"It's a start."

"And I'm workin' on the next step, which is to find you some medical attention."

"Please don't, Nick." She lowered her head, but this time she laid it on his thigh. "I really don't need a doctor."

Flummoxed, flustered and suddenly way too hot, he whacked at the heater control and cleared his throat. "How do you know?"

"I just know. I don't need one. I don't. Not now." She moved her head just enough to get a rise out of him. "Nick? You're making me a pillow, Nick."

He said nothing. He didn't dare. All she knew about him was that he'd nearly killed her. Either she didn't know what she was saying, or she really was Deer Woman. The supreme seducer in Lakota lore, that was Deer Woman. Nick focused every ounce of attention he could muster on the road ahead. Between windshield wiper whaps, a swelling of light served as a welcome distraction from the unwelcome swelling between his legs.

What the hell was this woman trying to do?

"Nick?"

"Okay, we're coming to a town. We're just outside of Mexico. Mexico, Missouri. But all I know about it is the motel where I was gonna stay tonight, which is coming up on the right."

"Go there."

"You're sure?" He was blinking. His blinker was blinking. The neon was flickering, and none of the signs were good. "No vacancy. No more rooms. I've got a reservation, but just the one room."

"I don't take up a lot of space, Nick."

Jeez Louise.

"I'll sleep in the truck if you want me to," she said softly. "I just need to be still for a while."

"Yeah, you're right. And there'll be a phone. I won't be driving up and down the street in the damn rain looking for hospital signs."

"No more signs, Nick. I've seen enough signs."

"Look, I'm not..." Not stupid? Not sure? Not horny, after she'd made herself known to his good-man-be-damned parts?

"Not what?" she chimed in.

He sighed. "You're safe with me, Joey."

"Thank you. You have no idea how good that sounds."

"But you're hurt, and I want to get you some help. I *have to* get you some help, Joey."

"You're all the help I need."

He parked in front of the motel office, shut the engine off and tried to shut himself down by staring straight ahead while she gathered herself over one arm and pushed herself up, sitting up, sitting close but no longer touching him. Thank God.

Curse God. Or Deer Woman. Or female parts and man parts and absurd accidents that planted the party of the first part smack in the path of the party of the second part. He did not need this shit.

"Nick, you didn't hit me. You *found* me."

He turned to her, scowled at her, tried to make sense of her claim. "There was something in the road."

"It wasn't me."

"I didn't knock you off the road?"

She shook her head.

For some reason, he didn't feel convinced. It made sense, but it didn't feel right. The woman had jumped over the fence and back again, playing him for what? Champion or fool?

"You coulda told me."

"I'm a little discombobulated right now."

"You and me both." He jerked on the door handle. "I'm going to check us in, and then—"

"Don't tell anyone *anything*, Nick. Please. You didn't pick anyone up on the road. Nobody's hurt." She grabbed his arm. "It's just you checking in here, okay?"

"Who the hell cares whether…?" He made the mistake of looking into those sad, badly bruised eyes again. He hadn't hit her. Whatever happened, he'd had no part in it, and he owed her nothing. He had to get that through his head. Right now would be the perfect time.

He shook his head, but the wrong words came out of his mouth. "Okay. Just me."

"You told me to make up my mind, and I have. I trust you."

"Yeah, well, now you've got more choices. You've got—" his gesture took in the lights of a town that was nothing to him but a handy stop and a catchy name "—all of Mexico."

"I trust you, Nick."

2

Nick returned to his pickup carrying a key and a promise kept. No one had asked, but if they had, he would have kept the woman on the other side of the rain-streaked glass a secret. *His* secret. He couldn't remember having one before. Not that he couldn't keep one, but he simply had little cause in his life for secrets.

Now he had one. Lying there on the front seat of his crew cab was one sweet little secret. Banged-up, dressed in tatters, stripped of everything but her instinct for self-preservation, she had become a major hitch in an otherwise routine trip. As a rule, he wasn't real big on sweets, but her sweetness was growing on him.

Nicholas Red Shield had his own instincts, too. The urge to protect the helpless ones had been bred into him from way back, or so he'd been told by people who were interested in the history of his breeding. He could go way back when the subject was horse breeding. As for what his partner called his "warrior instincts," he would take Dillon's word for it. So he hadn't hit the woman with his pickup. He could still help her out. It wasn't like he was going out of his way.

"The room's around back." He tried not to get her wet as he slid behind the wheel, but she wasn't giving him much margin for dripping. "You awake?"

"Sort of."

"When is this damn rain gonna quit, huh?"

Taking her silence for lack of interest, he checked the number on the key again as the pickup crawled past the bumpers of vehicles belonging to boarders presumably tucked in for the night. He was surprised to find a wide-open and empty parking space in front of the door with his number on it. He smiled, thinking the signs, they were a-changin'.

If Joey was at least "sort of" awake, then her claim that nobody was hurt was bullshit. When he hauled her off the front seat, she made sadly little effort to add her own steam to the task.

"I've got you," he told her, cradling her in his arms. "Just relax and pretend you're not somebody I picked up on the road."

"I'm your dry cleaning."

"Oh, yeah. I'm real big on dry cleaning."

"You're a good man. A big man. A man who isn't afraid to do the right—" He'd shouldered the door to the room shut and was about to lay her down, but she dug her fingers into his shoulder and told him no. "Keep the bed dry. I'm soaked to the bone."

He put her in a chair, turned on a lamp and sat on the corner of the bed across from her, waiting for his next cue. He still felt guilty. Responsible. It was rude, looking at her this way, like he had a butterfly trapped in a jar and didn't know what to do with her.

First off, man, get her some clothes.

She was wearing what had probably once been a nice dress. Like everything else—he was just noticing the blood on her legs—it was in bad shape.

"It's really not as bad as it looks," she insisted. She hadn't gotten close to a mirror yet, but she didn't need one as long as she could read him.

He glanced away.

"How bad does it look?"

He gave her half a smile. "Sure you weren't hit by a truck?"

"I should have kept quiet." Gingerly she touched her fingers to her swollen eyelid, bruised cheek, gashed chin. "I could've used it for blackmail."

"And asked for what?" He braced his hands on his knees. "What is it you need, Joey?"

"Joey," she echoed wistfully. "Funny name for a girl, isn't it?"

"People go by all kinds of names these days. I know

a girl named George." He leaned closer. "Are you in some kind of trouble?"

"Yes."

"How bad?"

"As bad as it gets."

He nodded toward the nightstand that stood between the two beds. "Listen, there's a phone here. How 'bout making a call?"

She shook her head.

"Nobody?"

"Do you have someone, Nick? A wife? A girlfriend?"

"No, not right now, not…" He arched an eyebrow. "You're really good at turning the tables. You're the one who needs somebody. Some family, some—"

"Right now I have no one except for one very good Samaritan." She closed her eyes, drew a deep breath and made a valiant attempt to smile for him. "Are you from Samaria, Nick? Did you walk straight out of the Bible?"

"I drove straight off the damn road," he reminded her. "I don't know what the maps call Samaria these days, but currently they're calling my country South Dakota. How 'bout you?"

"I've been to South Dakota," she said.

"I'd say just lately you've been to hell and back."

"And hell hath no phone number for a woman scorned."

"If you say so." With a sigh, Nick pushed to his feet. "Besides dry clothes, just tell me what else you need so I don't have to ask any more damn questions."

"I'd love a hot bath. But it's your room, so I'll wait my turn."

"Right." Three strides took him to the bathroom. "I'll come out and find you passed out in that chair."

"What are you going to do?"

"What any *good man* would do," he grumbled.

He glanced in the mirror above the sink on his way to the tub and toilet, which were tucked separately behind a door. Mud, matted hair, homely mug—not a pretty picture. It was a wonder the injured bird hadn't chosen to stay in the bush. He adjusted the bathtub faucets until he had a warm flow going. Then he treated his face to a sink full of hot water and plenty of soap.

She opened her eyes as he lifted her from the chair.

"How do you wanna handle this?" he asked.

"Just put me in the water, clothes and all."

"Good idea." She was shivering like crazy. Maybe the water would clear her head enough so she could start figuring out what the hell she wanted to do. "I'll be right outside. Here's soap and…Joey?"

Her eyes were closed; her small chin skimmed the water. Her torn green dress drifted around her like seaweed, and her yellow hair billowed about her shoulders.

"Are you alive?"

"Barely."

"Can you…?"

"I don't think so."

He would start with the hair. His knee cracked as he knelt beside the tub, and he knew that if he stayed in this position very long it would fill with fluid. The concern passed quickly as he filled his long brown hands with shampoo and water and mud-clotted hair. It occurred to him that he hadn't washed anyone else's hair since he was a kid. Being the oldest, he'd often been given charge of the little ones. But he was the first to grow up and move on, and he'd passed the job on to Louise, the next one in line. Louise had been followed by Bernadette, who had still been sitter-in-residence when Nick had joined the army. Johnny had never had to take his turn.

As quickly as his brother's name popped into his head, Nick pushed it back into mental storage. He had enough misery on his hands.

Namely, her face. He hated to touch it. He'd tended tender flesh in his time, but he'd never seen wounds such as these on anything so fair and fine. He took it slow, irrigating each abrasion with soapy water squeezed from a clean cloth, while she kindly kept still and quiet. She had to know he was feeling none too easy with any of this. He was no medic. Most of the supplies he carried with him were for the horses, but he was pretty sure he had a few medicines for people in his duffel bag. Probably been there for *tona* years, but maybe they were still good. There was one bad place on her scalp that he thought could do with a couple of stitches, but it wasn't bleeding much. Maybe it would be okay.

Or maybe not. But he wouldn't be the one to decide. It was no good pushing people unless they were pushing you.

Motel management had provided a small bottle of mouthwash—good ol' piss-color purge—that made her flinch when he applied it to the cut high on her nose. He flinched sympathetically.

"I know it stings, but that's supposed to show it's working."

"Don't use it all on my face." She pulled up her sleeves and exposed scrapes on both arms. "From hitting the road."

"Hell of a way to bail out of a car."

"And I forgot to yell *Geronimo*."

"Just as well. No yelling, and you got yourself a live Indian instead of a dead one." His glance skated across her face. "You got any more you want to show me?"

"Not until I know you a little better."

Her wan smile abruptly had him tongue-tied. The only wonder was that it hadn't happened to him sooner. Well aware of his limitations, he shut the lid on the throne, took himself a seat and jerked the shower curtain far enough across the side of the tub so he couldn't see anything above her knees.

"Give me those wet clothes and I'll hang 'em up."

The tattered dress came first, followed by a slip, bra, panties. He didn't know much about quality in women's underwear, but hers was a matched set, and it wasn't cheesy. He started to wring the water out, but on second thought he turned the sink into a man's laundry tub—clothes, bar soap and tepid water. He wagged his head at his reflection in the mirror. Nick Red Shield washing a woman's underwear. Hell of a sight.

Feeling edgy, he turned the TV on, flipped through the channels and turned it off again. A glance at the clothes rack inspired a search through his duffel bag. One of his T-shirts would cover her nearly to her knees. There were jeans, socks, a couple of Western shirts. Besides his favorite fixes for junk food cravings, he had an extra toothbrush, some aspirin, Band-Aids and topical ointment, some pink stuff for stomach trouble and a prescription drug for his weak knee.

Uninspired, he called out to her. "Take your time in there. I'll go out and get us something to eat."

"No, please." Real fear had insinuated itself into the voice beyond the door. "Don't leave me here alone. I might…I'm really sort of…unsteady."

"I'll wait, then. If you need anything, sing out."

She did. Screeched, more like. He'd gone to the outside door and barely touched the knob, which told him she had the ears of an owl to go along with the voice.

"Hey, I'm not going anywhere," he reported. "Just goin' out to the pickup to explain the lack of food to the cat."

Silence.

"Hey! I said—"

Disaster struck in the bathtub to the tune of slosh, clang, thud and splash.

"Shit." Nick strode from one door to the other. "Joey? I'm comin' in!"

"I got dizzy," said a voice beneath the fallen shower curtain.

"You okay?" He tossed the tangle of rod, rings and curtain onto the floor behind him while she splashed around, scrambling to clutch her knees to her chest. Then they were both still, staring eye to eye. Reflexively he reached, closed his hand tight and drew back, firmly persisting, "Are you all right?"

"No worse than I was."

A little better, he thought. At least she had some color.

She nodded. "More embarrassed is all."

"We're long past that." He snatched a towel off the rack above the toilet and then bent over her, flipping open the drain.

"Since I'm the one without clothes on, I think…" He'd already handed her the towel, but still she claimed, "I get to decide."

"Suit yourself. I've got a T-shirt for you."

"Thank you."

"One more dizzy spell and you're outta here, lady. I'll be callin' a doctor."

"Don't."

"One more." His index finger signaled *final word*. He

turned away, going after the promised shirt and muttering, "One minute she's dizzy, the next, who knows?"

"I'm not going to die. I know that much." She was on her feet now, one hand taking support from the toilet tank, the other clutching towel to breast. "Not tonight, anyway," she promised him softly as he slipped his T-shirt over her head. She gave a shy smile. "I'm past that, thank you very much."

She made slow work of getting her arms through the sleeves and letting the soft white shirt fall over her torso, as though she'd released the cord on a window shade. Whether she was putting on a show or truly struggling was the kind of question that could only lead to trouble. A smart man would back off, let it ride.

And a slow one would get himself caught by the arm before backing out of her reach.

"Thank you, Nick. I'm past that tonight because of you."

"Hey." He shrugged. "It wasn't a good day to die. So you live to fight another day."

"You've helped me more than you know. I owe you—" she glanced away blushing, disconcerted by whatever she imagined "—so much more than thanks."

"Truth is, you're indebted to some unidentified flying animal that also lived to fight another day. So it's all good." He pulled her away from the wall. In her eyes he saw her imagination running just as crazy as any wild animal that had ever crossed his path. "All I want right now is a shower," he assured her as he moved her toward the door. "Help yourself to the phone. You gotta know *some*body. Whatever arrangements you can make, I'll try to help you find a way to get there."

Once he'd lathered himself head to toe, he hung his head, letting the hot water run over the back of his neck and claim his spine for a riverbed. It felt like God's tears. One by one the muscles in his shoulders gave in, and he permitted his scarred body a rare indulgence in pity and pleasure. But it was an unholy image his mind's eye conjured for his pleasure. The only player in it besides himself was close at hand and dependent upon the mercy of that hand. She owed him. She'd said so herself. *So much* more than thanks. For his continued good grace, she'd hinted that she would favor him in return. Maybe the hint was more like a promise.

And the favor would be more like a payment, which he didn't need. He had to wonder how hard the woman had hit her head.

He *really* had to wonder what kind of demon she had dogging her.

She lay still beneath the blankets. He moved quietly, hoping she'd somehow managed to fall asleep. Silently he cursed his noisy knee as he pulled on his boots, but the chinking of his keys was the killer.

"Are you leaving?"

"I need to get my trailer off the road."

"Trailer?"

"Horse trailer."

"I didn't see any horses."

"Just an empty trailer. I'm picking up some horses tomorrow."

"But tonight…"

"I'll be back with some food." He moved a step closer. "You think you could eat something?"

"How long will you be gone?"

"An hour, maybe. Did you get hold of anyone?"

"I've told you, Nick, there's no one I can call." She jacked herself up on her elbows. "Maybe I could go with you."

"Maybe you could get some rest. Look, I'm leaving my gear." With a nod, he tried to direct her attention to his duffel bag and all the stuff he'd left around the sink, but he could see she wasn't buying. He removed a small red-and-white charm from his key ring. "Hold on to this for me. I'll be back soon."

Her fingers curled around the scrap of leather and beads. "This is important to you?"

"As important as keeping my word. I'm not gonna run off on you."

"And you're not…going to tell anyone."

"Joey?" He hated to wake her, but he had to be sure she was all right. There was always the chance of a concussion, which was nothing to mess with. He'd had a bad one himself once, so he knew from experience that you were supposed to keep waking a person up to make sure they could still cuss you out for not letting them sleep.

But all this woman did was open those big sad eyes of hers, which gave him an unwelcome hard-on. A guy had to be pretty hard up to get juiced by such a pitiful sight, even if she was wearing his own well-worn shirt and nothing else.

"You want something to eat?"

"I can't."

"I want you to try."

Jesus, talk about pitiful. When had he started wanting somebody else to do anything but suit herself?

The brown paper sack hit the small table with a solid *whomp*. "What I mean is, I think you should give it a try. It's just soup. If you can't hold anything down…"

"I can. If I show you, will you leave me alone about doctors and hospitals?"

"For now."

But he wasn't sure how long he would stay this stupid. If she went unconscious on him, who would back him up when he tried to tell some cop that not getting checked out right away was her idea?

They spoke little while they shared the meal he'd brought. He figured he'd probably traded in his cowboy boots for combat boots by the time she'd reached the age she looked to be right now, drowning in his T-shirt. Her small shoulders quivered with the breath she drew as she presented the cup to show him she'd finished more than half the soup.

He nodded. He needed to remember his own father's example. Kid shows you his small accomplishment, you hold back everything but that nod. *Yeah, kid, I see. It's no more than what's expected, and you damn sure don't want to come up with any less.*

She set the foam cup on the bedside table and closed her eyes. "Thank you. That was good."

He finished her soup. He'd paid for it.

And he went on paying.

Once the lights were out, Nick was doomed to lie still in his separate bed and pretend that her crying into her pillow wasn't keeping him awake. She was trying to stifle them, but those quivering, watery breaths of hers were deafening. Sputtering, stuttering, tearful little noises. He tried not to imagine himself crawling into her bed and finding ways to comfort her. A man asleep would have shifted and settled again, but Nick was afraid to move. *Afraid*, for crissake.

He was no good with women. He had no moves, no words, no charm.

You should have taken her to see a doctor, you jackass.

She wouldn't go.

Who was driving?

Absolutely. Take her to an emergency room and leave her there—that was exactly what he should have done. Leave the rest up to her. It was the only way to deal with people, the only way that made any sense. Own up to your own part and leave them to do theirs. Don't get stuck with anybody else's shit.

Now you're talkin', man. Nick Red Shield is back in the saddle, back in his own ugly skin.

Absolutely.

Anyway, what was one night?

3

It was oddly comforting to be called by her baby's name. Lauren Davis had been left for dead, but Joey was alive and well. The sound of his name, spoken to her by another human being, made everything else bearable. She had a connection. The physical cord had been severed, but her baby was still part of her. If Lauren was Joey, surely Joey still belonged to Lauren.

From the day he was born, little more than a year ago, until the day he was taken from her, she had not let him out of her sight for more than a few hours. Her father used to say that she was born to ride. She now knew that she was born to be her baby's mother. Every time she closed her eyes, she saw his little face. Birthing pain was nothing compared to a mother's pain for the child who had been ripped from her arms.

Her whole life, Lauren had shed tears maybe one night in a thousand, but tonight she couldn't stop. Lying in a cheap motel bed next to a second one occupied by a man she hardly knew, she worked a cold, shaky hand against hot tears and tried to stem her sniffling. The man knew too much about her already. Too much for her own good, and not enough for his. But she had run out of choices. She needed time and a safe haven, and this man was all she had. He seemed to be the kind who couldn't walk away from trouble without carrying a piece of it with him.

And she was trouble. She was a human train wreck. She couldn't think straight, nor could she shut her brain down and make it rest. Start with something simple, she told herself. Just lie still. Simply breathe. She steadied herself in her own embrace and rubbed the soft sleeves of the shirt that smelled faintly of horse tack. The taste of chicken broth lingered on her tongue. Joey loved chicken with noodles. Lauren had packed several jars of the stuff in the bag she'd prepared to take with them when they'd left.

But Raymond Vargas had other ideas….

Pulse pounding in her ears, Lauren glanced toward the top of the stairs. Everything she'd planned to take with her was packed and ready to be loaded in the car. All she needed was Joey. Vargas caught her between the garage and the stairs to the room where her baby slept.

"What do you think you're doing?" Anger reshaped

a face once handsome, now a daily horror. Before she even saw it coming, his punch had landed. He drew his fist back, opened his hand and flexed his fingers. "I think I made myself perfectly clear. You're not taking my son. End of discussion."

Lauren's left eye was tearing, but only because his ring had connected with that side of her nose. She refused to cry. She would not even touch her face in a way that acknowledged the blow. As long as she had breath in her body, she would not relinquish the strength of her will.

She stood her full five feet, two inches tall and maintained strict control over her voice, her stance and her wits. "Raymond, you have no more interest in Joey than you have in me anymore. Just let us go."

"Where?"

"I'm not sure yet. As soon as we're settled, I'll give you all the—"

"We're settled, you and me." His cold gray eyes challenged her to doubt him. "Like this discussion, which I settled days ago. Women come and go, but this is my only kid. He stays."

"You didn't want me to have him, Raymond. Remember? You told me to have an abortion."

"Yeah, with good reason. You haven't ridden since you found out you were pregnant."

"I haven't *raced*."

"And you were hard to replace. You get up on a horse, you're like some kind of Roman goddess—

waist-up woman, waist-down horse." A quick laugh brightened his eyes, but not with warmth, for which they had no capacity. "I half expected you to give birth to a little creature with four legs."

"He's a baby, Raymond, and he needs his mother. Being his mother…" It was useless to try to explain to this man how motherhood had turned the order of things on its head. All she knew was that her child was always on her mind, and his needs came first. He had gone from nonexistent to top of all lists.

She shook her head. "I'm not getting back into it, Raymond. I'm not immortal, and I'm not a dumb beast. If I'm trampled, I know what happens. I've seen it."

"You started thinking instead of riding. That's your problem."

"It doesn't have to be a problem for anyone, Raymond. Certainly not for you. I know that I'm human, and I understand the rules. If somebody puts a gun to my head and pulls the trigger, I'm dead. Exactly like George Kobe."

"He put the gun to his own head."

"He was riding for the wrong people, and he was winning."

"You're safe riding for me."

"I'm safer not riding for anyone." Without thinking, she touched her smarting cheek. "I'm finished, Raymond. *We're* finished. We've been finished for a long time."

"Finished fucking," he acknowledged with an easy

shrug. "That's fine. No shortage of replacements there. But I never thought about having a kid. Blood of my blood, flesh of my flesh and all that. Every time I look at him, I see more of myself."

"You'll always know where we are," she promised quietly.

"Damn right."

"Just let us go."

"Not on your life." Cold eyes, cold smile. "Not *with* your life."

Lauren knew all too well that it was a mistake not to take a Raymond Vargas threat seriously, but in the long run, staying with him would be more dangerous than leaving. Life with Vargas could never be good for her son, with or without her presence as a buffer.

Letting him make decisions for her had been surprisingly easy at first. She had become the breadwinner for herself and her father long before she was old enough to hold a job almost anywhere except a racetrack, where age didn't matter if you knew your way around horses and any chore that came with them. But her earnings increased when she became an apprentice jockey at the age of fifteen. During her apprenticeship, she was widely considered to be more than gifted. By the time she was eighteen, she enjoyed media as well as social attention. Her introduction to Raymond Vargas was inevitable. He found her attractive. She found him fascinating. For a time he gave her everything she wanted, including the chance to ride some of the most remarkable horses she'd ever met.

She'd never asked about Vargas's business dealings. After he'd taken her off the open market and mounted her handsomely on his horses and in his bed, she'd determined to stick with him exclusively in both respects. She'd thrilled to the notion that she could run with a dangerous crowd in the company of a daring man. She didn't concern herself with where his money came from. She suspected, in fact, that too much information in that regard might be bad for her health. She relished the newfound means to run and ride and spend and play. Within the course of a single day she was free to be womanly and childish, accomplished and dependent, careful and crazy. No more worrying about consequences. As long as Raymond was pleased with her, she was golden.

And as long as ever-serious, ever-silent strong man Jumbo Jack was around, Lauren was safe. She indulged herself in a short, sweet, overdue adolescence.

But she'd gotten pregnant, and again life had changed. Her insights and her outlook had steadily broadened, while her relationship with Vargas had withered quickly. Any affection they'd shared was gone, and with no legal ties to him, she was ready to go her own way. She'd told him as much. Since he had shown little interest in the baby during his first year, she hadn't foreseen his objection to her plan or the obstacle he would become. It was impossible to reason with him and dangerous to defy him. She'd tried both.

Now, having failed in her first attempt to take her baby and run, Lauren hardly expected a second chance to materialize the same day. But after the confrontation on the stairs, Raymond's power trip had taken him down the road, presumably for his regular weekend overnight with his latest girlfriend. He'd clearly figured he'd made his point. And he'd certainly made *a* point. Lauren's head pounded with it. She'd taken some nasty spills in her time, but getting punched in the face was a new experience. It was one she didn't intend to repeat. Her bags were still packed, and her car was in the garage.

Surely the man hadn't thought he could stop her from running the most important race of her life simply by punching her in the face.

He had not, as Jumbo Jack Reed's appearance attested. She had started up the stairs, and suddenly there was Jack, on his way down the steps in all his burly substance.

"You might want a raincoat."

There was no way she could get past him. "Where am I going?"

"This weather won't be lettin' up anytime soon." His response to her ricocheting glance was more direct. "Don't worry about Little Joe. He'll be taken care of."

"He's asleep in his…"

The big man's demeanor was imbued with a vague

sadness as he slowly wagged his head. Any display of emotion was rare for Jumbo Jack. His dark eyes, droopy jowls, stiff slit of a mouth and hulking frame were the parts of a wholly unexpressive man who never wasted a move or a word. But he'd always shown as much concern for Lauren as he did for anyone, and his sadness gave her a spiky chill.

She turned away, forced her way past him up the stairs and peered into an empty crib. Even his favorite blanket—his "binky"—was gone. Lauren dug her nails into her palms as she gripped the crib rail and drew deep breaths of baby-scented air. *He was just here!*

"Where's my baby, Jack?"

"We're taking your car."

"Is…is that where Joey is? In the car?"

"Yeah. He's in the car."

But not in Lauren's car. It wasn't a good fit for the big man, but he took her keys and wedged himself behind the wheel. Lauren had gone with him without objection, but she couldn't give up trying to coax him to tell her what was going on. True to form, he said almost nothing until she hit a nerve—something she was surprised to find he had.

"Are you taking me to my baby?"

His attention to the road visibly wavered.

"Jack? Who took him?" Getting punched in the face had left her a little pixilated. Somebody had slipped in and out of the nursery while she was loading the car. "Was it Raymond?"

The windshield wipers whacked steadily, barely staying ahead of the deluge. She glimpsed a sign— *Leaving Illinois*—whap, whap. Bigger sign—*Welcome to Missouri*—whap, whap. Her face ached all the way down to her teeth. Raymond had shoved her around a few times in recent months, and he'd let her know there was more where that came from, although not in so many words. No words at all, really, but attitude. Plenty of attitude. She'd been playing around with the wrong big gun, and now she was in Missouri, and her little boy was...

"Just tell me he's safe."

"He's safe."

"He needs me, Jack. He's only a baby." Taking her cue from the windshield wipers, Lauren whacked steadily at her rising emotions, barely keeping her own waterworks at bay. "Why is he doing this?"

"I don't ask questions. It's better that way."

"Better than what? Better than what's going to happen to me?" She swallowed hard. The fact that she was no stranger to the big man was her only potential advantage. She sought an effective tone. Not fearful. Not angry. Not accusatory. "Are you going to kill me, Jack?"

Her simple, straightforward curiosity was met with silence. But he blinked. She was sure he blinked.

"What's the point?" she asked quietly. "I'm nobody."

"When did you get to be such a talker? We're goin' for a quiet ride here."

"I'm not a talker, Jack. I'm really not. No matter

where I go, I will see no evil, hear no evil, speak no evil. So what are we doing in Missouri?"

"Ray makes the decisions."

"And he decided on Missouri. So don't cry for me, Illinois."

"You always had spunk."

"Not so much anymore. Once upon a time I wore spunk like designer spandex. Things change when you have a child. I've always wondered and never asked, Jack, do you have a wife or any—"

"Listen, I got one rule, and tonight is the first time I let it slide."

"We shouldn't be talking," she acknowledged quietly. But he had just extended her single advantage.

"Say what you want, but don't ask me nothin'. I'm just drivin' the car."

"I'm glad to hear that, because…" She shifted in her seat, willing him to see her, notice her face. "Because I've always believed that nothing bad could happen to me as long as you were around. You were there for Raymond, but you made me feel safe, too. I always knew—"

It all flew from her head the instant he pulled the car off the road. She knew nothing. She imagined nothing. The rain, the engine and the wipers blended into a high-pitched humming in her ears, and she felt cold, hollow, slightly sick.

"Get out of the car."

She stared at the big man, dumbfounded.

"Get out of the car and disappear while I'm not lookin'." He turned toward the side window and muttered, "I won't take after you or nothin'."

It made no sense. "I can't go anywhere without my baby."

"You're already without your baby. Get used to it." He turned to her again. His eyes had gone cold. "Get out of the car."

"It's my car," she said thickly. "If you're going to kill me, do it here."

"I'll make you a deal." He glanced away quickly, as though the very suggestion embarrassed him. "Lauren Davis is a dead woman, all right? This is your chance to run. Get as far away as you can. It's the best deal you're ever gonna get." He stared ahead, muttering, "Jumbo Jack's gettin' old. Gettin' soft."

She imagined the huntsman giving Snow White the famous fairy tale reprieve. Despite the royal decree, he couldn't bring himself to kill her.

"Please, Jack, couldn't you help me get my baby back?"

"Not *that* damn soft." He nodded toward the roadside. "Go on now. Somebody'll pick you up. You gotta forget everything and start over."

"What are you going to do?"

"Make it look good. They'll find your car, but as long as there's no body, your disappearance is a mystery. The news'll go ape-shit for a while, so you might wanna dye your hair and try to ugly yourself up some."

"You don't understand, Jack. Joey's my life now. I can't—"

A ham-fisted blow to the side of her face literally made Lauren bite her tongue. She gagged on the taste of her own blood. Ear-ringing shock numbed all other sensation.

But not for long. He jerked the car door open, dragged her out of the seat and dropped her on the steep slope at the side of the road. Up became down, dryness got wet, light turned to dark, and chaos was all bound up with pain. She slid over bruising gravel and prickling grass, words of warning tumbling over her, spiny bushes tearing at her clothing and flesh. It was a relief to give in to the fall and finally be still with her pain.

So much for gentle protectors and fairy tales.

4

Nick rolled out at the same time every morning, no matter where he was or how long he'd slept. When his customary time finally came, he was sure of only one thing: he'd heard enough crying.

He headed directly for the shower. He started with hot water for untangling the knots in his gut, followed by an icy blast to get his head straight. Tempted by the last fresh, folded towel, he made do with a damp one, all the while silently kicking himself for a fool on at least a dozen counts. He had a fuel-efficient route all planned out. He had business to attend to, meet-up times and places all arranged. What was he thinking, throwing an open-ended promise into the mix? He could only hope she had people somewhere close by.

Not that Nick put any stock in hope. Hope belonged in a holiday storage box, along with promises and polite manners. Whatever she could arrange, he'd said he would help her get there. But he hadn't offered door-to-door.

He found her dressed in her own clothes and perched on the edge of the bed as though take-off might be imminent.

"You got time for a shower. There's a dry towel left."

"I'm fine, thanks."

She was a sad excuse for fine, and the shower was the only remedy he had to offer. That and another promise.

"I won't leave you."

"I'll only be a minute, then."

She sprang to her feet before he had time or sense to back away, bringing her face closer. "It looks a lot worse this morning."

Jesus, since when had his tongue cut off all ties with his brain?

"It does?" Her small voice betrayed the added injury.

"I'll get you some more ice," he offered, for want of any way to take back the truth. Red-and-black eyes, puffy lips, one side of her face double the size of the other—what could he say? He'd seen bull riders headed for the hospital looking way better than she did. To boot, she grabbed his arm before he'd finished reaching for the ice bucket. He wasn't used to being grabbed, and he had all he could do to tamp down the impulse to jerk away.

"I'll be right back," he promised, falling back on

his old proof. "See? My gear's still here. The cat's here, too. I brought her in last night."

"I don't want to hold you up."

"There's time." Man, those little hands were like a vise grip. "The ice machine is only a few doors down, Joey."

"It probably won't help. Let's just—"

"Humor me." He turned the act of pulling her hand off his arm into twirling her toward the bathroom—a move he didn't know he had in him. "Dance on into that shower. We'll never know until you try."

By the time she emerged, he'd made the ice run and turned his attention to the road map he had opened up and laid across the foot of his bed. Without looking up, he directed her to the pillowcase he'd transformed into an ice pack. "It should cover your whole face."

"Are we borrowing or stealing?"

"Neither. We're paid up until checkout time. We have the use of the bed linens until then. It's called renting." He pointed to the yellow highlighter trail he'd applied to the map weeks earlier. "Any friends or relatives anywhere along here?"

"I doubt it." She lay there with her head beside the map and the folded pillowcase over her face. "But it's hard to tell with a bag over my head."

"You didn't look. Mind you, I don't mind going off track some."

"Is Canada on your track?"

"Hell, no." He glanced at the pillowcase. "You got relations in Canada?"

"I haven't had relations in ages and ages."

"I could put you on a bus to Canada. You got any ID?"

She gave a small chuckle as she peeked out from behind the pillowcase. "You are the sweetest man, Nick. Do you know how—"

"Cover your face, woman. That thing won't do any good unless you keep it on."

"I don't know anyone in Canada. I was just asking."

"I'm on my way to Des Moines, picking up five horses, then two more in Lincoln. I'm driving all the way across Nebraska, so anywhere along I-80, if there's someplace you wanna go, no problem. Right here, we take 76 into Colorado." He knew she couldn't see the map, but he said it just to give her an idea. "I wouldn't mind taking you to Denver. Wouldn't be too far out of the way. One more stop in Wyoming, and then—"

"Where's home, exactly? You mentioned South Dakota."

"No place you've heard of, but we'll clip past the Black Hills. Ever been there?"

"I've been everywhere, which is why geography is my best subject."

"Then pick a place where I can drop you off. You got your airports, your bus stations along the way. But I haul livestock for a living, and it's my business to connect these dots. And I'll be taking a horse home with me this time around, so I'll need to—"

"You're picking up a horse for yourself?" She was

peeking at him again. Something he'd said had put a little spark in her eye.

"Yeah, that's…I bought a Paint stud, and I'm picking him up at the breeder's in Colorado."

"I can tell you're excited about him."

Wait a minute, that was *her* spark. He was only telling her where he was heading. Deadpan, as always.

"I've been lookin' for the right stud for a long time."

"And you're sure you've finally found him. I know that look. My father was horse-crazy, too."

"I'm in the business of raising horses. If that makes me crazy…"

"It does. You're a gambler. You can never be sure with horses, and you've got a lot riding on this one. Am I right?" The ice pack slid to the bed as she propped her head up to take a look at the map. "That's a long haul. I could be useful."

"Your face looks a little better. The ice helped."

"I can help you with the horses." She glanced up, working on him with her bloodshot eyes. "Seriously, Nick."

"Seriously, Joey, where can I drop you off?"

"Anywhere. Nowhere. Nowhere would be better than somewhere."

"That's where I picked you up." He pointed to that very nowhere spot on the map. "Right there. Maybe you want to put up a marker."

"A memorial to my near demise?"

"The place where the turnip fell off the truck.

Look this over and come up with a plan for yourself while I load up. We'll take some ice along." Another quick appraisal of the bumps and bruises on her face satisfied him that she would live. "But it's not too late to change your mind about seeing a doctor."

"I don't believe in doctors." She swung her legs over the side of the bed and sat up. "Against my religion."

"Yeah, and picking up hitchhikers is against mine, but I make an exception whenever I hit one."

"You didn't." She turned her head, giving him a pointed glance, along with a glimpse of her wounded profile. "And I never make exceptions."

Nick didn't mind helping his customers load their horses into his trailer, but he didn't expect to handle the whole job himself, especially when the animals were barely halterbroke. He wasn't much of a fan of Arabians, and the five he'd agreed to haul out of Des Moines made him feel even less friendly toward the breed. They were flighty as hell. When the fourth knothead balked halfway up the ramp and jerked the lead rope through his hands, Nick was about to say the hell with it. He would be doing the buyer a favor if he unloaded the first three and left the whole bunch in Iowa. Save himself and his trailer considerable wear and tear.

And then Joey appeared.

"Thought I told you to stay in the pickup."

"May I?" Her nod signified the lead rope as she quietly approached the horse.

"He'd just as soon knock you over as look at you, but, hell, why not?"

"What's a few more scrapes, huh? Settle down, boy," she murmured. Remarkably, her whole body and bearing connected with the horse. Muscle by muscle, the animal relaxed, and the woman spared Nick a pointed glance. "Both of you."

She'd spent some time around horses, all right. A moment ago the gray gelding's ears were laid back, every hair on his body aquiver. Suddenly he was all happy ears and willing hooves, following the little woman in the flimsy shoes and tattered dress up the ramp as though she'd washed her hair in alfalfa juice.

"Watch your feet," he called out to her as he headed back to the corral for the last horse. Hell, all he needed to top off a trailer full of high-headed Arabians was a hitchhiker with a broken toe.

But the last horse was loaded without incident. Nick was back on schedule, and Joey was buckling herself into his passenger seat.

"I hope the buyer isn't a friend of yours," she said.

"Nope."

"Does he know what he's getting?"

"I know what I'm hauling. I know what he owes me on delivery." He turned the pickup onto the highway, putting the gravel farm road behind him with a signature dusty wake. "What would *you* say he's getting?"

"Nothing my father would have gone crazy for. I know that much."

"And that much makes sound horse sense," he observed. "I'd like to meet your dad. Any chance you could arrange that, say, today or tomorrow?"

"Not unless you're adding the Happy Hunting Grounds to your itinerary."

"Sorry."

She stared at him for a moment and finally shrugged. "Me, too."

From mutually sorry to blissfully silent would have been fine with Nick. What did it matter why she was sorry? The number of times he'd ever asked why could be ticked off on one hand. "Why has two ears and a long tail," he used to tell his brother, who would then punch him and try to rephrase the question somehow. *Quit runnin' your mouth, Johnny boy. Watch and learn.* But his little brother had never mastered the art of watch-and-learn. He'd been an oddball Indian, that one.

"You're smiling," she said.

"Am I?"

"Sort of." She gave a bruised-lip version of returning the favor. "I was about to promise no more clichés."

"Water off a duck's back," he said with a chuckle. "Here's another one—nothing personal."

"Right. Agreed. So tell me about these horses you're raising."

"I'm just gettin' into it." Which meant there wasn't much to tell, and she ought to take a rest. "You can lay that seat way back. The lever's on the side. There's a blanket and pillow on the backseat."

"Thanks." She ignored every aspect of his suggestion. "You're into Paints?"

You want me to talk you to sleep? So be it.

"Like I said, I finally found the stud I've been looking for. He's homozygous, so he'll throw color every time. And he's built like you read about. Leggy, nice head on him, solid hip, powerful chest—everything my mares want."

"Everything they're lacking, or everything they desire?"

"We'll see. He's young, so I don't know how desirable they'll find him. It takes more than good looks to impress a mare."

"Looks can surely deceive."

"Yeah." With a glance he acknowledged the truth of that. "You take my broodmares. Or not. At first glance you probably wouldn't take them, you or your dad. But if he's really got horses in his blood—if he did, I mean—he'd give them a second look. He'd say, wait a minute, there's something different about these girls. Something special."

"Are they mustangs?"

"Good guess, but they're much more than that."

"I'm not guessing. I hear it in your voice. You're out to save them."

"I've already done that. They belong to me."

"Were they feral horses?" On the tail of his nod, she added, "True mustangs, or just wild horses?"

"Wild horses can be anything. They can be descended from draft horses turned loose by farmers who didn't need them anymore. They can be from animals that escaped or from stolen horses, or—"

"Indian horses," she concluded. "That's it, isn't it? That's what's so special about them. But how would you know? There's no way to tell a horse descended from Indian stock from any other wild horse." On second thought, "Is there?"

"What kind of horses did your father favor?"

"The kind that run fast."

"Was he a breeder? Trainer?" He cut her a quick glance. "Player?"

"Some of each," she said with a dismissive shrug. "Tell me about your mares. Are they registered American Indian Horses?"

"I'm a registered American Indian, and they're my horses. Does that work for you?"

"I know there's a registry for the American Indian Horse, but you did say that your mares were feral horses that you rescued from—"

"Did I say that?" Relentless, this woman. "We'll be halfway to Lincoln pretty soon, and I still won't know where I'm supposed to drop you off."

She let the ball drop. For a moment it lay still and quiet.

Then, in a tone so humble it stung him, she asked, "How bad would it be if I rode with you all the way to the end of the line?"

"You know somebody there?"

"Not well, but give me the extra mile. When we get to the next stop, and I'm still riding with you, not taking up much space or anything, just—"

Relentless.

"Just looking like somebody rolled a pickup tire over your face."

"I told you, Nick, you didn't hit me. I don't know what you saw in the road. It probably *was* a deer. But I know it wasn't me."

"What were you doing on the road like that?"

"In the night," she echoed. "In the rain."

Familiar refrain.

She'd offered no clues the first time he'd asked, and he wasn't getting any this time around. Did he really want any? He did all his traveling in his own territory without taking side trips into other people's business. He didn't ask for directions, never gave any, worked hard for what he got and didn't expect bonuses. He didn't go around looking to help people, but a guy sees a bad need rising, what else can he do? Here he was, and here *she* was, and the need for information he didn't really want was becoming a pain in the ass.

He glanced at her with the words *answer me* poised to jump off his tongue.

Her blue eyes brimmed with apology, and he swallowed hard. What was a little pain in the ass compared to the depth of despair in those eyes? He hated pressing her, but he had wandered into unfamiliar territory and had no idea how to proceed.

"What kind of trouble are you carrying around with you, Joey?" When she didn't answer right away, he pressed with, "How bad?"

She stared off at nothing, biting her lip in defense of her secrets.

"Look, you asked how bad it would be, and I don't know how to answer that. I don't know you. I don't know what's behind you. I take you to my place, what are you gonna do there?"

"Have the tire tracks removed," she said with a smile in her voice. "Maybe you have some kind of rubber eraser at your place. Remove the tracks, replace with new skin, give it a few days to heal."

If she was looking to amuse him, she'd missed the mark. With a sharp glance he told her as much. Too far afield.

Too close to home.

"How 'bout you give me a straight answer?"

"I'm pretty sure this is as bad as it gets." She turned her face from him and spoke softly to the side window. "I was left there. In the night, in the rain, I was left there after…a difference of opinion."

The breath he drew too quickly pinched him deep in his chest. He scowled. "Your man did this to you?"

"My man?" She gave a derisive snort. "A man, yes, and thank you for not saying *your husband*. I was dumb enough to be with him, but not dumb enough to be married to him. I'll say this for you, Nick Red Shield, you're quite intuitive for a man, but you presume nothing." She turned to him again. "Except responsibility."

"You took your sweet time setting the record straight about my responsibility."

"I was scared."

"Can't the police—"

"No, please. That would only make it worse."

"If I gotta be lookin' over my shoulder, it would help if I knew what to look for."

"No one's looking for me right now. You picked up some roadkill is all." She gave him a chance to laugh, and when he didn't, she offered him that sad excuse for a smile. "I need some time, Nick. A few days to get my head straight. It feels as bad as it looks."

"Truth is, you cleaned up pretty good."

"I can do even better. You wait and see." She laid her head back on the headrest. "Tell me about your horses, Nick. Where did they come from?"

"You've heard of Sitting Bull?"

"You mean the Indian chief? Of course."

"Of course. Most famous Indian in the world. Geronimo is a distant second, even with all the fools who go around yelling his name."

"Before jumping out of some moving frying pan into…Why do they do that, anyway?"

"Who knows what makes white people tick, huh?" He winked at her—a pretty amazing gesture for Nick Red Shield, but there it was. "I'm from Sitting Bull's band. Everybody knows Sitting Bull because he kicked Custer's prissy ass at Little Big Horn. Actually it was Crazy Horse and Gall who did the ass-kicking, but Sitting Bull had the dream and made the medicine.

"The rest was a matter of doing what warriors do—what needed to be done. But Sitting Bull, he was the man. After it was all over but paying the price for defending ourselves, Sitting Bull took most of his people into Canada. But it was a hard time, and the people were so homesick after a few years that they came back and surrendered. The army took all the horses, and imprisoned Sitting Bull and his followers at Fort Randall for two more years.

"So what happened to Sitting Bull's horses?" he put to her finally.

"I was just about to ask."

"He comes back from Canada, early 1880s, surrenders at Fort Buford in Dakota Territory. The army takes the horses, keeps what they want, sells the rest. You heard of the Marquis de Mores?"

She shook her head, but he seemed to be holding her interest.

From amazing gesture to amazing speechifying. What had gotten into him?

"Just some guy who bought a bunch of the mares because, like your dad and me, he had good horse sense. But no business sense, apparently, because his cattle business went bust." He glanced at her and smiled. Her eyes were closed. "Long story short, the horses got loose. You want me to stop?"

"Please don't. I'm interested." And suddenly all eyes. "I want the long story with all the details."

"I was thinking more like a rest stop."

"I'm not resting; I'm listening."

He gave a skeptical chuckle.

"Really, I'm fine. I know how men hate to make too many stops when they're truckin' down the highway."

"You do, huh?" He took the turn he'd decided on a few miles back when he'd noticed a sign. By his standards, it was way too soon for a stop, but it would take more than a simple gas station to get the woman fixed up properly. "That's why we have truckers' malls. One stop fits all."

After gassing up and parking his outfit a safe distance from curious eyes and bumping vehicles, Nick pried the woman out of the passenger's seat. He knew she was embarrassed about the way she looked, but nature being what it was, he finally had to warn her straight out that if she didn't go now, he wasn't stopping again no matter how desperate her situation. Then he left her to think that one over, which didn't take her long. The sound of her quickstep coming up behind might have made him smile if he hadn't been angry with her for making him say the obvious. Bad enough he had to take on a passenger, but he'd be damned if he was going to travel cross-country with her acting like a kid.

Once inside, she took off from him immediately. No chance to suggest a bite to eat in the restaurant or a little shopping for personal items, nothing. He felt funny about hovering around the women's restroom, so he staked out the aisles he thought might be points of her interest until he started feeling funny about his stakeout. A guy knew when he was being watched. He grabbed some of the items he'd been looking at, took them up front and gave the cashier the legendary Red Shield evil eye.

Yeah, lady, I've got cash.

The transaction was completed without a word from either side. Not a please, thank you, or have a nice day. And still no Joey.

But he was blowing this unfriendly joint, with or without her.

Maybe she'd skipped out on him. He was really going to look like an ass, carrying this particular sack full of stuff back to an empty pickup.

How're you gonna look like anything with nobody there to see?

Nobody besides that know-it-all cat. One word out of her, and she was going back in the trailer with the crazy Arabs.

But the cat had made herself comfortable with the woman, who was staring straight ahead, fighting to beat hell to keep her bruised eyes open. No reason to get a mad on, Nick told himself, as he opened the passenger door. Presumably she'd done no more and no less than what he'd told her to do. And she made a sweet picture, cuddling the big orange, never-before-cuddly tabby.

"I see you didn't lock the door behind you. But here, drink this," he ordered, handing her a bottle of orange juice, followed by a chicken sandwich wrapped in plastic, which changed the cat's mind about springing into the backseat. "And eat as much of it as you can. I paid six bucks for it."

The cat took bumblebee sniffs at the edge of the sandwich.

"Will one make me grow and the other shrink me? Because I think small would be better. Small head, small headache."

He took the bottle of ibuprofen out of his pocket and held it up for display. "But you gotta eat at least half that sandwich first."

"Do you always act like a mother hen?"

"You're my first chick."

She laughed. "I'll bet you have children, though."

"Not a one." He tossed a large package into the backseat, and then he handed her a small one.

"What's this?"

"Ice pack. That's for later, after you eat. You break up whatever's inside, and it gets cold." He glanced back at the store. "The woman in there looked at me like I was Jack the Ripper."

Joey nodded as she unwrapped the sandwich. "She asked if I needed help, and I asked where the bathroom was. She leaned closer and whispered, 'I mean real help. Do you want me to call the police?'"

"Jesus." He gave the store a second glance and

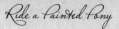

made a mental note to watch the speed until he was safely past giving the locals any probable cause to stop that Indian driving down the road in a fine rig.

"Yeah. Scary. I told her I'd been in an accident. I know you were trying to be helpful, getting me in there, but I really need to stay out of sight for a while, Nick. I'll just stay in the pickup with this bag over my head."

"I'll have to get you a bigger one." He pushed the lever on the side of the seat and told her, "Lean back. You wanna ride with me, you gotta eat, drink and then rest."

"What happened to *be merry*?" she asked when he got back behind the wheel.

"You missed the party truck."

He kept an eye on her progress, especially with the sandwich. She kept trying to feed bits of pricey chicken to the cat, but the Red Shield evil eye kept the activity to a minimum.

"What's your cat's name?"

"She's not my cat." He curtailed another food-slipping attempt, his critical glance meeting her wide-eyed claim to no blame. "She doesn't belong to me."

"Who does she belong to?"

"Herself. She wanted a ride. Never said where she was going. Guess we haven't come to *her* stop yet, either."

She gave a lopsided smile. "You're a very nice man, Nick Red Shield."

"Don't you believe it," he warned against that

injured smile. "And if you can't help yourself, at least don't tell anyone."

Later, just when he thought she'd gone to sleep, she proved him wrong again.

"Nick?"

Man, she was fighting it. He said nothing.

"Who was the Marquis de Mores?"

Who the hell cares? "He was just some rich French guy."

"What was he doing in—"

"Listen, there's nothing wrong with peace and quiet. You took some ibuprofen. I don't mind if you rest now."

"Do you mind talking to me?"

"I don't have much to say."

"Yes, you do. You have stories."

"Are you afraid to sleep?"

"Kind of."

He sighed. He knew the feeling. At least she'd picked a subject he didn't mind talking about. His sturdy, resilient girls.

"Okay, well, this de Mores married an American and built a big ranch in Dakota Territory, near the North Dakota Badlands. Have you heard of Medora?"

"Was that his ranch?"

"It's a town in North Dakota named after his ranch. He named it for his wife."

"Romantic," she muttered softly.

"Yeah, well, he was French. Built the woman a big house where they could have parties and entertain people by hunting big game, playing cowboy and like that. So he bought around two hundred fifty head of the horses the army had confiscated from Sitting Bull's people. Mares, all of them. De Mores was suitably impressed, claimed Indian ponies to be better than any other type of horse. Said he was gonna raise them. But the horses had other ideas."

"They ran away?"

"De Mores wasn't much of a rancher. He built a plant for processing the beef right there on the place, but his grand plan went to hell in short order. When he sold out, he only had about sixty horses left, and that was after only two years."

"And the rest of them…?"

"Took to the hills. The Badlands, where they roam to this day. And they've got the typical coloring, square build, fused backbone of the mustang or the Indian horse. They've got that heavy muscle and that big—" he glanced at her "—that big, heavy heart of the ones who were taken away."

She was looking at him, big, sad, blackened eyes eating him up as though his attention might feed her somehow. The heaviness in her heart was more than private, beyond ancestral memory. It was present. It was pressing.

It was killing her.

5

The second pickup of the day was no easier than the first. By the time they'd reached Lincoln, Nick had already made a liar of himself by making another stop. Any excuse other than puking, he would have played the smart-ass, but when the woman said she felt sick, his pickup changed course faster than a hummingbird. Not so much for her sake, but a guy had to preserve his dignity, and there was one smell that did him in every time, especially on the road. Before the vehicle had come to a complete stop, the door flew open, the woman bolted and Nick turned up the radio. He'd managed to head off a downturn in his own stomach, but by the time she took her seat again, she'd lost what color she'd gained.

She'd blamed the sandwich.

Rather than discuss the matter any further, he'd apologized for the meal.

On the road again, he'd given up on the idea of making up time in favor of a steady-as-she-goes plan. She goes to sleep; we keep a steady pace. No stops. No flying low. No cops. We won't make quittin' time, but we'll get there before closing time.

A safe six-horse delivery was bird-in-the-hand kind of money. He liked that. As long as she slept, there would be no more stops. Six hundred miles was an easy, average, normal horse-hauling day. And Nick liked normal. He thrived on normal. He would have dearly loved getting back to normal. But normal had flown out the window the night he'd plucked a certain mysterious bird from a Missouri bush.

Okay, so maybe he wasn't doing normal quite as well as he normally did, even if he didn't have a rider. But what did he expect when his own private Christmas morning was only a few hours away? Extra complications had added an extra wake-up to his plan, but no more. He was almost there. It was officially okay to anticipate, enjoy the gooseflesh, allow himself to do some secret smiling. Hadn't seen it yet, but he was close enough for the believing part to start kicking in.

He was finally getting his horse.

It hadn't been easy to come up with the final payment on Nick's dream. His name was True Colors, and he was a black-and-white tobiano with a family tree full of equine royalty, a face to make the angels cry and a body that would surely have old Sitting Bull standing up to make a song. He had a lot of running blood in him for a Paint. To boot, he was flashy. Color was what was selling these days, and True Colors would give his offspring the kind of color guaranteed to catch a buyer's eye. Once his babies' color had separated them out from the rest and they'd made the gate cut, their other attributes would make the sale.

Nick would have to stop buying and start selling really soon, and True Colors was going to help him by making a name for himself. The horse had earned some halter points, but Nick had no use for leading a horse around the show ring to be judged on conformation. Neither he nor his horses had time for politics. Performance, yes, as long as performance meant allowing his horses to be horses. Why would anyone ask such amazing animals to be anything else? Carefully coached and patiently coaxed, they would permit a man to mount, meld and experience every magnificent move they made. And they could do it without sacrificing their own God-given grace.

It was a fine balance, made more wondrous by its very delicacy. Big, brawny, sleek and shy meets brainy, bold, dicey and dangerous. How two such different creatures could come together in the incredible alliance called horseman was beyond reason. It was beyond natural. It was mysterious and holy, and it was pure magic.

It was the one trust Nick Red Shield indulged himself, and he held it sacred.

With True Colors, Nick would begin to fulfill his commitment to that trust. His sturdy horses and his worthy heritage—the best bones in the business—repackaged in twenty-first- century Paint skin. Heads would turn. Anyone who had any interest in horses would hear the story. And Nick would combine business with mission.

So the final payment had been hard to put together, but it would be easy to part with. The money order was burning a hole in his pocket. He was feeling it in his fanny. His gluteus maximus was pouring on the molten lead, draining it right down his right leg and into his gas-pedal foot. A highway sign told him he would make Ogallala in plenty of time to unload his trailer, hit I-76, and breeze across the state line into Colorado with daylight to spare.

But a siren told him otherwise. The no-stop promise he'd made to himself was about to bite the dust.

As he eased the rig off to the side of the road, his sleepy passenger stirred. "What's going on?"

"I got ahead of myself, I guess."

"Police?" She turned to the side mirror.

"I couldn't have been speeding. Not with this load." He reached across her, aiming for the glove box. "What's the matter, Joey? I didn't think you could turn any whiter."

She said nothing.

Nick wasn't sure how to go about reassuring her, seeing as he didn't know what he'd done. In his case, being "off the reservation" really meant something. And he didn't enjoy seeing his reflection in some white guy's sunglasses as he handed over license and registration—the signed, sealed and certified combination of his personal and prized documentation. It was especially nerve-racking when those papers left his sight in the hands of "the law." Nick tried to keep an eye on them in the side mirror, unconsciously tapping the steering wheel with his fingertips while the cop put his information through the legal strainer.

"I don't know about where you come from, Mr.…Red Shield, is it? But here in Nebraska we use lights on the back of both the pickup and the trailer. You don't have any trailer lights."

"Yeah, I do." Of all the accusations Nick had considered in his mental run-through, this one hadn't made the list. "This is practically a new trailer."

"It's a nice one," the cop said. "But no lights. You do the wiring yourself, Mr. Red Shield?"

"No. I had—"

"Who's this you've got with you?" Young, eager, feeling the weight of the uniform, the officer angled his fresh little face to get a better look past Nick's hawk beak. "Ma'am? Are you all right?"

"She's fine, except for feeling a little sick."

"I'm asking the lady. Do you need any help, ma'am? You look like you had a run-in with a tomahawk."

Nick tried to resist, but his pride wouldn't have it. He shot the man a glare worthy of war paint.

"Thank you for your concern, Officer, but…" She gave a little titter. "Tomahawk, I get it. He's joking, Nick. And it flew right past me. Oh! Flew past me. Get it?" She punched his arm. "Oh, it hurts to laugh. But it helps, too, after the day we've had. No, sir, everything's all taken care of."

"Did something happen today? It looks like it just happened."

"She had an—"

"I spooked the horses when Nick was trying to get them loaded. Sooo stupid. I've been around horses all my life, and nothing like this has ever happened to me before. I don't know what I was thinking."

"You're taking her to a doctor, right?"

"I'm—"

"He already did. Turns out, it looks a whole lot worse than it really is." She touched his arm, easy this time. "I'll bet that's what happened to the trailer lights, Nick. When those two geldings… Officer, you can't believe what a ruckus I caused. The wonder is that we even have a trailer, after the way they kicked—"

"Is this your wife, Mr. Red Shield?"

"This is—"

"Oh, no, I'm just…Nick's hauling my horses for me. I'm so sorry about the lights. We had no idea, did we?"

"They were working," Nick said doggedly, be-grudging her not so much her quick thinking as the play itself, the role she'd carved out for herself and the one she'd left for him.

"They were working just fine. I'll pay for the repairs, Nick, I promise. And the ticket, if you feel you have to cite us, Officer. What's one more headache after all the trouble we've had today?" She gave an over-the-top sigh. "My own fault, I know."

"I didn't—"

"I know you didn't, Nick, but I can say it. It really was all my fault. You didn't bargain for some ditz getting all panicky over…" She turned in her seat. "Officer, I would be so grateful if you could let us be on our way. We don't have far to go, and I really don't feel well. The doctor said I might have a slight concussion."

"It could be a short in the wiring," said the shiny young fellow, copping a whole new tune. "You'll have to get this fixed, but get her home first. Ma'am, you let Mr. Red Shield take care of unloading the horses for you, all right?"

"I will. I promise."

"You're sure you'll be all right?"

"I'm fine, Officer. Thank you so much."

"She's not fine," said the officer, just between us men.

"No shit," Nick grumbled.

"You were going a few miles over the limit, but under the circumstances, I'm gonna look the other way on that one, too."

Nick watched in the side mirror as the patrol car pulled a U-ie across the median and headed east.

"Are you always that quick with the bullshit?" he asked as he maneuvered the rig back onto the road. He still occupied at least one driver's seat.

"It worked, didn't it?"

"Didn't even make any sense."

"Of course it did. If I didn't come up with something, he was going to think I was afraid to talk."

"You look like you've seen a doctor like I look Irish. If he really fell for it, he needs to get himself a different job."

"He did his job. He's not a detective. All he needed was a reasonable explanation."

"Why didn't you tell him the truth?"

"Because the worms must be kept in the can. At least for a while." She turned her attention to the side window, where the view of plowed fields hadn't changed much throughout the day. It was springtime in Nebraska. "Where are we, anyway?"

"Like you said, we don't have far to go." Hell, he could match her for questions dismissed.

"We'll be stopping soon?"

"The Arabs are gettin' off the bus at Ogallala. We're almost to the state line."

"I must have slept quite a while."

"What about you, Joey? Where's your stop?"

"You passed it."

"Right."

"But I'm not complaining. I'll catch it next time around."

It was almost funny, the woman acting like she'd done him some big favor. He didn't mind seeing her get a little wind back into her sails, even if she'd done it at his expense. Anything was better than standing by while she'd puked up what little she'd eaten.

He'd planned to pick up the stud and finish his run without another stop, but he was fast learning that plans were made to be broken with Joey tagging along. His customer in Ogallala seemed happy with his new horses, which only proved to Nick that one man's herd of knotheads was another's dream team. But he kept his opinions to himself, pocketed the man's payment and accepted his help with fixing the trailer lights while Joey listened to him for once and stayed in the pickup. In return, he decided that she deserved a comfortable night's rest. They were back on the road with enough daylight left to allow him to see his stud, pay off his debt and maybe hit Joy and Gwendolyn up for a night's lodging for the two fillies he'd picked up in Lincoln.

Comfortable with his new plan, he took the turnoff to the Painted Ladies Ranch.

"Well, okay." Joey stared as they passed the sign. "So I'm definitely staying in the truck this time."

"It won't take long to do my business and pay my bill. These ladies are a lot of fun. Friendly, real hospitable. I'll leave the fillies, and we can go get a room…or two."

"Which road did we take when it forked back there? Are we in Nevada?"

"What happened to geography being your best subject?"

"Wyoming, then? Are places like this legal in Wyoming?" He questioned her with a look. "The sign says 'The Painted Ladies Ranch,' for Pete's sake. You think I don't know what this is?"

"You can't see my stud if you don't get out of the pickup." He raised an eyebrow. "Who's hackin' on who here?"

"If one of us were teasing, it wouldn't be me. I did my show for Mr. Policeman. Even if I had the heart right now, it would hurt my face too much. And it's impossible to tell about you, Mr. Red Shield, since you hardly ever crack a smile."

"I've got my face to consider, too."

"I'm considering it as we speak. Solid. Stiff. Quite studly, yes, but you might get a reduced rate from your friendly, fun-loving ladies if you could soften that serious—" Her eyes brightened. "There you go. I'll see your stud now that you raised me a smile."

"How you talk, woman." Eyes on the road, he shook his head. His mouth would not stay straight. "How you talk."

But once again she hid her face in the pickup while he took care of his business. The Painted

Ladies' owners, Joy and Gwendolyn, were expecting
him. Joy ignored the hand he extended, forcing a wet
kiss on his neck, while Gwendolyn appraised the
new trailer and asked him straight out how much he'd
had to give for it. The fillies were granted a pen and
hay on the house, payment and papers were exchanged, and Nick turned down the offer of a night's
lodging for himself on the excuse that he had
someone with him.

"You go out there and get him, bring him on in,"
Joy suggested with an expansive gesture. "We've got
plenty of room."

"He didn't say if it was man or mare," Gwendolyn scolded.

The ladies peered at him, waiting for clarification.

"She's asleep."

Still they peered.

He lifted a single shoulder. "She's had a rough time
lately. That's all I know."

And it was more than he felt like telling, but there
it was, just in case Joey stepped out of the pickup either
looking like a woman on her way to losing her cookies
or acting like one determined to win an Oscar.

Truth was, Nick didn't know too much about
anybody, including Joy and Gwendolyn. No more
than he needed to. The ladies ran a nice little operation, raised good horses and knew how to treat a
customer. Collecting unnecessary information about
people had always struck him as a rude enterprise.

"She doesn't want to stay?" Joy asked.

"She's asleep." That was all they would get out of him. He glanced out the dusty office window toward the barn. "Is he around?"

"Of course he's around. You think we'd let him out of our sight with you on your way to close the deal?"

"The man hasn't seen his horse in months, Joy. Can't you see he's dying here?" Gwendolyn slapped him on the back. "Come have a look. You're leaving him overnight, too, right?"

"If it's no trouble. Just wanted to stop in and take care of all the details. I'm planning on getting an early start," he said as he followed the pair across the sage-dotted yard.

Typical of serious breeders who lived with their horses, the best facilities on the place were built for the animals. The small ranch-style house had an office and a comfortable front room, with slip-covered furniture where the ladies had served him strong coffee and white bread sandwiches a time or two. But, man, they had a nice setup outside. They wasted no time growing anything just for show. The only grass that wasn't native was a half section of alfalfa. There was a fence around their vegetable garden, which hadn't been planted yet, a henhouse and a pretty little pond. The rest was maybe half a million dollars worth of housing for horses.

"It doesn't look to me like your friend is sleeping," Gwendolyn said as they passed his pickup on the way to the paddock on the west side of the barn. "She's sure welcome to come in and make herself—"

"I told her all that." He noticed some movement in the cab. Looked like lazy ol' Alice had taken on a new life as a playful kitten, boxing with some toy Joey had rigged up for her. "Like I said, we're not really friends. She's just hitchin' a ride."

"Maybe I should go say—"

Gwendolyn grabbed Joy's arm. "Maybe you should help me mind our business and reassure our buyer that you won't be stickin' your nose into his."

Nick was past caring what any woman was up to at the moment. He had only one thing on his mind, and that was the horse he'd gladly traded the equivalent of the skin off his back to get. He knew exactly what that meant; he'd done it before. Hell, for the papers in his hand and the dream-come-true standing in front of him, no question, he would do it again.

The lithe and leggy boy had filled out, slicked off and turned himself into a prince among horses. In Nick's eyes the two-tone beauty wore the plush black tail and silky mane as royal attire and carried his head as though he'd been born to rule. Nick's involuntary chuckle was part appreciation, part pure wonder that an image of anything as foreign to him as royalty would spring to mind, that Nick Red Shield would actually feel giddy, and that he could barely resist the urge to tip his head back and unleash some weird, wild and winning howl.

The stallion turned his glossy head and pricked his ears in a show of mutual interest.

"Are you going to run him?" Gwendolyn asked.

"Race?" It wasn't the question so much as the sound of an ordinary voice that surprised him, and he spared it only marginal attention. "Haven't decided."

"I almost named him Roll Your Own. He's got all the makins'. Of course, you know that. I've been impressed from the first with all you know about bloodlines."

"As far as horse sense goes, you're almost as impressive as Gwennie," Joy said. "I'm not a particular fan of horse racing myself, but it would be fun to see what this one could do."

"Main thing for him to do is make babies."

Gwendolyn laughed. "Most males would kill for that job."

"Some would. Some have." He couldn't stop smiling as he waited for the horse to complete his majestic, if shifting, approach, weighing curiosity against caution. He spared Gwendolyn a glance, and his chuckle could have passed for a nicker. "How's that for awareness?"

"Student of history, are you?"

"My partner's the history man." He could almost hear Dillon having himself one hell of a laugh over Nick offering even the slightest comment on the nature of man. Like he cared. "I'm all about the horses, and this is as good as it gets. Get him home, get to know him, then we'll see." He offered his palm for the horse's inspection. "No rush, huh, boy?"

"We'll leave you two alone," Joy said. "If I miss you tomorrow, stay in touch with us, Nick. Let us know how this big boy's doing."

Distantly aware of their departure, he credited the Painted Ladies for delivering perfection—the perfect horse and the perfect private moment. It was sunset at the edge of the prairie. In the cool coming of evening, warm breath filled the space between the mouth that would take a bit and the fingers that would ply the reins. But this was a moment to be savored in its purity, before the testing of strength, wit or trust. It was like a mother finally face-to-face with her newborn after all the waiting and the work. All things were equal now. There were no names, ranks or numbers. Velvet muzzle nuzzled veteran hand.

Hello, you.

His next action came as instinctively as the last. *Get Joey over here.* He turned and found her standing near the pickup, watching and waiting. She'd draped his denim jacket over her shoulders, and the sleeves dangled nearly to her knees. With a nod, he beckoned her to join him at the fence.

The horse took as much interest in Joey's hand as he had in Nick's. Maybe more. Envious, Nick imagined walking his own lips over the same small hand.

Looking for what, for God's sake?

Indulgence, maybe a little petting. No more than any stud would enjoy.

Nick felt a smile coming on.

"This big boy's going to have plenty to say for himself," Joey was telling him. "You won't have to send out announcements, Nick. You've got yourself something quite special."

"I do, don't I?" He didn't need assurances, but he liked the warm way her words struck him, like the sun's last rays spiking a puffy cloud. "I wanted you to meet Joy and Gwendolyn, but they can be kinda nosy."

"I'm not feeling especially presentable."

"All banged-up, you still look twice as good as any woman I've ever brought along for the ride."

"I knew it." She punched his chest with her fingertips. "That business about me being the first, that's such a line."

"Let's say, any I've ever *imagined* comin' along with me."

"Thank you," she said quietly. "I don't need any more questions about my face."

He knew the feeling. "The fillies are on their way up to Casper. Ever been there?"

"Oh, yes. Many times." She caught him before he could ask. "But I don't know a soul there."

"You're pitiful, you know that? You've been lots of places, but you don't know anybody. No family…"

"No friends," she finished for him. "Pathetic, I

know. And shameless. Quite ready to take advantage of your willingness to pity me."

"You've got a way of looking up at me with those big black-and-blue eyes that's hard to resist."

"If you've got it, flaunt it. That's my motto."

"You hear that, True?" *True.* The name had a strong feel. Nick was suddenly all smiles and sharp wit. "When a female starts in with the flaunting, just you remember—what you want, they've all got it."

"You're onto us, huh? And you said I was the first woman you'd taken for a ride."

"Ain't exactly what I said."

"Close enough. I can't wait to see True's harem," she enthused, and Nick questioned her with a look. "You know, the mares you've got lined up at home, just waiting for him. Painted ladies in waiting."

"If you're ever in the neighborhood, stop in and we'll show you around."

"I'll do that."

He nodded. "Be sure to call first. I'm on the road a lot, and my partner's the kinda person you wouldn't wanna be dropping in on unexpected."

"Man or woman?"

"Don't matter."

"Your partner," she insisted. "Man or woman?"

"Depends," he said, feeling playful. "Sometimes it's hard to tell. It's just the two of us out there, so we're not too picky."

"About what?"

"I'm just sayin', be sure to call first."

She tossed her hair, catching a glint of sunlight. "You're a very mysterious man, Nick Red Shield."

"Yeah, real mystery man." He chortled. "I still don't even know your full name."

"Don't matter," she muttered. A poor mimicry of his deep voice, it nevertheless won her an unintended smile. The instant she tried to return the favor with a look she probably imagined as cute and saucy, he wished he'd held back. She reminded him of a black velvet painting of a mock-happy clown.

He was glad she was nowhere near a mirror.

"So you're inviting yourself for a visit to the Wolf Trail," he surmised as he walked her back to the pickup and opened the door for her. Figured it wouldn't hurt to practice some white man's gallantry now that he owned a prince of a horse.

"Is that your ranch?" she asked, and he dipped his head to confirm. "I'm pretty sure you invited me. *If you're ever in the neighborhood, stop in.* Wasn't that an invitation? Not the most enthusiastic or heartfelt one I've ever received, but in your case, I'll take what I can get." She gave a coy smile. "Especially since I'm planning to be in the neighborhood."

"And when will that be?"

"Depends."

"On…?"

"Weather. Road conditions. The good working order of this vehicle and the good humor of its driver."

"Sadly, lady, you've got me pegged all wrong. No humor. Don't even try tellin' me a joke." With Joey settled in, he closed the door and thumped the open window frame. "But the vehicle seems to be working just fine. Nothin' short of a miracle, with all she's been through. So you've got your vehicle. Don't be lookin' for humor on top of it."

Circling the front of the pickup, he sensed that he had a tail. Sure enough, the cat jumped in ahead of him as soon as he opened the door.

"Hello, kitty, what's that you've— Yikes!" The cat bounded onto the front seat, up to the top of the backrest, pausing long enough to display her find, and then leapt down into the back. "Nick, I think she's got a mouse."

"She's a cat."

"But she just brought a mouse in here."

"Supper's pot luck tonight," he told her as he busied himself with his keys, ignition and seat belt. "But don't worry. I'll get you something else. Wanna try some more chicken?"

"You know what's missing from your humor? You're so funny, you forget to laugh."

"So does everyone else, which is why I don't tell jokes. I've been warned." He chuckled as he pulled out onto the road, remembering one of Dillon's empty offers. "Hell, I can get paid not to tell jokes."

"By somebody who has nothing better to do with his money? Who would that be?"

"My partner loves to throw money around. Crazy pastime, if you ask me, stuffing your money in other people's pockets."

"For not trying to be funny?"

"He says it's worth it."

"Settling the earlier question of gender," she pointed out. "What's his name?"

"Dillon. After the cowboy, not the singer."

"And it's just the two of you out there together," she concluded. "You don't have a family?"

"I've got a partner," he repeated with exaggerated patience. "And he's family."

"That's all you've got?"

"Hey, I'm one up on you." He glanced askance. "All right, yeah, I've got some younger sisters and the usual relatives. But I'm on the road a lot. They see me when they see me."

"Lucky them."

"If there's a need, they know they can call me. Like when somebody gets left out in the rain and needs a place to stay."

"Yes," she said softly. "Lucky them."

"Lucky us." He set his turn signal toward a vacancy sign. "Room at the inn, or so it appears. Wanna go in with me and see which face gets the most stares?"

Joey declined Nick's invitation, as well as his offer to get her a separate room. Both passes pleased him. Staring eyes made his skin crawl, and the two of them together—a small, beat-up white woman in the company of a big, mean-looking Indian—they'd already drawn their share. So much for being presumed innocent.

Not that he had any illusions left about the way most of the world viewed his face. He stood out in a crowd, which was plenty of excuse for not being anywhere two or three were gathered, no matter what the purpose. He wasn't like Dillon. Wherever there was a fight so Indians could be heard, Dillon would be there, speaking up like the mighty wind. Nick would be keeping mightily to himself. It hadn't always been by choice. Thanks to endless days and nights in a hospital bed, he'd read all the books, he'd seen all the movies, and he knew all the lines. But he rarely spoke them. He'd done way more prattling in Joey's presence than he was used to.

Even before doing his "big empty" time in the hospital, he'd been inclined to keep his thoughts to himself. Going all the way back to junior high school, he'd been tagged "big Indian." Not only because he was big, which he was, and dark-skinned—great for scar cammo—but mainly because he wasn't one to run at the mouth. He wasn't out to prove anything. Figured as long as he wasn't bothering anybody, he shouldn't have to.

And neither should the tiny woman with the big fresh hurt. With nothing of her own to haul into the room, she'd settled on the cat. Walking tall and feeling like he'd won the lottery, the Nick he never knew

followed along chanting some lame verse about the woman taking the cat and the cat taking the mouse. But he got no laughs, no credit for being the only show in town. Didn't matter. He was on a roll. He unloaded his baggage, shooed the cat away from the bag of take-out food they'd detoured to buy, glanced up and realized the problem.

Joey had discovered someone in the mirror above the sink. She leaned closer, peered for a moment as though she wasn't sure who the woman was, and then closed her eyes. *Oh, yeah, it's me. I remember now.*

He tried to imagine her with the kind of a man who would do this to her. He'd known a few. There wasn't much to them. A big temper, but nothing much otherwise. One of his sisters had been with a guy like that. Hard to understand how a woman could be too unhappy over losing something so worthless.

But Joey was feeling bad over something more important to her than her face, and that something was probably a man. He would be some sharp-dressed, sharp-looking, sharp-tongued white dude, and right now the woman was looking at her face in the mirror and worrying whether it would sicken this guy, the spineless wonder who'd left her beside the road. He'd be sorry, she was thinking. By now she was probably hoping for a knock on the door. That would be *her* miracle.

But when she opened her eyes, she looked not at her own reflection but at Nick's. She gave a small smile, squared her shoulders and tried to fix up—rearranging her hair, wetting her puffy lip with a careful tongue.

"Does it still hurt?" he asked quietly.

"Kind of a dull ache. Not throbbing as much as it was this morning. But it almost looks scarier now than it did." She turned to him. "It scares you, doesn't it? My face scares you."

"Hardly." He stepped back, away from the mirror and the light, unwilling to lend his own face to such close examination. "It did at first, but knowing I wasn't the cause of it makes it easier. Not for you, of course, but for me."

"It looks worse than it feels."

"You're talkin' to a guy who knows better." His hand itched to touch her, but he didn't know where or how. "You'll be okay."

She nodded.

"Even better if you stay away from him." He turned to the jumble of paper bags he'd just set beside the TV, which was bolted to the dresser, which was nailed to the wall. "It's none of my business," he muttered into his shirtfront as he leaned over to pull some of his purchases from one of the bags. "Just a suggestion."

"A good one. Getting away and staying away was exactly what I had in mind. But my plan didn't work out quite the way I wanted it to."

He turned to her, a pair of small jeans and a long-sleeved cotton T-shirt in one hand, and a pair of clunky shoes that probably wouldn't fit her in the other. The stuff he'd bought earlier was nothing compared to the challenge he had no right to make.

How about a plan for putting the bastard behind bars?

She glanced away quickly, as though she could see the question in his eyes and it embarrassed her. Like she was to blame for something.

Rarely did he feel like asking for the details of anyone's life. Anything most people volunteered was more than he wanted to know, and he knew damn well this should be no exception. Asking personal questions was a way of implying that you had a free shoulder and you didn't care if it got wet. Damned if he would ask. She could tell him what she wanted him to know. He didn't need to be saying shit like…

"You wanna tell me about it?"

She shook her head.

Good. He'd made a once-in-a-lifetime offer, and she'd rejected it. He should have been relieved, but he stood there hanging his head like a kid ready to say please.

"I don't know if this stuff will fit." Thank God for the small favor of something even less appealing to talk about. "I wanted you to pick something out at the truck stop, but you disappeared on me. They didn't have much in the clothing department."

"Oh, Nick." She took his gifts without any inspection. "You are the sweetest man. Thank you."

"Yeah, well, wait till you try them. Don't be offended if they're too big. I was way off my turf."

"But I…"

"You can't get around the horses dressed in what you've got on. I don't want that whopper you told the cop to come true," he said as he released what had begun to feel like hot potatoes into her hands. "You want first crack at the shower?"

"You go first." She looked up at him, all teary. "I'd love a long, hot soak."

His throat went prickly on him. *Damn her eyes.*

He took the bed closer to the outside door to give her proximity to the bathroom. She'd eaten only part of a hamburger—he knew what part because she'd asked him to finish it for her—but if that didn't agree with her, he wanted to let her think she could sneak off to the bathroom any time without bothering him. The fact that she was bothering him more all the time was his problem, not hers. He did what he could to make things easier. He wore jeans and a T-shirt to bed, faced the outside wall, sheltered his head with the extra pillow in an attempt, however futile, to cover the second base of bother. At least he would see none and hear none, and he promised himself that if he spoke none, he would have all three bases under control.

But she crossed him up completely. At the touch of her hand on his shoulder, he stiffened like a deer headed home on the roof of his ol' man's Chevy.

"Do you mind if I sleep with you tonight, Nick?"

He pulled the worthless pillow down and rolled onto his back. "You mean…"

She sat down on the bed. "I'll be very quiet and very, *very* still. I promise."

By way of invitation he tossed the pillow past his head to the empty space next to it, staring all the while at the ceiling. The mattress gave so little beneath her weight that he couldn't be sure exactly what she was doing unless he looked, which he wouldn't. He could feel the length of her beside him. Head-to-toe warmth. Head-to-toe itch. Head-to-toe bother.

Toes, he didn't worry about.

"Joey? I'm not gay."

"Okay."

One small word in the dark. One giant statement to hold up to the light.

"When I told you about my partner, that's what you thought, wasn't it?"

"Isn't that what you wanted me to think?"

"I was putting you on. Kidding."

No comment.

"I just want to make to make sure you understand that I'm…not gay."

"Whatever you say, Nick."

"It's not only what I say," he explained patiently. "It's the way it is."

"What I don't understand is why it matters." She gave a soft laugh. "Your partner's right. You shouldn't try to be funny."

He hadn't been trying to be funny; he'd been trying to have fun. He was pretty sure he knew the difference. And he was damn sure it mattered.

6

Even with his glasses on, Dillon Black could not believe the sight unfolding on the ground below him, right in front of his sore eyes. The big blue dually had just rolled to a stop, the doors had opened, and what to Dillon's wondering eyes should alight but a tiny woman. Nick had brought a woman home.

A little bit of a thing wearing somebody else's clothes, but she sure walked like a woman. Dillon couldn't hear much from where he stood atop his makeshift painter's scaffold, but he could see the way she was talking, just like a woman. Nick wasn't doing much talking back, but that was just Nick acting bucky. Once a big Indian, always a big Indian. He was the last of the great Indian hand talkers, that guy, sparing the woman a slight nod and a heavy-handed gesture, something about the barn and the hills out back.

But since his partner was supposed to be coming home with an essential piece of their business plan, there damn sure better be a horse in that trailer, Dillon told himself as he set aside his paint scraper. Not that Nick was the kind of guy who would trade the cow for magic beans—a move like that would be more like Dillon's own style—but there was a first time for everything. As far as Dillon knew, this was the first time Nick had ever picked up a passenger on one of his stock-hauling runs. Not only picked one up, but brought one home. And a woman to boot.

Dillon couldn't wait to have a closer look. Bracing a hand on the platform, he took the five-foot hop and made a solid two-foot landing next to the big front door of his transplanted church. Good landing, good score, good first impression. Embarrassing Nick in front of a female guest, whatever their connection, would not do. It was one of many considerations Dillon took upon himself out of respect for the man he loved like a brother. Not that Nick would ever see Dillon as a brother—anybody claiming that particular chair at Nick's table risked losing more than his seat—but Nick's tunnel vision was no harder to deal with than Dillon's myopia. Except for the part about the ugly glasses, which he furtively tucked into his shirt pocket.

He approached the couple with his usual swagger,

but nobody seemed to notice. Beyond any topic of conversation, they had a considerable togetherness going on between them. Dillon had a nose for such things. But he also had eyes, and the closer he got, the clearer his focus, and the queasier he was feeling about the look of Nick's woman. She'd been worked over, and the damage was fresh.

"Joey, Dillon Black," Nick said. "My partner."

"Pleasure, ma'am." Dillon gave the lady a handshake and his partner a theatrical aside. "Tell me you didn't do this."

"She says she doesn't have anyplace to go," Nick explained.

Dillon could have predicted his comment's flight path. Straight up and over his partner's head.

"I had an accident," the woman recalled in a voice whose echo came across as its own astonishment. "It was crazy, really. Nick stopped to help me, and then, when he couldn't figure out what else to do with me, he let me ride along with him."

Dillon appraised the cuts and bruises with a deep whistle. He could feel Nick's disapproval, but knowing Nick…"You figured out she needed a doctor, though, right?"

"Right."

Dillon got the point. Nick was ready to step between prying eyes and pitiful injured party. But this was no time for Nick to be taking a person at her word, not a female-type person. Half the time they didn't even want to be taken at their word, as anyone who'd ever been married to one could verify.

"It's really not as bad as it looks. Really," the woman insisted, making it two *really*s, which canceled each other out, according to Dillon's math. But she smiled and flashed her rescuer a look so appreciative that Dillon had to wonder whether the ol' boy might have permitted her to thank him properly somewhere along the road. "I was just lucky Nick found me," she enthused. "It was dark and desolate, and it was raining cats and dogs."

"That explains it." Dillon slapped Nick's chest with the back of his hand. "You took her for a stray."

"I took her for a deer," Nick said.

"Are we talkin' the sweet kind of dear, or the kind with hooves?"

"Hooves."

"Ah, Deer Woman." Dillon slipped the woman a subtle wink while he made a pretense of counseling his partner. "You realize we'll both be dead by morning, cuz, but what a way to go."

"You go away with your damn mythology," Nick said, holding firm against the threat of a smile. "Unless you're interested in having a look at a real stud."

"He's a beautiful animal," the woman confided, giving Dillon a tentative glance to let him know she didn't quite know what to make of him but was willing to give him a temporary pass. "Excellent choice."

"Thanks. You, too." He chuckled. She was still half

a beat behind, but catching up. "No kidding, you've got good instincts. Most people would wait for another ride rather than get in with this guy. He's got a helluva bark on him, but he don't hardly ever bite."

"She knows that," Nick said over the rattling of trailer latches. "Better than you, looks like, for all your talk about good instincts." He shot Dillon an unmistakable warning glance before he disappeared into the trailer. *Keep your mouth shut until I come out.*

But Nick had to build a little suspense, leaving Dillon to stand at attention in the rutted hardpan driveway. Man and horse shifted around inside the trailer, where small talk was permitted—easy boy, ho, easy—while the man fussed over the horse's appearance with a degree of attention he would never afford himself. Nick was probably the one person Dillon knew who never made an entrance. Ah, but give the man a horse… Not until the travel kinks were combed out and the dust brushed off the animal's sleek hide did Nick make his presentation.

"Now, that's what I'm talkin' about," Dillon crooned as Nick led the Paint in a circle around his audience of two. "That picture of him you've got hangin' in the kitchen? I thought sure it was airbrushed. But he's even better lookin' in person." With an easy approach, Dillon invited the horse to check him out before offering to pet him. "You sure know your horses, Nick."

"That I do." Nick turned to his new friend. "It'll

only take a minute to make this boy comfortable, and then I'll figure out something for you."

"You need help?" Dillon asked.

"I'll help," the woman said quickly.

Nick almost smiled. "That's two more offers than I know what to do with."

But the woman knew. Without a word, she claimed the lead rope and looked to Nick to show her where to go. She wasn't letting the man out of her sight. What was the old womanly wisdom? When you go to a dance, stick with the man that brung you. This one was sticking, all right, following that man straight to the barn. Maybe for a little Lakota two-step?

Dillon hung back and took in the strange show. It pleased him on the one hand; on the other, maybe it rankled a bit. People usually took to Dillon right away. It was Nick they were never too sure about, and Dillon had made a habit of preparing the way. *He won't seem too friendly at first, but once you get to know him…*

Be damned if Nick hadn't gotten something going on his own this time.

Maybe Dillon should have bitten his tongue on his usual *helluva bark* remark.

Nick was fond of Dillon's cooking. Of course, he preferred almost anyone's cooking to his own, and he never offered a hand when better hands were available. But Joey-on-the-spot was a different story. She pitched right in with the potato salad, looking for

alien components like a rubber spatula and celery. This was the Wolf Trail, for crissake. But Nick didn't have to say anything. As long as Dillon had all the answers, Nick was free to sit at the kitchen table with a book and wait for his supper.

It was good to be back. His trailer home was no palace, but it met his needs. It was a warm, comfortable place to come home to. He had his bed, his books, all the necessary facilities and then some. A little company once in a while didn't bother him, either. The picture would have been perfect, except that with all the chatter going on in the galley, a guy couldn't possibly keep track of what he was reading.

Dillon had his ways of doing things with whatever was on hand, but could he just shut up and get the job done? Hell, no. He had to try her way. Don't cut the root end of the onion off first? How clever. Man, he'd have to put this knife to the whetstone, but be damned if her trick wasn't working just slick. No tears!

Just chop the goddamn onion, Dillon. It's the knife that's working.

More precisely, it was Dillon's hand working the knife while he jacked his jaw and kept Joey entertained. No glasses, Nick noticed. Dillon was always pretty vain when it came to the glasses. Joey had pulled her hair back and tied a towel around her waist—no vanity there, but she only had the one shirt—and the two of them were standing hip to hip, or close to it, merrily making supper for the real man, who didn't hang out in the kitchen. Not in how many years?

Plenty.

"That's plenty," Nick barked. He wasn't sure when he'd left the table and stationed himself behind the island divider where he could see what was so damned exciting about this onion. The two faces turned, questioning his judgment. Hell, he knew what he liked.

But he rarely felt the need to tell anyone. Committed, he lifted one shoulder. "Too much onion spoils the potato salad."

"You're kidding," said Dillon, eyeballing Nick as though he'd just shaved his head or something.

"No, he's right," Joey said. "Let me finish the potato salad. We'll wrap up the extra onion, and you'll have it already chopped for something else. I did find some pickles. What about the eggs, Nick?"

"Lots of eggs."

"How about a touch of mustard?"

"I never use mustard." Dillon interjected.

"Mustard sounds great." One by one the muscles in Nick's shoulders unraveled. *When had he tensed up?* "But you make it your way. I'm not picky."

"Never used to be, anyway," Dillon muttered. "I suppose I should ask you how you want your burgers. Knock off the horns and wipe the ass?"

"You don't want to get E. coli from rare beef," Joey warned.

"You hear that, partner? You go poisoning me,

you'll never be able to live with yourself or my share of the business. Cook 'em up healthy." He turned to Joey. "Do they have to be burnt?"

"Cooked through," she instructed. "Brown is better than pink."

"Hear that, partner? Brown over pink."

"Have you tried it yet?" Dillon spared him a pointed glance as he tossed a red patty into the iron skillet. It hissed at him like a snake in the garden, and Dillon chuckled. "Brown over pink? Once you get started, you'll be coming back for more."

"As long as it's healthy," Nick said. "No time to be gettin' sick. I've got plans."

"Oh, it's healthy, cuz. And it's about time you got picky about what you eat. Time you got some new cooking stuff, too, like maybe one of them rubber things Joey was lookin' for."

"You make a meal in the kitchen you have." Nick slipped Joey a deadpan glance. "Not the kitchen you wish you had."

"Like he's some TV show cook," Dillon said. "Not that he ever watches TV."

"I watch the news."

"Not anymore," Joey put in. "Now that True Colors has come into your life, I can't see you wasting even a minute in front of a television set."

He shook off the impulse to ask how she *could* see him wasting his time.

"When do I get to see True Colors' harem?" she

asked. "Or should I say brood? They're broodmares, right? But a brood would be like chicks or something, wouldn't it?"

"This is a ranch, not a farm." Nick reached across the counter and plucked a hard-boiled egg from the small pan in the sink. "We don't do chicks."

"Speak for yourself, partner," the burger-flipper advised.

"I like *harem*," Joey said. "True Colors definitely deserves a harem."

"What you're tellin' us is, you're not a country girl."

"Not at all." Joey exchanged glances with Nick. He was rolling his egg between the counter and his palm, while she was a whacker-cracker. She smiled, amending, "I mean, that's not what I'm telling you. I'm saying a glorious specimen like True Colors has every right to expect them to be lining up at the barn door."

Dillon laughed. "Better yet, he has every right to herd his mares around and take his pleasure the way God intended. Can I get an amen, brother?"

"Amen." Nick slipped the shell off in one piece and laid the egg in Joey's hand. "Let's just hope they don't kick the hell out of him."

"If they did, then he wouldn't be much of a stud, now, would he?" Dillon judged. "There's a couple of 'em out there he'll have to show who's boss, but he looks like he can manage. Pretty soon he'll have 'em backin' up to him like a parade of tankers taking on liquid gold."

With a glance, Nick warned Dillon not to go there. Anything to do with trucking oil was not to be mentioned under Nick's roof. "He's young," he said aloud.

Dillon shrugged. "So were we, once upon a time."

Bowl cradled in her left arm and spoon in hand, Joey turned to Dillon. "Maybe you'll clear something up for me. What's your relationship to each other? Partners, cousins, brothers, what?"

"All I know is, he gets all pissed when I call him Uncle Nicky."

"Uncle Nicky?"

"Or Grandpa. He's such an old man. You try to show him how to have a little fun, you're wasting your time. Believe me, we tried back when we were kids, but this guy—"

"You need to remember we're business partners and make sure you're takin' care of business," Nick said. "Did you fix that stock tank?"

"To me, he's like my older brother." Dillon caught Nick's glance as he moved the skillet off the hot burner. "Okay, *bigger* brother. You're bigger than I am. Hell, she can see that." He turned back to Joey. "And, no, I'm not his real brother." Loading up a platter, he gave a wave of the spatula between burgers. "I don't claim to *be* him," he said firmly, turning back to Nick. "I said *like*.

"And, yes, I got the parts for the stock tank. I haven't quite gotten around to fixing it yet, but in case you haven't noticed, it's spring, and every streambed in the country is filled with runoff." He switched tones for more delicate ears. "He forgets he's not the only one who has a real job."

"What do you do?" Joey asked as they carried supper to the table.

"I'm a dealer."

"A dealer?"

"Drugs. Name your poison, dear lady."

Nick groaned.

Dillon chuckled. "See? I've got the best poker face in the state."

"I knew you meant card dealer."

"I had you goin' for a second. Admit it. I know that look." Dillon gave a self-possessed look of his own. "Haven't seen it for a few years, but I know it well."

Joey set out a mixture of plates and utensils that had clearly served long and well, but she arranged everything on the table in a homey way. Nick gave Dillon credit for cleaning off the table somewhere along the line—it didn't get eaten off much—and decided to return the favor by fixing the stock tank.

"I'm sure I don't know what you're talking about," Joey was saying as she chose the chair across the table from Dillon.

"She even sounds a little bit like Monica, doesn't she? *I'm sure I don't know what you could be talking about.*"

"Your wife?"

"My ex-wife. Had a wife, but couldn't keep her. She wasn't much of a country girl, either. Hey!" A spoonful of potato salad had somehow inspired Dillon. "Here's one for you: What's a cowboy without a girlfriend?"

"I'm sure I don't know," Joey said, already smiling.

"Homeless," said Dillon.

"But you're not homeless."

"Ain't no cowboy, either," Nick informed her as he thumped the bottom of the ketchup bottle, unloading half the contents on his hamburger.

"Used to be," Dillon insisted. "I hung up my spurs for that woman, but she left me, anyway. Didn't want her babies growin' up to be cowboys. She got real nervous when our boy said he wanted to be a cowboy when he grew up. 'You have to choose,' she said to him. 'You can't do both.'"

Nick filled his mouth with overcooked hamburger and cold, runny ketchup while the two of them laughed.

"How old are your children?" she asked.

"Emily's almost eighteen and Dylan is thirteen. *Fourteen*. They sure don't stay babies very long. The growin' up part happens real fast."

"So I've heard."

"It's like one of those little sponge toys they get at a carnival. You put it in a glass of water, and the next morning it's full grown. You turn your back for a second, and those babies disappear. Little people turn into big people. When Emily was born, she was so small, she fit—"

"We get the point, Dillon." Nick wiped his fingers on the paper towel Joey had thought to put next to his plate. For all the red stuff dripping off them, he might have been the one who'd gone at the onions with a dull knife. "Aren't you working tonight?"

"Yeah. Late shift." Dillon was still staring at the empty cradle his hands formed.

"How far away are they?" Joey asked.

"Minneapolis. Less than a day's drive, but the days pass, and you get to makin' the drive less and less."

"How long has it been since you've seen them?"

"Emily came through here last fall on her way to start college. She's at U of M Western." He grinned. "Dillon, Montana."

"Also named for Matt Dillon?"

"I don't know if I'm named for…" He chuckled. "Yeah, I guess I am. I think my parents ran out of apostles."

"But your son is named for you."

"Actually, he spells it with a *Y* in the middle. Or his mother did."

"Like the singer," Joey said.

"Like the poet. And she named Emily for a poet, too. Monica likes poetry. You gotta be named for something, right? Ol' Nicholas here was aptly named for a saint."

"First Nicky, now Nicholas," Joey said, with a smile.

"And a man's name is his bond, right, partner?"

"Word," Nick grumbled. "It's his word, not his name."

"Aw, hell, words are a dime a dozen, but a name

says who you are and where you came from. My daughter found out about Montana Western because she saw her dad's name on the map and found out there was a college there. So she got to checking it out and found out they had this horse program, and her mind was made up. I mean, there was no more discussion."

"A woman after my own heart," Nick said as he pushed back from the table. They'd hardly touched their food, and he was finished. "I'm going out to the barn."

Pausing only to grab his hat, he made a direct but unhurried exit, gently closing the back door behind him. A deep breath of the South Dakota evening cleared his head. Standing there on the wooden step, ostensibly surveying his spread, he could hear their voices through the open window. He wasn't listening, but he had ears.

"He likes you."

"I don't think so. I'm afraid I'm a bit of bother."

"Oh, you're a big bother. A major bother. And nobody ever needed bothering more than good ol' Saint Nick."

It was just Dillon being Dillon, Nick thought. He was damn lucky Nick was immune.

Nick tossed his hat over the nearest saddle horn and plowed his fingers through his hair, one palm skimming over the scar he'd dubbed Dragon Lady. In its early days, it had looked like a brutal lover's long red fingers crawling up the side of his neck. It was one of many souvenirs of the day his waking memory all but denied. If it hadn't left its marks, he might have been able to strike that day—hell, strike the whole twenty-ninth year of his life—right off the books. But he had his indelible reminders. Each to his own form of body art, he reminded himself as he rubbed the crinkled skin.

He felt better now that he'd made a firm pact with himself. Every part of him, body and soul, was on notice. Other than keeping the one promise he'd made—and he wasn't sure anymore just how far he'd said he would go—but other than that, Nick Red Shield was not available. His mama hadn't raised no fool, and only a fool would offer himself up to be strung along by a woman with no last name. If Dillon wanted to take over where Nick had left off, so be it. If she expected Nick to help her get to a safe place, she needed to pick a dot on the map pretty damn quick. He had work to do.

He'd parked the trailer, unloaded some gear—not a pressing chore, but something to do—and set about stowing it in the stall he'd dubbed his tack room. Every halter had its hook, every saddle its rack. Before he knew it, he was singing, "Every cow…boy…"

A funny feeling stopped that noise cold. He had company. Smug, smiling and prettier by the hour.

A guy couldn't even warble in private.

"True Colors seems a bit disgruntled," she

reported, stepping out of the soft evening shadows into the cone of light cast by the bare bulb affixed to a rafter. "He's running the fence."

"He knows they're out there." Funny feelings ran true to his gender.

"His harem." She moved in on him, pushing her interest in his horses ahead of her. "When will you take me out to see them?"

"When I get time."

"The chores never quite get done, do they? Is there something I can do?" Skirting the rack of bins he'd built to create a divider for his sanctum, she affected a telephone voice. "How may I help you, sir?"

"You got the wrong number, lady. I didn't call for any help."

"So. You can dish it out, but you can't take it."

"Don't need it. Thanks, anyway."

Sooner or later he had to clear horseshit out of the trailer. If he'd done it sooner, she might have been quicker to get out of his way. As it was, he couldn't even get to the shelf behind her without nudging her over to one side, then back the other way. The woman's determination to take over his space had rankled since day one.

What day were they on now?

"Dillon's quite a guy," she said.

Sounded like a song to go along with the dance. Nick felt no obligation to join in.

"Your partner. Dillon."

Ignore her, and she'll go away.

"Partner and some sort of blood relative other than—"

"I know who you're talkin' about," he said patiently. "Yeah, he's a guy. I'm pretty sure I told you that."

Patiently? What happened to the good ol' Red Shield bark?

His better instincts—the ones that kept people at a distance—seemed to have deserted him.

"I was going to say, you're quite a pair, but I was afraid you'd…"

"That's two brilliant observations. Can't think of a thing I could add either way." He reached over her head and slipped the rings of two cotton cinches over one of the coat hooks he'd inherited from Dillon's church. "I mean, the word *quite* kinda says it all."

"You don't make it easy, that's for sure." She was peeking up at him from under his arm, her little nose inches from his beak.

Man, he could kiss her so easy right now….

He rubbed his chin on his denim jacket sleeve, staring into those disquieting blue eyes, letting her know she shouldn't expect any change. But since he had her cornered, he had to be the one to back off this time.

"So how does this work?" she asked artlessly. "Do you share everything fifty-fifty? Property, labor, expenses…"

"Women?" He challenged her innocence with a passing glance as he lifted the lid on the footlocker he'd taken with him along with his army discharge. "Sure way to kill a partnership."

"I should think so."

"Everything but True Colors. I bought him on my own."

"He's a gorgeous animal. I don't know much about breeding in Paints, but I do know something about syndicating horses, and a good stud—"

"That horse is mine." *Thwap* went the trunk lid under his hand. "One partner is more than my limit."

"You remind me of my father," she said, unfazed. Her attempt to get a look inside the trunk—on purpose or not—had been purposefully cut short. "He loved the horse business, and love was his reward."

"I've heard that love is its own reward. Personally, I wouldn't mind turning a profit." Nick planted one booted foot on the old G.I. chest and braced a hand on his troublesome knee. "Dillon's the romantic. He'll do anything for love. He's been workin' on that crazy old church building over there God knows how long, God knows why."

"For the love of God, maybe?"

He gave a dry chuckle. "Maybe. A little white town north of here wanted it moved, so he got it for practically nothing."

"A *white* town?"

"A town that belongs to white people. No offense. You got a better term?"

"I never thought of a town…" She laughed. "I had this image of a whole town painted white to match the church. Sorry. I'd never heard of a white town."

"Yeah, well, you're on the rez now. You're the minority. We gotta call you something." He squeezed the flesh around his stiffening knee. "So, Dillon, he can't resist a deal on something he calls 'a piece of history'—God knows whose history—and he buys himself a church. Movin' the damn thing, now that was another story, but he did it."

"With a little help from his partner?" she asked, and he lifted a shoulder. "That sounds like love."

"Real funny."

"Like a brother," she pressed. "Not a *real* brother because we seem to be touchy about that distinction, but helping him move a whole building, and a crazy one at that, well…" She gave him one of her benevolent smiles. "With some people, the love goes without saying."

"Guess you've got it all figured out."

"Not quite. I think Dillon misses Monica quite a bit, even though she broke his heart when she left and took the kids."

"He told you that?" *What a bullshitter, that guy.*

"Not in so many words, but like you said, he's a romantic. And he doesn't seem the type to swear off women and become a priest or a monk."

"You got that right."

"So I think he's building a house. He's making a house out of that church because he wants Monica back. It's like one big ongoing prayer. Am I on the right track?"

Nick lifted a shoulder. "You'd have to ask him."

"But he still cares for her, doesn't he?"

"You know what?" He didn't realize he'd been kneading his knee until he caught her glancing at his hand, which froze instantly. "I wasn't around him much when they were together. Their place was across the road, and he burned it down after she left."

"Burned it—"

"And if you want any more details, you'll have to ask him."

"I was only…" She stared at the hand on his knee. "What about you, Nick?"

"What *about* me?" He straightened his back, drawing his hand up to the middle of his thigh. "Are you gonna get personal with me now?"

"Not if you don't want me to." But she was closing in on him, thinking like any small creature sensing weakness in a bigger one. "When you lose someone you've been with…someone really close, like a wife or…someone like that, you know, it makes you a little crazy."

"So you're looking for a little company for your misery because you lost somebody on the road back there in bum-fuck Missouri?"

"No." She looked surprised, even wounded. "Not Missouri."

"Yeah, it was." It was his turn to press. "I found you in Missouri."

"That's not where it happened."

"Where *what* happened?" He leaned down, nose to nose, daring her to own up or back off. "I'd like to know, because I must've taken the wrong turn somewhere. I'm going down the road one minute, next thing I know I'm flyin' off course and then blowin' off my best-laid plan, all because I ran into you."

"And you didn't even run into me."

"Which means it makes even less sense." The look in her eyes was a serious source of irritation. Did she think she had some big dumb lug all set to roll over and play best friends? "I don't know who you are, and I have no idea why you're here."

"I'm here because you're a very sweet—"

He grabbed her by the shoulders.

"Stop it with that shit. I'm not sweet. Okay? I'm not—"

He had to kiss her. He had to put his lips against hers and taste that sassy mouth, tease that sharp tongue, give her the kiss they both needed. She met his mouth, caress for caress, stroke for stroke, measure for measure, and, God, how he wanted to hold every part of her against every part of him, pull out all the stops and grow this thing.

The sound of her protest was so small, he nearly missed it, but there was no mistaking the tears in her eyes. Touching her tongue to her bruised lip, she hung on to his jacket like a cat climbing a curtain.

"I'm sorry."

"No," she whispered. "Don't be."

He released his grip on her arm and touched the corner of her mouth with a blunt fingertip. "I wasn't thinking."

She held his apologetic gaze with the force of her own. Somehow she knew how hard it was for him to stand for this kind of exchange, how unnatural it felt for him to look her in the eye, the way he was feeling. It was an act that took his power away, but not his strength. She knew it, and still she played her hand. She released half her hold on his jacket, trailed her fingers along the path of his thigh, took his knee in hand and rubbed his deep-tissue ache like toothpaste from one part of the tube to another.

God help her when the cap came unscrewed.

"It's okay." She slid her other hand around his neck and drew him down, whispering against his lips, "Let's try gentle."

7

Nick loved morning light and spring chill mixed together. The world was golden, every old familiar thing renewed by the rising sun—chirpy sparrows and whistling hawks, thirsty dogs and curious cats, steam off his dream horse's fresh droppings and his own laughter as True Colors sprinted from pen to paddock like a kid distancing himself from the mess he'd just made. Never let it be said his majesty's shit didn't stink.

He noticed a light on in the kitchen as he headed back to the trailer. Something else was on the rise, and the absence of Dillon's car perked up even more promise. The aroma that blasted through the back door put Nick into a holiday frame of mind. If it was spring, this must be Easter.

"I hope you like pancakes."

Joey stood watch over the same cast-iron skillet Nick's mother had used, the one she'd given him the first time he'd set up housekeeping on his own. Joey smiled at him as she tucked a strand of butter-colored hair behind her ear. She'd clipped most of it high on the back of her head, but there were jaunty bits brushing her cheeks and the back of her neck. She had the look of a doll, made for play.

"Every red-blooded American boy likes pancakes." He set his cowboy hat on its crown on the shelf above the two coat hooks beside the back door and finger-raked his own shaggy hair. He kept it long enough to shield the back of his neck from cold air and colder eyes, but it was probably time to get it shaped up some.

"I believe it," she said, her tone turned wistful.

"Did you sleep all right?"

"I did, thanks." Busy pouring batter into the skillet from a glass bowl, she lifted one shoulder. "Well, I took a bunch of your ibuprofen."

"A bunch?"

"Three. Or so. Whatever, it was just enough and no more." The report was directed at the front of her shirt, and he wasn't sure whether she was uncomfortable with the fact that she was using the stuff or that she'd taken it from him. Before he could let her know that it was fine either way, she looked up and smiled. "How's True Colors this morning? I'll bet you were up at the crack of dawn."

He nodded, surprisingly pleased with her awareness of him.

"Did you try him out?" she persisted.

"He's green."

"And?"

"And it's the prettiest green you've ever seen," he confirmed, slipping her a smile on his way to the coffeepot.

"I'd love to take a turn around the track on him. I'm a pretty good rider."

"Soon as I get the track built, I'll give you a call."

"A turn around the pasture?" She flipped a pancake and tried again. "Maybe just one teeny circle around the barn, then."

She wasn't getting what *green* meant. "I've got a couple of nice saddle horses out there. We can take a ride after breakfast."

"Thank you for…last night."

"Did I miss something?" He figured she was playing some kind of trump card from a woman's personal deck. A couple of kisses were supposed to add up to gratitude on somebody's part.

"I don't think so. My guess is you rarely miss a beat. You gave me a bed last night. I'm not sure whose it was, but I'll try not to wear out my welcome."

"This is my house. The beds and everything else belong to me. I'll let you know when you're not welcome."

"Where's Dillon?"

Ah, there it was. The new attraction.

"I expect the boy's in church by now."

"Is it finished inside?" she asked offhandedly as she shoveled a big golden pancake onto a blue enamel tin plate.

"How do you mean, *finished*? There's electricity, but so far I only know of one junction box. The water's there whenever he settles on a place to run the pipes."

"Did I push him out of *his* bed?"

He raised his brow over a slurp of hot coffee. "Now, that I wouldn't know."

"You're the one who told me to take that room, but I didn't know—"

"Did you see him around here when we came back inside last night?"

"No."

"Well, there you go." He sipped again, giving her a moment to figure out where *there* was. "He went to work, remember?"

"That's right. The late shift." She gave a self-conscious laugh. "I wasn't sure what to expect, and the part about him working completely…" She tapped her temple wither index finger.

"You were afraid we'd be lookin' to go two on one?"

Her shoulders stiffened as she flashed him an icy look. "Where I come from, it's called *ménage à trois*. And it's not my sport."

"I agree. I got enough trouble with English." His smile was as tight as his gut. "I gave you the room I cleaned up before I left."

"Your room," she finally concluded. "You gave up your bed."

"Like I said…" He shook off the notion of repeating himself. Either they dropped the subject, no matter what the language, or get it on and get it over with. The welcome and its wearing out worried her, and the game with all its nuances wearied him. He stepped closer and peered into the skillet. "These are some interesting pancakes."

"You like those?"

"What's this?" A face with ears covered the bottom of the pan. "A bear?"

"Or a mouse. I guess it's pot luck."

"This one looks like a train engine." He pointed to the variety of shapes that had already been off-loaded onto a plate. "And a horseshoe."

"Made especially for red-blooded American boys. Oh, and I almost forgot." She shoved her hand into her jeans pocket and came up with his beaded key chain. "Thank you for humoring me. I was a little nervous about getting dumped again." She pressed the trinket into his palm and gave him a blue-eyed heartbreaker of a look. "I was actually pretty scared."

"You're not anymore?"

"Not like I was. I don't think I've ever met anyone quite like you before, Nick. I wish my father could have met you."

"Am I *quite like* him?" A little mocking, a little teasing—best way for a guy to keep his head on straight.

"Not *quite*." She flopped the mouse on top of the train. "You're more sensible. You have your dream, but you're going about fulfilling it in a practical way. My dad trained and raced his own horses on small tracks for small purses. Lots of claims races. He'd have a good horse one day, and the next day it would get claimed."

"Isn't that the name of the game? I haul all kinds of horses, so I hear lots of stories. Running horses through claims races is a gamble, just like anything else in the horse business. It's all about picking the right one."

"That's true. But my dad never got a chance to develop anything. When you're small-time and it's your whole livelihood, you tend to turn the horses over pretty quickly. You can only go so long without a paycheck.

"Dad would put a price on a horse in a claims race, and you'd have to keep a poker face around the paddocks before the start. You never knew who was betting, who was buying, and who was a tourist coming out to admire all the pretty horses. Dad was good at it. He could be friendly, easygoing, just as open and honest as you please without ever giving anything away."

"Like what?" He braced his butt against the sink and sipped his coffee. "What would he hold back?"

"Whether he was desperate for a win or a sale. The one thing you can't afford to be carrying around with you at the race track is desperation. And if you are, you can't let it show."

"A guy shouldn't get himself cornered like that."

"Really?" She raised an eyebrow, connecting with his hard-line stare. "I'm here to tell you, it happens to the best of us."

"Is *that* why you're here?"

"Yep. Your own personal messenger, sent by the Fates. Stay away from corners, Nick. Don't let anyone box you in," she instructed, punctuating with a wag of the spatula. "Room to maneuver—that's the key."

"You wanna see *room to maneuver*, you've come to the right place. Look it up in the encyclopedia, you'll find the Wolf Trail."

"I'd rather look at it from the back of a horse."

"You say you're a pretty good rider?"

"The truth is, I haven't been on a horse in quite a while. But I used to ride a lot. My parents split up when I was pretty young, but I spent a good deal of time with my father. I learned a lot from him."

"Like how to converse with somebody without giving anything away?"

"I don't think you need any lessons in that department," she said as she turned off the gas burner.

"Yeah, but my way, you just don't converse."

"That's hard to pull off in most circumstances."

"It was workin' pretty good for me until I ran into you." He reached over her to claim plates from the cupboard, so close that the edge of his jacket brushed her hair.

"You didn't—"

"Didn't run into you, I know. But somebody sure did."

"But I look better today, don't you agree?" She reached past him for the plate of pancakes, noticed her image in the shiny toaster, paused for closer scrutiny. "The swelling's gone. Cuts are scabbing over." She tilted her head, and the image ballooned. "Huge nose, tiny eyes, rubber-band lips."

"Right. This is a fun house, and you're the lead clown."

"The bruises are turning some pretty colors." Her quick turn surprised him, and he stepped back, little realizing that he was in for another surprise. "I have some doozies underneath my clown jeans. Wanna see?" She filled his free hand with the plate of pancakes, turned and pulled her shirt up and her waist-band down, exposing her black-and-blue hip. "This one looks like a map of Florida tattooed on my butt."

Nick caught his breath. The soft curve of her hip, the narrow waist, the slope to her spine, so smooth, so tender, so terribly discolored.

The back door swung open.

"Morning, buckaroos! Do I smell…uh…" The end of the narrow counter was all that separated Dillon from the examination going on in the kitchen. "Am I interrupting something besides breakfast?"

"The answer is yes." Nick shouldered past his snick-ering partner. "You're buttin' in, and you stink like—"

"I thought so. Because I've seen that look before.

I'm the father of two teenagers. Quick release is what that move is called." Dillon lifted the front of his white dress shirt to his nose. "I stink like what?"

"Fish bait. What are you angling for this morning?"

"I stink like smoke. In the casino biz, that's the smell of money." Leading with his nose, Dillon followed the plate in Nick's hand. "Mmm, pancakes are just about the best breakfast there is. Did you find the grape jelly? There's a new jar in the cupboard." The plate clattered to the table. "Hey, cool. This one has ears."

"Purely decorative. Kinda like those fry breads you're wearing." Nick said, indicating Dillon's ears with a jerk of his chin.

"Looks like there's plenty. I'll fill up a plate, take it to church with me, let you guys get back to what you were doing." He glanced over his shoulder as he reached for a fork. "Hey, can I have this Volkswagen? I've always wanted my own little bug."

Joey laughed. "Another red-blooded American boy."

"Yeah, great mileage on those suckers. I've heard a tank of gas and a good tailwind will get you halfway to Florida in one…"

Nick shoved the edge of an empty plate into Dillon's gut.

"What? What'd I say?"

"Did you just get off work, Dillon?" Joey asked sweetly. "You don't have to—"

Making a production of straightening his shirt as

though he'd just been accosted, Dillon grinned at Nick. "Yeah, I think I do."

"Let me make some more coffee," Joey said.

"Not now, thanks. It's bedtime. Breakfast, then bed."

"I was just asking Nick whether your church is finished inside," she said, taking Dillon at his word and a seat at the table. Nick followed suit. "You're turning it into a house?"

"Haven't decided exactly what it's going to be yet, but I've got some rooms framed out. When I'm working nights, I like to bunk in over there where it's quiet during the day. Kinda like when we were kids, we'd sleep outside all summer. Remember, Nick?" He pummeled Nick's shoulder, jogging his syrup-pouring arm. "As soon as the trees leafed out in the spring, we'd cut some branches and thatch the shade. Some people call it a 'squaw cooler,' but Nick's sister, Louise, she'd kill us if she heard us use that word. Remember how Louise was all politically correct after she started getting involved in stuff at school? But she was right. It's an insult. You know what *squaw* means, Joey?"

"I know what a white town is," Joey said.

"It is what it is, right? It's not a slur. It's just a town on the rez that belongs to white people. And white women, like you, we don't call you anything. Is she white? Is she Indian? Either way, it's the same word for woman. But *squaw* is what the old fur traders and mountain men used to call Indian women, referring to their, you know…private parts. It's like calling someone a—"

"Jeez, Dillon. Who wound you up?" Nick sliced a butter curl off a stick and tucked it between two smiley faces. "I'd like to eat these while they're still warm. Nothin' worse than cold mice."

"Engine in these things is in the rear," Dillon said as he rolled his VW into a cigar. He dipped the end of his creation into the syrup on Nick's plate, chomped it off and smiled. "Still warm."

"Just sit down and eat," Nick said. "You're like a bird on a wire."

"It's from working the graveyard. You're just gettin' started, and I gotta decompress."

"Getting started? I've been up since—"

"Yeah, I know, around here we don't waste daylight. Let's build us a shade this year, huh? Breezy spot to kick back and swat flies. This trailer house gets to be a bitch by about July the fourth." Dillon polished off the pancake roll and eyed the shrinking stack on the table. "One more, and then I'm outta here. What's this? A train? Monica used to do this for the kids. You got any—"

"Oh!" As she reached to pass Dillon the pancakes, Joey bumped her cup and sent a river of coffee streaming across the fake wood tabletop. "I'm sorry. How did I do that? I was just reaching for the…"

"I've got it." Nick tipped his chair back and snatched the upended roll of paper towels off the counter.

"The pancakes," Joey said quietly. "I must have been feeling nostalgic this morning. My dad was into pancake art. He'd make a contest of it. We used to eat a lot of pancakes."

"I knew this wasn't Uncle Nicky's recipe."

"How about my breakfast recipe for the man on the go?" Nick offered as he made a paper dam for the coffee river.

"Bring it on, man."

"Put an egg in your boot and—"

"—beat it," all three said in unison. But only Joey laughed.

Dillon slid off with a groan. "There's a reason why the straight man doesn't get to tell the jokes." He gave a parting salute on his way to shutting the back door. "You need any more Indian humor, Joey, you come to me. I'll be sleeping in church."

The ensuing silence was shared awkwardly by two people eating cold pancakes. Nick almost wished Dillon would come back. His yapping had served to keep some of the uncertainty at bay. He couldn't shake the image of that beautiful black-and-blue hip from his head, couldn't stop wondering how much it hurt and why she thought so little of showing it to him. He tried to concentrate on the chore at hand, soaking up syrup to help choke the pancakes down. He looked up from his plate as he finished. On cue, she did likewise. Like prisoners handcuffed to each other, they had become inescapably connected. He gathered dishes and got up from the table, obliging her to make the same move.

"You're not smiling," Nick said. "Dillon usually leaves 'em smiling."

"I'm lookin' at you, kid." She slipped her plates beneath his, and they stood with the plates between them, fingers brushing fingers, neither taking nor relinquishing. Handcuffed.

She applied a bit of pressure and won the plates.

And smiled. "You won't take off without me while I'm cleaning up the kitchen, will you?"

"Who's a kid? Lady, this old face don't belong to no kid." He touched her cheek with a wind-chapped hand. "But this one might. I thought about it last night after you went to bed. Pretty risky for a guy to be kissin' a girl who looks like you without carding her first."

"You knew I was cardless. I thought that was why you were checking my teeth."

"Busted." He chuckled, his eyes tracking her every move between stove and sink as though she were performing a task he might have to replicate.

"Dillon might well be the silver-tongued devil in your family, but I'd venture to say yours is golden. Not that one kiss earns you any medals, but so far you've scored very high." She turned her back on the running faucet and bubbles building in the sink, presenting him with a warning finger. "And I know what you're thinking. *She hasn't got her wisdom teeth yet.* Rest assured, they've already come and gone."

"That explains a lot."

"So," she said, slapping the faucet down in a behind-the-back play, "turnabout being fair play and all, it must be my turn."

"I'm forty-three, and I still have all my teeth."

"Dillon's right. You are a killjoy."

"Maybe, but there's a lot of things I'm not, and one of them is easy." He closed in, one slow step at a time. "'Course, that don't mean I can't be had. It's happened before."

"Had by a woman?"

"Oh, yeah. You're a hard-hearted bunch. I know that much." He cupped his hand around her face, dark skin over light. "Now it's your turn."

"Twenty-nine. Almost. Missing only…those… four…"

He kissed her softly, exchanging his essence of Karo for hers. She slid her hand over his shoulder, tucked it underneath his collar against his neck and measured his hair between her fingers

"What happened here?" she whispered when given scant space.

"I just told you." Such word games were not his way, but neither was explaining the scar that lay beneath her hand. "I got burned."

"Burned…by a woman?"

"Left a handprint." He actually tipped his head to one side to improve her view. "See the fingers?"

"How?"

He took her hand in his and took a step back, assessing the look in her eyes. It was an ugly scar, and it wasn't the half of it. She was looking to him for a story that would profit no one in the telling.

"A woman really did that to you?"

"I really got burned." He squeezed her hand. "Let's leave the dishes to soak. You ready to ride?"

She laid her hand on her chest and the long-sleeved blue T-shirt he'd picked out for her. "This is as good as it gets. My whole wardrobe."

"You might need a jacket. Man, I've got nothing that small." He drew her by the hand to the tiny closet that formed a room divider for the dining area. "Let's see what Dillon has hangin' in here. How's this?" He pulled a green plaid shirt jacket off a hanger and gave it the sniff test. "Prairie hay and fry bread."

She grabbed the shirt, sniffed, shrugged. "It's fine. Your nose is way too sensitive."

"Thought about goin' to work for the DEA, but I don't do well on a short leash."

He found her a cap, and she used the adjustable strap as a ponytail holder. Once they were outside, she took the lead, a newfound vigor pumping some bounce into her step. Could have been the hat, he thought. Big honkin' tractor above the bill. His sister had pressed it on him with the claim that it had brought her luck at the slots one night and she wanted to share. He'd suggested a share of her winnings, but

Bernadette had told him to take the hat and get his own. He never had. He wasn't a gambler.

A blue roan pup bounded across the bone-dry yard as they approached the barn. Joey spun on her heel and greeted her with outstretched arms.

"Hello, puppy. What's your name?" She scratched the dog's head and patted her ruff, encouraging vigorous dog-style dancing and prancing. "What's that? Wags? Oh, Paw-Paw." The two shook on it. "He's trying to introduce himself, Nick. Can you help us out?"

"I've been callin' her Mama."

"Oh. He's a she. How did I miss that?"

"There's another one around here somewhere. We call him Buzz, short for Buzzard Bait. He's real shy when strangers come around. There he is." Nick tucked his tongue against his teeth and whistled louder than necessary, he-man enough to impress. The black shepherd hung his head and approached warily. "He was skin and bones when he moved in."

"Moved in?"

"People don't want a dog anymore, they drive out in the country and drop it off. I guess they figure if there's a house anywhere in sight, they've found the animal a new home."

The dog took a slow turn, closing in guardedly before taking a seat right next to Nick's boot. Nick rewarded him with an affectionate head scratching.

"Somebody found one for Buzz."

"Nobody did him any favors. Buzz found his own way." He liked to give credit where it was due. Survival deserved big points, the fancy two-door doghouse she was noticing on the south side of the machine shed notwithstanding. "Yeah, Dillon built that. Made it into a duplex when Mama came along."

"She was Mama before she met Buzz?"

"She whelped within a couple of days after she moved in. Somebody got rid of five dogs in one. The pups all went to relatives—mine and Dillon's—and Mama got fixed. Nobody gets to reproduce around here without my say-so." He slid the big white barn door along its overhead track, making a mental note to get up there with a can of WD-40 and lubricate the damn thing. "Wild horses are one thing. Wild dogs, that's something else."

"Is it a big problem?"

"Sometimes."

During last spring's foaling there had been a bloody "for instance," but he'd taken care of both newborn kill and vicious killers, keeping all but the simple statistics to himself. *Shit happens. Bury it and move on.*

"Hey, kitty." Joey seated herself on a small stack of square bales inside the barn door, where the mouse-bearing tabby dropped in from a higher vantage. "Another successful hunt, I see."

"We've had breakfast already, but thanks for the thought, Alice."

"Alice?"

Nick gave a diffident smile. "You know you've been on the road too long when you're having two-way conversations with a cat, callin' each other by name. But she's still not my cat."

"You just feed each other."

"What're friends for?" He headed for the racks in the first stall. "You see a saddle you like? This fourteen-inch is the smallest seat I've got."

Joey joined him in the search, soon settling on the oddball in the bunch. "This one suits me better."

"Dillon picked that up at an auction. Says it's Australian. I tried it out, but it's too damn flimsy for my taste." With his long reach, he easily hauled the hornless lightweight down from the top rack. "I suppose it's a little closer to what your dad used."

"A little."

They brushed the two saddle horses he'd penned earlier. By tacit agreement, she bridled and he saddled. The docile sorrel was his choice for her.

"Rusty's no plug, mind you, but I trust him out in the hills with my five-year-old nephew, who thinks he can…" He caught her disapproving glance. "Well, you said it's been a while."

"I'm sure Rusty and I will get along famously. A leg-up?"

The request was a little foreign to Nick, but she was small, the horse was tall and the stirrup was well beyond her reach. He took her bent-knee cue and managed the hoist without popping his own knee out of place.

"What's your horse's name?" she asked as they put the last of the corral gates behind them.

"Nothin'." He patted the buckskin's withers and greeted Joey's frown with a smile. "That's his name. One of my nieces hung it on him when she was about two. Which is probably why he won't let her near him."

"Sounds like you're everyone's favorite uncle."

"Don't have much competition." He adjusted his hat against the sun as they headed down the well-worn trail that led to his favorite place to ride. Nothing but sage and buffalo grass as far as the eye could see, easy draws and hills rolling out to the bases of buttes that rose to support the overriding sky.

"It's so beautiful here, Nick," she marveled. "Such enormous peacefulness."

"A little livelier where you're from?"

"Sometimes." She shrugged. "Okay, most of the time."

"I have another run scheduled for next week. Think you can stand this much peace for that long? Then I can maybe take you—"

"Is that an invitation?"

"To what?"

"Stay?"

"It's bad enough, people putting dogs out on the roadside," he said. "No choice, I guess. I have to let you stay until you tell me where you belong."

"I promise not to move in." She turned to him, squinting into the sun, her ponytail fluttering like a yellow flag. "Unless Dillon wants to add on to the duplex."

It was a pleasure to watch Joey merge her mental and physical motion with that of the horse. She was a natural. Clearly, no amount of time away from riding had weakened her gift. Nick gave himself over to simply enjoying the ride. No checking on the thirty head of stock cows he and Dillon had bought one at a time whenever they had cash to spare simply because they needed a practical reason to lease range land. No riding fence or fussing over the windmill pump that mostly never worked on the stock tank that had sprung another leak. Today was all about saddling up and taking a girl for a ride—something Nick hadn't done in years, unless the girl was missing at least one tooth and sported blinking lights on her tennis shoes. As hard as he worked, he figured he had a real joyride coming to him, and today was the day.

They were both pleased to discover his much-discussed mares enjoying the mid-morning sun atop a breezy ridge. She loved the picture they made against the blue sky, and he was surprised to see the first foal of the season—a frisky buttermilk filly. He challenged Joey to help him chase the herd into a pasture closer to the home site, where men and dogs would more easily deter predators. With everything working for her but the whistle, she took to the task like a seasoned hand.

Back at the barn, she found fault with her own dismount, complaining of "jelly legs," which surely didn't show. She promised Rusty a rubdown, but she climbed between the rails to pay True Colors a visit while Nick pulled the saddle.

"Come, let me tell you about the beautiful girls I saw waiting out there for you," Nick heard her say as he approached. She turned, eyeing the saddle he had pulled off the sorrel and was still carrying. "What are you doing?"

"You got enough left in your legs to try him out?"

"I've been found worthy?"

He said nothing. The notion had just hit him, and hit him hard—the handsome sight they would make, one on top of the other. He couldn't wait to make it happen. The way he was dancing around, True Colors had to be pretty keen on the prospect, too, and Joey could barely contain herself. Before he gave her a leg-up, he took off the baseball cap and buttoned every button on the shirt jacket. Nothing would be flapping or flying off.

He was not disappointed. He stepped back to admire the way the pair fit together, both visually and physically. It was perfection. He opened the gate to give them space to stretch, remounted the buckskin and followed them into the field. It took a few strides to catch up.

And he caught her smiling.

"Would you say he's a Cadillac compared to Rusty?"

"At a walk?"

"All right, kick it up a notch, but let's not—"

A trot.

"Ah, yes, definitely more action," she said. "Not a Caddie, though. More of a high-performance vehicle, say a Ferrari or a Porsche."

"How about a Mustang?"

"I don't know cars, but I know this boy wants to go."

The easy canter lasted a few strides before Nick lost touch with *easy* in his futile attempt to coax the buckskin to keep pace. If she didn't watch out, the stallion was going to take off on her.

"Hold him, Joey," Nick said calmly, even as his pulse began to race against accelerating hoofbeats. "Shit."

He couldn't tell whether the horse had run away with her or she was trying to give him a heart attack on purpose. If he gave chase the stallion would only run harder. The buckskin could be hotheaded, but ol' Nothin' had *nothing* on the Paint. He followed, but made a wide circle, hoping to direct the stallion and avoid disaster. He knew the ground. No holes to speak of—the flat had been worked with a plow. If the horse tripped…if Joey lost her seat…

But the speed began to diminish, the direction gradually changed, and Nick released his breath. They weren't going to hit the fence. The rider was in charge.

Damn her purple hide.

Nick rode in close and ponied the stallion to help Joey settle him down. She gave a thoroughly exhilarated laugh, as though she did this every day, taking off across an open flat on a galloping stud, and wasn't it fun?

"That wasn't cute," he told her as he steered her through the gate he'd left open.

"My dad was in the racehorse business, for heaven's sake. Nick, do you—"

"Your dad wasn't riding my horse. What business are *you* in, lady?"

"I knew what I was doing. And Nick, he's—"

"You say it's been a long time since you've been on a horse. What the hell...?"

"I warmed him up first, Nick. A little bit. Do you realize what you have here? The spirit, the spark, the motion, all channeled in—"

"Crazy woman," he snapped as he swung down from his saddle. "I thought he was running away with you."

She dismounted with the ease of a gymnast, handed him the reins and peered up at him, amazed. "We scared you?"

"Damn right you scared me." And confused him. He glanced back and forth between horse and rider, both of whom, if he wasn't mistaken, were feeling pretty cocky at his expense. "*What I have here* is the *spark plug* I need to ignite the engine to drive my dream. And what you have here is...is a hell of a nerve."

"Were you scared for me or scared for him?" she asked softly.

He couldn't say. *Shouldn't have to say.*

"You're right, Nick. I had no right to breeze him like that. But look at him." She gestured eagerly. "Such quick recovery, you could put him in an endurance trial, Nick. He didn't even break a sweat. This boy is golden!"

"Not with a broken leg, he won't be golden."

"We rode this ground earlier. I knew there weren't any holes."

"Worked it last fall," he admitted. "We're putting it into oats."

"Is there a track around here? We should clock him."

"*We?* You got Alice's mouse in your pocket?"

"I'd almost forgotten what it was like," she enthused as she patted the stallion's muscled neck. "Discovering that promise for the first time. Owners and trainers might see it in the breeding or the anatomy or whatever, but for a rider, it's less reason and more rhyme. You know?"

Disgusted, he shook his head. "Tell me."

"You do know. You just want to hear it from someone else. Confirmation, right? Do you know what I know?" She delivered the last part in a little singsong.

"Tell me," he insisted, his brain juggling the new pieces of the far-from-complete puzzle that was Joey.

"You know what it's like when you're perched up here on top of the world with everything in place, and you know there's nothing missing in this one, that it's all right here between your legs, every essential element tuned to perfection. You know what it's like to be right there, on the verge of ignition. There's no holding back. Takeoff is inevitable, and when it happens, you get to share in the flash and the flow." She grabbed his hand. "You've been there. I know you have."

He couldn't say. All his juices were rushing southward.

"The reason I know is because you own this horse. You chose him." She eyed the horse. "Maybe he chose you."

"Were you a jockey? Is that what you're telling me? Did you ride your dad's horses?"

She turned to busy herself with the saddle, undoing, unfastening, unburdening. "I rode a few times for my dad," she said offhandedly, "but by that time he was getting out of it. He couldn't afford it anymore, and his health was deteriorating. He was working at the track, living on the backstretch. When I was with him, I took whatever jobs I could to help out. Horses are a lot of work, but it's a good life for a kid, being around them every day."

"You gave it up for something better?"

She turned her face away from him, letting the wind brush her hair out of her eyes. He'd brought up that sore subject again. Not something but some*one*. It was written all over her face. He wasn't one to pick at scabs, and he didn't know why he persisted in worrying hers.

"All right, look, I have to go into town today and pick up some supplies," he said. "What do you say we look for some clothes that fit you better?"

She looked down, pinched at her jeans. "You did very well. Nothing's too tight. Nothing's falling off."

"I'll do better when nobody's runnin' off on me."

"I don't want you to…" She touched his hand. "You don't have to buy me any more clothes, Nick."

"Should we steal them?" He laughed at her expression of mock horror. "No? Then we'll buy you what you need, and you can work off the bill. Like you say, horses are a lot of work. You can't be wearing the same clothes every day." He glanced down at her as he lifted the headstall over True Colors' ears. "I've got a sensitive nose, remember?"

8

Lauren had lost count of the fine horses she'd ridden over the years, but True Colors could certainly prove to be among them, given the chance. His power and speed hadn't surprised her. What she hadn't expected was the surge of excitement she'd felt the instant she'd sighted a stretch of flat ground through the notch of an eager horse's ears.

And now she was excited for Nick. He'd picked himself a winner. She didn't know what he'd paid, but she was sure he'd gotten the kind of bargain her father had chased after most of his life. For the average player, the trick was getting the right horse at the right time and having the resources to make the right moves. Not that Nick was a player—and this was probably no

time for him to try to become one, given his agenda—
but, damn, he had the horse.

A horse like this doesn't come along every day, Laurie-girl.

After a two-year respite, one morning's ride had her
thinking like her father's daughter. Or, worse,
Raymond Vargas's—

Don't go there, she told herself as she gazed out the
pickup window at an endless sea of grass that was still
more winter brown than spring green. One rainy
night and a couple more days of sun would bring the
prairie to life. Before her time with Vargas, she had
watched a lot of countryside fly past the window of
many a pickup. Just about the time it had become un-
bearably boring, she'd gotten old enough to help with
the driving. She, too, had been a partner once, before
she'd allowed herself to become a piece of Raymond
Vargas's property. His piece; and his property. *How
disgusting.*

She stole a furtive glance at her new driver. It
seemed a crime to entertain any thought of Raymond
Vargas in Nick's presence. Nick was a good man. He
was a *real* man. He was nothing like Vargas, and if it
weren't for Joey, she wouldn't even crowd the two
names into her head at the same time. But she had to
find a way to get Joey back without getting herself
killed, which would do her son no good. She wasn't
much—she'd done enough of Vargas's bidding to
compromise any self-respect she'd once had—but she
was Joey's mother. One worthwhile role in life—not

a piece, not a property, but a mother. She had been racking her brain for options, and Nick's goodwill was all she had going for her.

He was a man of rough-hewn features, obviously forged by hard knocks. His hair covered his jacket collar but didn't hide the scar on his neck. He said he'd been burned. Probably an understatement. Tall and lean, with strength earned on the job instead of a weight bench, and she'd noticed that he favored his knee at the end of a long day. He didn't complain or demand, embellish or boast, and she found him more attractive with each passing hour.

God help her, she had no business bringing the man her kind of trouble.

He glanced at her, his eyes seeking clues to her thoughts. He seldom asked, rarely challenged. Played his hand close to the chest, earning him a smile.

"Are we going to a white town or an Indian town?"

"We're crossing the bridge." They'd topped a rise, and he nodded toward the road and the river basin below. "This side is Indian country. On the other side, you've got your stores, your restaurants, your banks and ATMs. That's where we're going."

Welcome to Mobridge, South Dakota, home of the Sitting Bull Stampede.

Lauren had tried to tell him that all she really needed was a change of clothes and a few personal items, but once inside what he termed "the closest thing we've got to a general store," Nick behaved like a man who only saw his kid on holidays, offering to buy every little thing that caught her eye. The boots were the biggest extravagance, but he told her she wasn't getting on his horses again without them. And he shouldn't be giving her Dillon's jacket, couldn't take her up on her offer to help with chores unless she had a decent pair of gloves, wouldn't mind seeing her in another dress if she wanted one. He declined to give an opinion on underwear, and when she held up a box of tampons and asked—*shouted*, he later insisted—"Can I get some of these?"…well, she succeeded in shifting the balance of power.

"You said you had sisters," she teased.

Taking refuge at the paperback book rack, he gave his signature chin jerk toward the cashier. "Let her ring up whatever you want and call me when it's time to pay."

"How about—"

"If you need it, get it."

She spotted a display of telephone cards. A pay phone, she thought. A way to place an anonymous call. Yes!

And then what?

She wasn't sure, but she slipped one of the cards between the antiperspirant and the tampons. Even as the scanner beeped it onto the bill, she felt like a thief. It was a need she didn't want to explain, mainly because it was more gut than reason. She knew what she had to get done, but she hadn't figured out how to go about doing it.

But she knew the telephone card was safe from his

notice as long as it went into the bag with the tampons. He would undoubtedly consider examining the receipt to be an invasion of her privacy. Or an embarrassment. Either way, for whatever it might be worth, she had her phone card.

Following Nick's suggestion, she left the store wearing all new clothes, and she felt like a new woman. She availed herself of the sun-visor mirror, dabbed some cover-up on her cuts and bruises, applied a couple of licks of mascara and a swipe of drugstore lipstick, toss-fluffed her hundred-dollar haircut, and turned to find him watching her, bemused.

"Better?"

"Is that *you*?"

"Of course it's me."

He chuckled. "How about the new you and the old me go get some supper?"

"Anything but chicken." One more glance in the mirror and she folded the visor, satisfied with her minute's worth of handiwork.

"You got your drive-in, your phone-your-order-in and your walk-in-and-have-a-seat."

"The last one sounds good."

"That would be the Dew Drop Inn," he said as he hit the turn signal. "Best beef anywhere."

"You're sure I look okay?"

"Good enough to get me arrested." He surprised her with a smile.

The restaurant's dark interior was a relief to any

eyes coming in from the unremitting brilliance of
Dakota daylight. Decor that had not been touched
since the place was built—Lauren was guessing
1970s—seemed straight-street clean and flat-town
practical. It was early, the place was quiet and the
booth was cozy.

And the *Restrooms* sign in the far corner also read
Telephone.

"Will you excuse me while I…?" She gestured in
the direction of the sign and then pointed to the
menu. "Order me this salad."

"What else?"

"Skim milk and a glass of water."

"What about some meat and potatoes? Around
here nobody orders a salad for a meal, so you're
probably in for a disappointment."

She tapped the menu with a persistent finger. "It
says 'chef salad.' That's a meal."

"Maybe when it's made by a chef, but this is…"
He turned a plastic-coated menu page. "Be adventurous. Ever tried chicken-fried steak? It's got nothing
to do with chicken."

"All right."

"With fries, or mashed potatoes and—"

"All right, I'll have a cup of soup with the salad. Soup
of the day, whatever it is. How's that for adventurous?"

She followed the sign behind a room divider and
found the phone on the wall next to the door to the
ladies' room. Just a quick call, she told herself. A

woman's voice answered, and Lauren hung up, her hand shaking. She'd charged ahead and broken her own ice.

It would be easier next time. She would keep trying until she heard the right voice, she promised herself as she pushed through the next two doors on a tear. Inside the toilet stall she wrapped her arms around her middle and held on until she stopped shaking. She could only think of one possible inroad, and it was the one who had put her out on the road. It was a long shot. But what other shot did she have?

She returned to the table and drank most of her water before she noticed the way Nick was watching her. She had stopped trembling. Hadn't she? She drew a deep breath and slid the glass across the table, feigning disgust.

"I know beggars can't be choosers, Nick, but I've gotta say, the water around here sure tastes funny."

"Good well water is hard to find. Around here it's mostly artesian. This tastes better than the stuff at my place." He sipped, smiled. "And you…I gotta say, you ride better than I do."

"Oh, no, I'm really rusty." She gave a smile for a smile. "Like the horse. Rusty is as Rusty does."

"Rusty *is* reliable, and he *does* well by me as long as I do the same in return."

"I should not have done what I did." The admission applied to several impulsive moves she'd made, and the day wasn't over yet. "But, oh, Nick, that horse is something else, and I wish you'd let me do it again."

"I'll see if I can locate a grandstand for you."

"It wasn't like that." She leaned forward, peering, pondering. "You have no interest in racing him? You strike me as someone who might value performance, and your boy is a runner."

"That's what Gwendolyn said, too. I could tell she didn't want to sell him to me at first, because I'm not into that part of it. I know she'd like to see him get some points for something. But she likes my mares. She warmed up to the idea of crossing a gorgeous Paint with a piece of history.

"Some people just don't see it, you know?" He leaned closer, as though some of those people might be listening. "Those horses still know what it really means to be a horse. Even now... Hell, I don't have that much land, but what I do have is right for them. It isn't a habitat that somebody created for them. They're natural horses."

"They can't be natural if they're broke to ride?"

"Sure they can. Indian ponies were broke to ride, but it was more like a partnership. Horses aren't like dogs. They're a lot happier hangin' with their own kind, and that's what mine are doing most of the time. But there isn't much freedom left in this world, not for any of us. If you don't serve a purpose, you don't get to take up space, except maybe as a specimen."

"But your stud has been carefully bred for color and performance. I wouldn't call him a natural horse by any stretch."

"Carefully chosen, too. If we can breed the best of both worlds into his offspring, we'll get respect. We'll have value."

"Space permitted," she said. No matter what else was on her mind, she could always talk horses. *Whither goes the horse, so goes the rider.* Or so went Daddy's horseshit philosophy.

"Yeah, when you're as common as dirt, there's no value, so you get squeezed out, start dyin'. You finally get to be a rare specimen, people take notice. Plus, you can't take up much space anymore, being a rare breed." He shrugged. "It's a crazy world you've got here, Joey."

"Look again." She spread her hands. "I've got nothing."

"Hell, you've got new boots and a change of underwear." He leaned back to accommodate the waitress. "And the soup of the day. What more do you need?"

"I could help you, Nick."

"With what?"

"I know a little something about horse racing. We could try him out locally and see what happens."

"Locally?" Hungry for blood, he tested his ribeye with the stab of a fork. "We're gonna have to do some driving just to find you that grandstand."

"We'll get your map out, and we'll check your next itinerary against the racing circuit. Paint horse races are a little harder to find, but Paints are permitted in lots of Quarter Horse races. We'll find out which ones." She tasted her soup. Bean du jour. "I'm telling you, Nick, this horse will make the kind of a splash your plan needs."

"Are you a trainer now?" He eyed her.

"I learned a lot from my father. It was valuable experience, and it, um…" She picked at her salad. "It's not as complicated as you might think. You're already halfway there, and it can be fun, which is something I think both of us could use."

"According to my partner, *fun* is mostly a state of mind." He chuckled. "Kinda like, rusty is as rusty does. Jeez, one shithouse philosopher in my ear is bad enough."

"Well, just think about it." She choked down two more forkfuls of iceberg lettuce. "You're right about the salad. It's obviously not the specialty of this particular house. Will you excuse me again for just a few minutes?"

Studiously avoiding his eyes, she slid across the vinyl seat and tore away. The series of numbers kept repeating itself in her head, and she had to try it again while she had the chance.

This time the numbers yielded pay dirt.

"Jack? Jack, is that you?" Silence scared her. "Don't hang up! Please, Jack. I need to know what's going on with my baby." More silence. "Jack? You're the only one I can trust."

"Whatever gave you that idea?" came the deep, hushed response.

"The fact that I'm still alive."

"You won't be if he finds out."

"Or…maybe you won't be. Don't hang up, Jack. I don't want you dead. You're much more…*valuable* to me alive."

"Don't be a fool, girl. Don't be trying to twist on the tiger's tail. You won't get anywhere with that."

"Where's Joey?"

"He's with his father. They hired a woman to look after him. He's okay."

"I miss him. I know he misses me."

"Probably."

"You been seeing him much, Jack? Does he get to go to the park and the duck pond and all his other favorite—"

"Little Joe doesn't go anywhere without me." Jumbo Jack gave a very un-Jack sigh. "It's not the best job I've ever had, I'll tell you that much."

"You're a bodyguard. What difference does it make?" *Wrong thing to say. Try again.* "He should be with me, Jack. I'm his mother. He's hardly…" Hardly weaned from her breast. She'd known little more about breast-feeding than what she'd read, arbitrarily planned to nurse him for the first few months and then, possibly for the first time in her life, actually enjoyed letting nature take its course.

"Look…you shouldn't call here," her former protector was saying. Even hushed, his voice evoked the image of a human tank. She imagined gaining control of the turret and turning the gun. But the fantasy faded with the words "You wanna stay alive, you shouldn't call here. It doesn't matter about me."

"Let me call your cell phone, Jack. Just so I can find out about my baby. Give me the number."

"It changes."

"I know, but what is it right now? Please, Jack, give me this much. Some connection, some peace of mind." *He was still there. He was listening.* "Without that, it doesn't matter about me, either."

He gave in. She flagged a waitress down, borrowed a pen and wrote the number on her palm. When she looked up to return the pen, the waitress was gone. Nick Red Shield stood in her place.

"Thanks, anyway," she said. "I'll try again in a day or two."

Nick said nothing after she hung up the phone. He watched her pocket the phone card, must have known he'd paid for it, but he made no comment, posed no question. Not even with his eyes.

"I'm sorry to keep you waiting. I just thought of someone who might be able to help, but…"

"Didn't know if you'd fallen into the john or flown out the window," he said flatly. "I've paid the check, and I'm going out to the pickup."

"I'm coming."

She had to redouble her pace to keep up with him after the waitress got between them carrying their plates. He'd barely touched his steak. She wouldn't blame him if he slammed the door and spun out, leaving her standing on the sidewalk in front of the Dew Drop Inn with her precious phone card in her pocket and her boots too stiff for walking.

But she knew he wasn't like that. She was depending on it.

"I don't mind if you use my phone," he said quietly after a silence that nearly brought her to tears.

"I'll pay you back," she whispered, too embarrassed to do anything but hang her head.

"I'm not worried about that."

More silence. She tried to think of something else she could offer, but nothing came close.

"Is Jack the guy who—"

"Please, Nick, don't go there. It could mean trouble for you, worse than I've already caused. I mean, right now I'm a nuisance, which is bad enough. If they knew..." She closed her eyes, mentally rephrasing. *Keep them separate.* "It's better for both of us if I don't make calls from phone numbers that can easily lead to me."

"I'm not afraid of some weasel who beats up on women."

"That's the problem, Nick. You have no idea."

"Try givin' me one," he suggested without taking his eyes off the road.

"It's very complicated and very...painful. Inside and out."

"What's that supposed to mean, Joey? You wanna call him, go ahead and call him. If he shows up at the door, you can go or stay. I'll back you either way." He spared her a glance. "Just be straight with me."

"I've never met anyone like you." She meant it. She felt it so deeply, she had to turn away. "The last thing I want to do is cause trouble for you, Nick. What was…done to me was…could…" She shook off the notion of playing the for-your-own-good card. It would be the ultimate lie. If she cared enough to spare him, she would not be asking, "If you could just give me a couple more days…"

"Take your time. You're no trouble." He gave a wry chuckle. "Not much, anyway."

It was as plain as the damage on her face. True Colors was born to run.

By the time Nick had parked the pickup in the gravel driveway at Wolf Trail, Lauren had secured his blessing to try the stallion out on a lunge line. She wasted no time attaching a generous length of nylon to his halter and putting him though his paces. The horse was green, but he'd clearly been handled and was no stranger to working the circle. He seemed to enjoy showing her his stuff as much as she appreciated the view. He was a stretchy, stylish, two-toned eyeful and he moved like a wish with wings.

Lauren's best mounts had been Raymond's Thoroughbreds, but she had also ridden her father's Quarter Horses, which were a step down only because her father had never acquired the horse among horses.

Even though Paints were not major players in racing, they were gaining recognition, and more and more race tracks were making room for them, either in a class of their own or running against Quarter Horses. Nearly half a century of selective breeding had produced a registry of horses that many in the business considered to be the source for the next crown jewel in the horse world.

Lately, even Raymond had shown some interest in the growing popularity of the breed. A few months past he'd mentioned seeing one he liked at a track. Lauren had paid little attention to the remark at the time, but watching True Colors switching directions and changing leads like an old show horse brought the comment to mind in a new light. A Paint racehorse had caught the eye of Raymond Vargas, but he had yet to possess one.

Raymond was no horseman. He wasn't even comfortable around horses, but they were among the effects he had taken to collecting. He considered himself to be a major player, and he was obsessed with owning the best of whatever was in play. Gambling with what he owned excited him, particularly when it moved him a step up on the ladder of ownership. Any kind of ownership. He relished long shots, took special pleasure in getting in on the ground floor or discovering an unknown, be it a dark horse or a nameless jockey. If the horse became a winner or the jockey made a name for herself, he was on to the next venture. But always on his terms.

Lauren's decision to take herself out of the game before he was finished with her had been her first mistake, but by the time she understood the gravity of that first one, she had compounded it several times over. She had misjudged the man at every turn. She should have known better. He owned a stable, but from day one she had known that he had no love for horses. He owned lush property, myriad toys, and maybe as many people, but he showed no contentment with any of it. There was only his obsession with owning more, securing control, spreading his power. He'd extended his obsession to include the child he hadn't wanted. Immersed in her newfound joy, she hadn't seen it coming.

And she called herself a mother. What kind of a mother would allow such a thing to happen to her baby?

"One in a million."

Lauren turned to discover a spectator. Dillon swung his leg over the top fence rail and settled in.

"You just don't see that kind of action every day," he said.

"No, you don't," she called out over her shoulder as she continued her turn, following the line that connected her to the cantering horse. "He's very special."

"Nick says you rode him."

"I did."

He dropped down from the fence and ambled closer, joining her at the center of the horse's circular course. "You got to ride him before I did."

She laughed. "Sorry."

He moved to stand directly behind her. "No, I'm just sayin'…" It took him a moment to decide. "I never could get the hang of this. Not that I ever saw much point in it."

"Lunging?"

"You might as well take 'em for a spin."

"Lunging has its uses. Here." She handed him the line and the long, supple willow branch Nick had cut for her to use as a whip. "It's just a matter of getting him to keep the line taut."

"I get the idea, I just don't…" He kissed at the horse to keep him moving, but he didn't seem to know what to do with the willow.

She took it back from him, gave it a quick flick and made it whistle. The horse drew the line tight again. She glanced up, offering Nick's handsome partner an equally tight smile. "I thought you were in the horse business."

"I'm a rider, not a trainer." He chuckled. "Kinda like, I'm a lover, not a fighter."

"I get it," she assured him. She worked the willow, but left him the line. This way, he wouldn't be standing right behind her making her nervous. "Somebody has to do the training."

"Just like somebody has to do the fighting. That would be Nick." They exchanged glances—hers doubtful, his knowing. "Again, not something you'll see every day, but he'll fight if he has to."

"And you?"

"Me? I'll call Nick." Without taking his eyes off the horse, he grinned. "Tell you what else you don't see every day. Nick's sittin' in there workin' on his books. That part isn't unusual—he's just as particular about his business records as everything else, including who gets to ride what horse. He comes back from a run haulin' stock, usually does his books the same day. But this time he's sittin' in there by the window."

"Let him trot now," she instructed. "He doesn't like to sit by the window?"

"His desk is in the bedroom. He's a creature of habit, is our Nick. He does bookwork at his desk. Always." He glanced toward the trailer house as he turned the lead over to Lauren. "Tell you something else. Those expenses ain't gettin' entered in that ledger with him watchin' out the window."

"I'm surprised he isn't out here keeping close tabs on my every move," she said as she reeled the horse in, greeting him with pats and praise.

"Then you don't really know the man," Dillon said. "He's got no time for anyone he has to keep tabs on. If he didn't trust you with this horse, you wouldn't be out here."

"But you say he's keeping an eye on me."

"No, I didn't. I said *he's watching*. What I'm tellin' you is, he's enjoying the show."

"Why doesn't he come out here and enjoy it up close and personal?"

"Because he's generally distant and private. I don't know where you came from or how you've gotten this far with him, but my hat's off to you."

"It's not like I have any designs on him."

"Then what are you up to?"

She answered with a scowl.

"Hey, I'm not Nick. I don't mind askin' the tough questions point-blank."

"I'm not up to any…" True Colors nudged her shoulder, as impatient with Dillon's interrogation as she was. Time to walk. "You're trying to protect Nick. *From me?*"

"I'm glad somebody found a crack in the ol' shell," he said, following along, one of a pair of human bookends bracketing the prancing horse's head. "Just be careful how you poke around in there."

"I don't intend to…" She peered past True Colors' long face. "Aren't you the one who's poking around at the moment?"

"Sure, but you're the one who's trespassing here. It's only right I should be asking you what you're up to."

"What I'm up to with Nick," she clarified. "Not quite the same as asking what I'm doing here."

"Yeah, it is. Unless you're researching a book or playing the slots, Indian country is flyover territory. *He's* the reason you're here."

"Because he brought me here. Because this is where he lives. *Because*…" She glared at him for emphasis. "I had no place else to go."

"Like I said, Nick allows very few people into his life beyond a certain point. If you've passed that point—I'm not askin' for any details, mind you, but I'm just sayin', whatever it is you're looking for…"

"A safe place," she assured him. "And only for a little while. And if I can, I want to find some way to be useful while I'm here."

"He'd kill me if he knew I was talking to you like this. I'm probably way out of line, but it wouldn't be the first time." A blessed moment of silence passed as they reached the fence. "You could tell him, you know," Dillon suggested. "Whatever it is you're running from, you can trust Nick with it."

"It doesn't matter." She turned her back to the fence and began winding the lunge line carefully around her gloved palm in measured loops. "It really isn't…that important."

"See, now you're lying, and that's what I'm gettin' at. Whatever happened, whatever you've done, he's not gonna throw you out."

"I haven't done anything, and look at my face." She looked at him, giving him the total eyeful. "I don't want this happening to anyone else."

"Are you married?"

"No. And that's all I'm going to—"

"Wouldn't matter. Nick wouldn't care if it was a husband or boyfriend. I saw what he did to his sister's husband—now ex-husband—even when she begged him not to. You wanna beat up on women, you make sure they're not related to Nick Red Shield. Do you have any kids?" Dillon braced his back against the rail fence. "I asked you before, and you never answered. See, I've got kids. My kids were taken away from me. I know what it's like."

"You're guessing, and you have exactly zero to go on."

"I'm a blackjack dealer, Joey." He reached out to rub the Paint's cheek. "He's been good to you, hasn't he?"

"He's been very good to me."

"I'm askin' you to return the favor. He ain't half as tough as he makes out to be." Dillon shoved his hands into the front pockets of his jeans. "What happened to your kids? *Kid.* Which is it?"

"I take it you're the tough half of the partnership. Funny. Nick said you were the romantic."

"*Romantic?*" He gaped at her. "He really said that?"

"Said you'd do anything for love, including turning an old church building into a place for your family to come home to."

"He wouldn't say that. I haven't said what it's gonna be. Haven't decided yet. Too big for a house." Sun in his eyes, he squinted in the general direction of his white elephant. "Too hard to heat, too open. Too damn churchy."

She smiled, pleased with herself. She had his number.

"Why did you buy it?"

"It was cheap." He shrugged. "Seemed a shame to tear it down. It was an Indian mission at one time, before the farmers moved in and built a town around it. There was a schoolhouse, too, but somebody else bought that. There were stories about one of the missionaries and how she tried to speak up for us Indians. Gotta love that. She was friends with Sitting Bull. She built the first YMCA in the Dakota Territory right here on Standing Rock."

"What's Standing Rock?"

"Standing Rock Indian Reservation. That's where we are." He laughed. "You don't even know where you are."

"I've been to South Dakota many times, but not this part."

"See? Flyover territory."

"All right, you got me there. But you did buy an old church building just because you fell in love with the history of it. You're definitely a romantic."

"It's not just the history. Hell, that ol' church is built to withstand a buffalo stampede."

"But you don't know what you're going to use it for."

"I've got some ideas. I don't like to tell anyone about my plans while they're still formulating."

"Cautious and coy," she teased. "Typical of the true romantic."

"No way. Charming, sure, but romantic? I don't believe Nick would say I was—"

"A hopeless romantic," Nick confirmed from behind the fence. Lauren and Dillon turned toward each other like a pair of interlocking gears and peered over the rails. "I said it. It's true."

"How does somebody as big as you manage to sneak up on a person like that?" Dillon asked as Nick scaled the fence.

"It's easy when the person loves the sound of his own voice as much as you do." Nick dropped to the ground. "This woman is tryin' hard to make herself useful, and you're out here bending her ear."

"Lemme see." Dillon made a pretense of examining Lauren's ear. "Don't look bent to me."

"We lunged twenty minutes," Lauren reported, handing Nick the coiled nylon line. "Somebody's obviously been working with him, Nick. He's ready and willing. If you'll give me the go-ahead, I'll set up a conditioning regimen for him."

"Conditioning for what?" Dillon asked.

"Takin' a run at those mares." Nick slid Lauren a pointed glance as he raked his fingers through the Paint's mane. "You got a harem to satisfy, you get yourself in top form before you show up at the gate."

"Well, sure." Dillon folded his arms and scowled at the horse. "But it sure wouldn't take me no twenty minutes."

9

The three of them had shared a moment, but Lauren had no idea where she'd stood with either of the men when it ended. Dillon made his suspicions abundantly clear, but at least he was friendly, while Nick did his best not to be. In the end, he'd walked away again, and she knew exactly which of her remarks had been the stinger. They'd all been smiling when Lauren offered to make Dillon something to eat before he went to work, tossing off easy regret that he'd missed out on the early supper at the Dew Drop Inn. Dillon shrugged it off, saying he never went hungry at the casino. And the smiles evaporated as Nick walked away with his horse.

He had work to do, he'd said, and he'd left her to

squirm in the presence of Dillon's glib charm and perceptive misgivings. For all his efforts to keep to himself, Nick was easy to read, and unlike any man from her previous life, he had a giving nature. He couldn't help himself. He'd found her with nothing, and he had to provide. Even more imperative, he had to protect. All he asked was honesty. *Be straight with me.*

He asked too much.

At the very least, she could give him some space. Over at the barn right about now, True Colors was probably getting an earful about female treachery. Lauren imagined herself as a fly on the wall. She would happily flit from the man's shoulder to the tip of the horse's ear and back again. Or become the mouse in his pocket or the cat in his hayloft—anything but the woman he'd left alone in the house.

The sun had set, but darkness had yet to set in. Spring daylight was wondrously stubborn on the high plains. But so was solitude. She turned on the TV for company, cutting into the middle of a news broadcast. "Missing is three-time Breeders' Cup-winning jockey Lauren Davis, whose car was found in the river after—"

She turned the volume down and huddled close to the speaker. Her picture appeared on the screen. It was an old one. She was wearing silks, and sported short blond hair and no bruises on her face. The old Lauren. The one who had taken time off "for personal reasons."

"—Vargas, owner of those horses and others ridden by Davis, said in a statement that Davis had been suffering from depression since the birth of their child, who is now in his father's custody."

Depression?

"—called off temporarily due to heavy rain."

Lauren snapped the TV off, turned and stared at the phone.

Don't call from here.

But she didn't know when she would get to a pay phone again.

And you don't know who's going to answer.

Jack was her only chance, and how much chance was that? How much leverage did she have with him?

There was a job not done, for one thing. She wasn't dead.

Blackmail?

How would a person go about blackmailing a henchman? She had to understand what was in his head, why he'd let her live. And she had to be right on the money. If he was capable of feeling anything, she had to know what it was. Sympathy? She needed more. Guilt? He needed more. Affection? In his dotage, maybe, and he was probably getting there. Old enough to be her father, and no family or friends to speak of. Loyalty to Vargas was all Jack knew. That and the two innocent lives assigned to his portfolio. She had to know whether she and Joey counted for anything with Jumbo Jack.

Which meant talking to him.

The first ring sent Lauren flying off the floor. She snatched the receiver on the next ring.

It was Dillon with a message for Nick. Irrational guilt prompted her to handle the call with extreme care, even going so far as to take notes. Dillon laughed when she asked him to repeat the highway number. He reminded her that there was only one.

She had just hung up when Nick walked in the door. New guilt. Or maybe just guilt hangover. Whatever it was, it showed. Nick looked at her expectantly, but he wasn't going to ask.

"Dillon called," she said quickly. Even the truth felt like a lie. "He said that some of the horses got out on the highway."

"Where?"

"He said he ran them back into the pasture, but he says the fence is down."

"Did he happen to say where?" he asked with exaggerated patience.

"Exactly three-quarters of a mile north of the bridge. He said it's hard to see from the road because it's in a low spot. There's a post rotted out, but the wire is still strung." She handed him her silly notes, jotted on the back of an envelope. "Wanted to make sure I had all the details."

"And Dillon gets points for running them in," he allowed, turning to go back out the door.

"So where are you going?"

"If they try it again, they could get hung up in barbed wire. Might as well take care of it now."

"In the dark?"

"Nope." He jacked his eyebrows, mocking her. "I've got headlights."

"How long will you be gone?"

"An hour, maybe." He nodded toward the TV, as though he'd decided to play host. "That thing only gets two channels, but it'll keep you company. And you can use the phone." On second thought, he flipped on the TV himself and handed her the remote. "There. Catch up on the world—"

She pressed the power button, quickly cutting off the news. "I'd rather go with you."

"In the dark?" he mocked.

"With you." She grabbed her new jacket off the back of a kitchen chair. "If you don't mind my company."

"Guess I'm gettin' used to it," he allowed as he followed her out the door.

He was getting soft. He knew better, but he didn't seem to be doing much about it. Getting used to her company was just too damn easy, and there would surely be a price to pay down the road. For now, he had a fence to fix, had himself some company, and it was all good. He caught her watching his every move, caught himself feeling good about being the object of her attention, spotlighted by the headlight beams.

She stood close to him while he pounded a new post into the ground with the steel post driver. Almost in his way, but not so much that he couldn't deal with it. She could stay and ask her questions, oblige him to speak the answers, self-evident as they might be. He liked the sound of her voice. Maybe she liked his. Maybe it was no different from the racket the crickets were making in the darkness beyond their pool of light. It might be the same sound every night, one someone else wouldn't think bore repeating, but it wasn't a racket if you were a cricket.

The mares stood watch on the ridge above them. Hard to see them in the dark, but Nick knew they were there. He wondered how they compared notes as they watched him plug the hole they'd discovered. *Can we go now, Mama? Can we go now?* They were geared up for overdue spring grass, and the lead mare had to be planning her next move. *Just as soon as the man gets out of the way.*

"The days seem longer here," Joey was saying. "Even at night, it doesn't seem so dark. I like that." She dodged his elbow as he switched tools, trading the post driver for the wire stretcher she'd been tending for him. "I think I've turned into a big chicken."

"No surprise after what you've been through. Hell, we don't mind having a chicken on the place, long as it's just one. Otherwise, we don't—"

"—don't do chickens, I know. This is not a farm." She gave a nervous giggle. "Why did the chicken cross the road?"

"What chicken?"

"The one who's always crossing the road."

"It's the horses I don't want crossing the road. The

chicken can build a nest in the passing lane and lay eggs for all I care."

"Work with me, Nick. I'm the big chicken."

"Then tell me." He cranked the handle on the wire stretcher. "Straight from the chicken's mouth."

"To find a place to hide."

"From…?"

"From what was on the other side, which was—" she smiled when he looked up from his wire stretching "—the guy who does do chickens."

"I gotta meet this guy."

"What would you do?"

"Well, any guy mean enough to do a chicken—" he stepped back, eyeing the newly planted post and tightened wire for a moment before he slid her a sly glance "—guess I'd have to challenge his little cock to a pissing contest, huh?"

Pleased with himself for getting a real laugh out of her, he laid his gloved hand high on her back and guided her up the slope to the pickup, which would not be crossing the road just yet. Reluctant to put an end to the night's outing, he turned toward the ridge rather than the highway.

"Where are we going?"

"A place I didn't show you this morning."

The mares took the hint. They fled the headlights, following the fence line for several yards before turning suddenly like a school of fish and darting off into the darkness. The horses would take the short way, while the pickup would ply the long way. But all ways led to the river.

He had a favorite place. It was a piece of riverbank lined with scrub oaks and carpeted with tall grass. It wasn't a secret any more than anything else on the place was a secret, but it was a place he sought these days only in solitude. Pretty much the way he lived his life.

But not tonight. Tonight he was walking through his grass, underneath his trees, along the banks of his cresting river, with a woman. The sky was velvety and thickly dotted with stars, and the crescent moon lent the river a silvery cool sheen.

Like children rushing for choice seats, the horses had beaten them there and were already calmly grazing, as though there had been no escape, no chase. But their quick breaths made telltale steam. Nick had given Joey a flannel throw, which she carried at her waist over folded arms as she walked close to his side. When he asked, she said she wasn't cold and nothing more.

He stopped, laid his hand at the base of her neck and pointed across the water. "My great-grandfather's cabin stood over there."

"On the other side of the water?"

"Before they dammed up all the rivers out here, this water was much narrower. It's a tributary of the Missouri. The dam they put in south of here created all this backwater, mostly on Indian land. Drowned the trees that provided the firewood, the best home sites, the sweetest garden plots." Reaching over the water and into the night, he was mapping it out with his hand, like the Indian in the pictures, showing Lewis and Clark the way. "But it's been like this since I can remember, all fat and full, especially in the spring. We used to come here to swim when we were kids. It's not the best for fishing, but sometimes we'd catch bullheads and crappies."

"You and Dillon?"

"Whenever we could get away from the girls, this is where we'd come."

"The girls wouldn't leave you alone, huh?" She sidled in close, and he gathered her closer as she tipped her face up to him and smiled. "Must have been tough."

"Sisters. My two and Dillon's whole gaggle. We pretty much scared them off from swimming with stories of snapping turtles and water moccasins."

"Water moccasins don't live this far north. Do they?"

"Johnny swore he found a nest of them right down…" He caught himself and the curiosity in her eyes. "My little brother, John, he got to tag along. We'd come out here on horseback, meet up with some other friends sometimes. We built a raft one year. Good times."

"Good times," she echoed softly. "Would you go back?"

"And be a kid again? If I could pick one of those days I would."

"Just one day?"

"The days were longer then. The bad ones were

endless, but on the days when everybody's cool and things are goin' right, man, when you're a kid you can turn bread into cake and water into honey."

"It sounds like you had a pretty glorious childhood. You and Dillon and all those sisters. And Johnny? Where's your brother now?"

"John's dead," he told her. He squeezed her shoulder, hoping she would get the message. *Not right now.* "How 'bout you? What was little Joey like?"

"Little." She shrugged. "I was a little girl when I stayed with my mother and a little tomboy around my father. But I've always been little."

He wondered whether she'd always offered so little, or was it just him? And while he was wondering, she claimed his hand, placing hers against his, palm to palm. He slipped his fingers between hers and considered the weaving they made—dark alternating with light, rough with smooth, strong with slight. Slowly he bent his fingers and clamped them firmly over the back of her hand.

"Little Joey meets Big Indian. People stare." Oddly, the idea made him smile. "Strange pair."

"And how."

"I can make poetry, and you can talk Indian. *Hau.*" He chuckled as he lifted the blanket from her arm. "Hello, Joey. Who would name their girl Joey?"

"You would."

"You're not my girl." He shook the blanket open with one hand and draped it around her shoulders, bringing the ends together beneath her chin. "Did I name you?"

"Sort of." She rose on tiptoe. "Kiss me, and I'll be your girl."

He looked her in the eye. "For how long?"

"How long can you make a kiss last?"

Long enough to make her quit teasing. But he held back.

"Not long enough?" She stepped back, giving her head a little shake. "Then how about one of those perfect, endless days you were talking about? For that long. I don't think I ever had a day like that."

"We used to have them. Must have been before you were born. I'm a lot older than you."

"In some ways, maybe. At least you got to be a kid for a while. I've had a very long adulthood."

"Can't tell by lookin' at you."

"What can you tell by looking at me?" She closed in again. "Look at me, Nick. Please, look at me and tell me what you really see."

"I see you. You're a beautiful woman." He touched her cheek. "Scared, hurt, feeling lost, don't know whether you're comin' or goin'. The one thing you must know for sure is that my eyes see a beautiful woman."

"I'm afraid to look in the mirror," she whispered. "It's not about the cuts and bruises. It's about…being all undone, you know? Coming apart in so many places. I'm scared I'll find big chunks of myself missing." She grabbed his hand. "How much is left, Nick?"

"More than you think."

"How do you know?"

"I know because I've been there. What's left is a body caught in a trap and a big pair of eyes lookin' for a way out." He drew her hand to his chest, tucked it against his shirt. "But your body is still beautiful. That's the only part I can tell by lookin' at you."

"And yours?"

"Mine never was."

"Are you willing to let me be the judge?"

"If this keeps up, you *will* judge. It won't matter whether I'm willing or not."

"You're the sweetest man I've ever known." She lifted her chin. "If I'm so beautiful, why won't you kiss me?"

He took his time, first pressing her hand to his lips before drawing it over his shoulder and taking her in his arms, all the while locking in on her eyes, searching for clues. He didn't care who she was right now, but he cared what she felt. He touched his lips to hers without pressing, and she opened them, willing to receive him. But still he took his time, tasting without consuming, nipping and sipping and helping himself to bits of her lips without betraying his hunger, until she lifted herself to him and gave herself through her lips. No longer did his time or his mouth or his breath exist. Everything was *theirs*.

Arms pulled; knees and tall grass cracked with their bending. They sank to the ground together, exchanging kisses on the way down. He lifted her onto his lap, thinking to cradle her, but she swung her leg over his hips and straddled him, taking his breath away. He wanted to do the same to her—kiss her too hard, hold her too tight, press her too close to allow for breath or thought or doubt to seep between them—but even as she took his hat and tossed it aside, he kept his head.

As long as she's giving, let her have her way. Let her back off when she's had enough. Don't scare her. Don't do anything to scare her.

Gently he caressed her strong back and her small bottom, moving her clothes without taking them away, reveling in the feel of his mouth against her perfect skin—her velvet earlobe, satin neck, the silk stretched over her collarbone. She tried to sneak her hand past his shirt collar and down the back of his neck, but he caught it, kissed it, slyly drew her hands to his sides. She leaned into him, her thighs cleaving to his hips like a rider preparing for a jump. A little elevation on his part and he would take her up and over.

If she would take him in.

He lifted his head, glimpsed the wet gleam of her parted lips and caught them with a kiss that drove every part of him and drew against her secrets. She countered with her tongue in his mouth and her hands at his back tugging at his shirt. He groaned and pulled them away, but the kissing went on as she reversed his hold, laced her fingers with his and pressed him. He gave in, allowed her to push him over. By the time he lay all the way back in the grass, she was laughing.

"Ride me, then. Where do you wanna go?" He rolled his hips, knocked his aching cock on the door between her legs. "Wanna go home? I'll take you home if you—"

She stopped laughing.

"I…don't…have…a home." She drummed each word into the ground with their clasped hands. "I don't," she whispered hotly. "I don't."

"Okay." He drew her down into his arms, and she stretched out her legs and slid down next to him. "Okay, Joey, okay."

"You said I could be your girl."

"Okay."

"You did say it, didn't you?"

"Probably." He pulled the forgotten blanket around her shoulders and tucked his free arm behind his head. "You've got me saying all kinds of crazy things."

"I know you don't trust me, Nick, and I don't blame you, but give me a chance to show you…that…"

"That what?"

"That having me here isn't such a bad thing."

If he spoke, he would say something foolish. It would be about having her, about the fact that he would like nothing more. Trusting her was another matter, but why bring it up? They were just two people hankering for a good fuck, which really didn't require too much…

"What happened to your brother, Nick?" she asked quietly. "Tell me what happened to Johnny."

Too much in the way of trust.

"It was an accident." He didn't know why he answered. It wasn't like him. It was even less like him to elaborate. "A fire."

"A fire," she whispered. "Oh, Nick, I'm so sorry."

"It was a long time ago."

"What kind of—"

"The bad kind. We were workin' in the oil fields, Dillon and my brother and me. Explosion on a rig."

"Were you there when it happened?"

"I was there."

"Was it—"

"It was a long time ago." He placed two fingers over her lips. "You lost your home in a bad way. I lost my brother."

She slid her arm underneath his jacket and around his middle, and they held each other. For a long moment Nick lost himself in the stars overhead. Johnny wasn't lost. He had traveled the Wolf Trail— the Milky Way—the road to heaven. On nights like this Nick imagined reaching for the sky and finding John's hand in that river of stars. They didn't look like balls of fire from here. He'd survived a ball of fire, and it looked nothing like a star. Had he lived, John would surely be telling about it. Hell of a storyteller, that guy. He would have been thirty-five. Unbelievable. He would have had his own family by now. He would be tribal chairman or manager of one of the casinos. An artist, maybe, or a musician.

Joey would have liked him.

They might have been a pair of grouse cozying up in the grass for the night. Unconcerned with the nesting pair's presence, the horses went about the night's pleasant business, snatching mouthfuls of tall grass, spanking themselves with their tails, swishing and sliding, shadow through shadow. The new foal suckled, loud and sweet.

"I've been thinkin' about letting you earn your keep," Nick confided. "I was planning on putting True Colors with a trainer for a month or so. I had a guy in mind, but—"

She pushed herself up and hovered over him. "I can do it, Nick."

"I usually train my own horses, but I've never had one like this before. You seem to know—"

"*I do.* I know a lot about training and conditioning horses. Seriously, this is something I really can do."

"I figured you could be good for something." He pulled a piece of grass from her hair. "Besides making goofy pancakes."

"And following you everywhere you go."

"You start gettin' in the way, you can be sure I'll let you know."

Nick lay nude on his stomach, kitty-corner across bed sheets that smelled of smoke. Cigarettes and sage. Dillon's job and his romance with the past. Nick liked sleeping in his own bed—looked forward to it after

being on the road for days and nights on end—but he'd given his bed away out of pure-D mortification. He knew the spare bed would smell like Dillon. He should have added in a stop at the Laundromat on the trip into town.

He liked his own bed, but the nude part felt strange. No one ever had his back. He kept it covered all by himself. He'd spent so damn many days and nights lying in a hospital bed on his stomach, just like this, with nothing touching his back except the Dragon Lady's evil fingers. They had put up a tent to protect his raw flesh from the outside world, but there was no keeping her away.

He'd made his peace with her, let her melt into him, agreed to carry her on his back for the rest of his life. In return, she'd agreed to let up on him enough so that he could bear to go on living. With time, walking around in his fried hide had become less of a chore. Time and the family he'd driven back time and again. Family and the few friends his lifelong preference for solitude had permitted. Friends and the splendid four-legged creatures who didn't care what a man looked like as long as he wasn't bent on harming them.

But there would always be the Dragon Lady. He could feel her with his hands, but he never had to look at her, and he hardly ever did. He kept her covered. Nudity was reserved for the kind of Dakota summer heat that settled in and stayed heavy, even after the sun went down. Times like that, the Dragon Lady didn't want anything touching her. Other times, he kept her covered. It was part of their truce. Once the fire had gone out of her, she'd shriveled into a homely old thing that couldn't stand to let anyone stare at her. Privacy was a condition for any peace in his life.

But there in the dark he lay, back exposed, door ajar, brain abuzz.

What kind of person tempted fate this way? A masochist? An idiot? Maybe a character in one of Dillon's eternal fables or infernal history lessons. Whoever, whatever, Nick didn't know what he thought he was doing.

The hell he didn't.

Joey was still prowling around out there. They'd done the you-go-ahead, no, you-go-first, routine with the shower, but now that all that was done, she ought to be in bed. Nick's bed. Where he dearly wanted to be.

But first, maybe she would stop and tell him goodnight. And if she did, she would push the door open. She would peek in and think he was sleeping, but she would come to him, anyway. She would see the way he was, *but she would come to him, anyway*. He would tell her to go away, but she wouldn't listen. He would warn her not to mess with the Dragon Lady, but nothing would scare her away.

Damn you, Red Shield, you're so funny, you forget to laugh.

She probably thought there was something wrong with him. The night was clear, the stars were perfectly aligned, and she'd given him all the right signals. He should have done what they'd both been dying for and then some. The hell with tricks, trust or Trojans, sometimes good judgment was nothing but a pain in the ass. And it was bound to hang on for days.

She had to be thinking there was something wrong with him.

And there was. But it had nothing to do with performance. Underneath his scarred hide, Nick was the real thing—not much for show, but he could sure perform when he got the chance.

Or took advantage of an opportunity.

Next time.

10

Nick could hear his sisters coming from *tona* miles away. Once upon a time, it had been their little-girl voices. Nowadays, the noise was always motorized. Both of them went through used cars like most people changed socks. At any given time there was usually only one functioning vehicle between them, and today Louise was driving.

"For a quiet woman, you sure have one loud tailpipe," Nick teased his sister as she emerged from next month's trade-in. She'd parked it dead center in the gravel driveway, letting him know that he could put anything he was thinking of doing on hold for now. The girls would have their due.

"Too much beans in her Indian tacos," their

younger sister Bernadette said. She was the little one with the big mouth and the parade of kids. "And you, my brother, have a funny way of keeping your promises to your nephews," Bernadette scolded while she unloaded the two ambulatory kids from the car. "You told Tony he'd be the first to see this super horse you were getting, and he marked it on the calendar when you'd be coming back. You've been back how many days?"

"It took me a little longer—" He greeted his nephew with the handshake due every visitor. "Hey, cowboy, what's up?"

"Is he here yet, Uncle?"

"He sure is."

"When is Dillon gonna stop scraping that church and get to painting?" Bernadette planted fists on ample hips and gave Dillon's eternal project a disdainful once-over. "He's been scraping on that thing for, what, two years? Pretty soon he'll be scraping through to the studs."

"It keeps him out of trouble," Nick said. "You kids want some pop?"

"We came to see your new horse. Can we ride him?" the one they called Bubbles wanted to know.

Another child's voice in the backseat of the car drew Nick's attention, but all he could see was an ample butt on toothpick legs in stretch pants. "Louise! What are you doing to my namesake?"

"It's the buckle on that old car seat," Bernadette explained. "I need a new one. They say those things go bad after a while. Even if you haven't wrecked, which I haven't. Only barely bumped that one farmer's truck that time backing out of the post office."

"So that car seat's been through one run-in with a farmer and how many kids?"

"Four. Five? But they weren't all mine. To boot, my car died, but I'm getting a bigger vehicle pretty soon."

"Bigger?" The childless sister backed out of the car with her arms full of fussy baby. "Are you pregnant again?"

"No, but I've gotta be able to fit two car seats plus all the rest. Tony was fussing to come out here, and Bubbles had to go to the clinic, so I had to leave Bernie and John with Tina because I couldn't fit them all in."

"You think you've got enough brothers and sisters, Nicky?" Nick took the baby from his sister and settled him on his hip. "You wanna see what your uncle brought back from Colorado?"

They were on their way to the barn, Nick leading the way with Tony at his side, keeping pace like a jumping bean. "I can ride him, can't I, Uncle?"

"No, but you can take turns on Rusty."

"But I wanna ride the super horse."

"We have to get to know him a lot better before we can trust him that much." Who'd come up with *super horse*? Had he said that? "We know Rusty, and we know he'll take care of you."

"I can take care of myself," Tony grumbled.

"Who's the woman?"

Bernadette couldn't have caught more than half a second's glance at Joey through the open barn door, but she had an eagle eye, that girl.

"She's…" The sisters gaped at him, hungry for a shocker. "She's my new trainer."

Both faces fell.

"You've got a trainer?" Louise was quietly amazed.

Bernadette wasn't buying. "So who was your *old* trainer?"

"Eddie Arcaro," Nick deadpanned.

"He was a jockey."

"It was the only name I could come up with. Hey, Joey, can you name me a famous trainer?" She appeared again, pausing in the doorway, and he gave an invitational nod. "Actually, Joey's father was a famous trainer, but the name escapes me. Joey, meet my sisters, Louise and Bernadette," he said, indicating each one with the customary jerk of his chin. "And Tony, who came to see his uncle's new horse. And the cheeky one over there, we call her Bubbles. I can't remember if that's her real name or—"

"It's Barbara Ann," the little girl said.

Bernadette snorted. "If you wasn't gone so much, you'd be able to—"

"Every time I see her, she's added another one to the brood." Nick shifted the baby for Joey's inspection. "This handsome fellow is Nicholas."

Joey greeted each one in turn, but the baby quickly

claimed her full attention. She pulled the leg of his miniature blue jeans down, smoothed and patted. "How old are you, little one?"

"Nicky's one year and one month," Bubbles reported as the baby, taking equal interest, reached for Joey. Her eyes lit up as though she'd been asked to dance. She offered open hands, nodding eagerly, and little Nicky went to her as if they'd been friends for life.

"He likes everybody," Bubbles said. "But watch out. He leaks. And he pulls hair."

"And he's almost as big as she is, brother. Bubbles, you take—"

"Oh, no, please." Joey bounced the big boy on her hip while he angled for the bill of her cap. "Yes, he likes my hat. Don't you, Nicky? I borrowed your uncle Nick's hat. Let's see how it looks on you. Oops." Nicky's mop of black hair and half his face disappeared beneath the cap. Laughing, Joey adjusted it. "There. It's big for me, too. I have it on the tightest notch."

"He just wants to get at your hair."

"And once he gets hold of a handful…"

"Hair's too much fun, isn't it, Nicky? Such a big boy," she cooed. "Are you walking yet?"

"Trying, but he's too fat," Bubbles said.

"Tony!" Bernadette aimed her command toward the corral fence, which her five-year-old had decided to scale. "That's a stud horse. You don't go in there without Uncle."

Stripped of one charge and duly reminded of the

other, Nick headed for the corral as the Paint poked his nose between the rails to see what the boy might be offering besides fingers.

"Joey's the one who can really show him off," he told the group. "He's broke better than I thought, and, man, can he run. E'en it, Joey?"

"True Colors is amazing. He really is." Making baby talk with his namesake, Joey hardly spared Nick a glance. "You wanna ride the horsey, big boy? Or walk first? We have to learn to walk first, huh?"

"Where're you from, Joey?" Bernadette asked.

"Nick brought me up here from Missouri."

"Sort of a package deal," Nick supplied. "Brought them back together, horse and trainer."

"She staying in town?" Bernadette persisted.

"We were listening to Bobby Big Eagle's radio show on the way over." Louise flashed a shy smile. "He wants people to call in with news tips."

"You girls're killin' me," Nick said, chuckling as he slid the bolt on the corral gate. "You wanna throw a saddle on him, Joey? Give my sisters their news flash."

"You go ahead, Nick," she said. "I just worked him out, rubbed him down, the whole bit. It's your turn."

Bernadette offered to take the baby.

"No, please go ahead. I'll watch Nicky for you."

Nick rested his chin on his arm, casting a furtive backward glance while he held the narrow corral gate open for the family parade. Bent over with a baby hand fastened to each of her thumbs, Joey was already testing little Nicky's progress on two legs. Nick didn't want to move. He wanted to hang on the gate and watch her, the better to learn her. But he had family to attend to.

They all trooped into the corral behind him. Nick put Louise in charge of the box of horse treats after he gave Tony and Bubbles two apiece, the better to make friends with the stallion. The sisters acknowledged his beauty—*eeez*, said one, and *ahhh* said the other—but neither of them had ridden a horse since she was in grade school, and then rarely. Once every Indian kid's birthright, horses were disappearing from reservation life. Nick meant to do his part to keep his sister's children interested, but he'd been busy lately.

Hell, he'd been putting them off. Old habits were hard to break. His sisters knew about his plans, and they never called him crazy when he said he was going to bring the Indian pony back. And not just any Indian pony. Lakota stock. The children would hear the stories and know that not only were the Red Shields Sitting Bull's descendants, but their horses came from his horses. These were the details that lived in growing minds, along with size and beauty and speed.

They should see how this horse could run.

But a quick peek past the corral rails gained him no glimpse of his horse trainer. He shook his head. Women and babies. *Put a baby in a woman's hands and she forgets everything else she signed on for.*

"Your sister and me, we agree," Bernadette buzzed

in his ear as he took a seat beside her on a homemade feed bunk. He questioned her with a look. "It's good to see you taking an interest in a woman."

"You think I don't have any interest in women?"

"Not since that Kay Mart woman."

"Her name was Kay Martin, and I barely saw her a few times before you two drove her off with all your snooping around, checkin' up with your friends at Turtle Mountain."

"And we found out about her steppin' out on you," his sister reminded him. Keeping an eye on the children and an ear on the adults, Louise nodded surreptitiously. She stood three feet away and didn't say much, but neither did she miss a word.

"She was just a friend," Nick said. "I didn't have that much time for her. Hell, I'm a busy man, and women are a lot of work."

"This one you brought here looks pretty young."

"And white," Louise said quietly.

"She's *really* white. Way young, and too skinny. More like Dillon's type," Bernadette said. "Looks like the wind blew her into a wall or something. Did she get into a fight?"

Nick leaned forward, braced his arms over his knees and shook his head.

"She's really a horse trainer?"

"See why I don't come around that much? You two girls, you're one big wind." He lifted his chin, squinting into the sun. "Lou, I'm counting on you to put a sock in this one so none of this discussion or your speculation gets back to Joey. She's having a rough time, and I'm helping her out. End of story."

"I'll ride Rusty. Uncle?" Nick turned to connect with Tony, who was standing at his elbow. "I said *okay*. I'll ride Rusty."

"Me, too," Bubbles said.

"You'll have to ride double, then."

"I get the saddle," Tony said. "You gotta ride behind me."

"Quit your bossing. You can each have a turn in front." Nick pushed to his feet. "It's all about keeping the peace between brothers and sisters."

"Uncle's right. No bossing," Bernadette ordered.

"Or meddling," Nick added, eyeing the children's mother.

"Don't worry. We've given up looking for a woman for you. As long as she's nice and you like her, we're not gonna mess anything up for you, brother."

"Besides," Louise added coyly, "we don't have any informants in Missouri."

Dillon woke up slowly from a peaceful day's sleep in the rudimentary loft he'd created in his church, the beginning of an ever-changing plan for a place to live and dream. He dreamed big, and because he also dreamed often, he didn't object to an awakening, as long as it wasn't overly rude. And this one wasn't, not really. After all, he was the one who had left the front door open. But he'd only meant to invite the spring breeze inside.

He rolled to his side and braced himself on one arm. It was Joey, wandering into what she no doubt took for an empty building and a source of entertainment for her charge. He gathered her latest assignment must be baby-sitting. The baby had to be one of Bernadette's kids. At that age, they all looked alike to everyone but the parents.

He opened his mouth to speak, but then closed it in deference to the winning sound of woman conversing with a baby as though she were having a two-way exchange. Perched on his mattress and still half asleep, Dillon fancied himself a bit of bric-a-brac on a shelf. Better yet, the casino's security camera, the "eye in the sky." He would keep quiet—no evil could be found in this sweet little scene—enjoy the view and leave them to their play. They'd already discovered the workbench stool with the swivel seat and caster feet.

"I won't let it get away from you, sweetie. Oh, big boy, look at you, walking it across the floor. Oops!" She tucked the stool between her legs and pulled the boy onto her lap. "Here, let's take a ride. Isn't this a fun car?"

Not too fast, Joey, that thing can get away from you.

But she spun and rolled into the wall, pushed on the wall and spun around again, filling the rafters with the kind of baby giggles Dillon couldn't think of cutting short. Finding a spy on the wall—now that would be a rude awakening.

"Your uncle Dillon has some really cool stuff here, huh? What's that?" Back on the floor, the baby had discovered a block of wood. "Another car? Oh, look, Joey, here's a whole bunch of blocks. We could build a house."

Joey?

"I mean Nicky. I'm sorry. Watch, here's one for you, and one for…"

Dillon tuned in with new interest in the woman sitting cross-legged next to a box of scrap wood. She chattered away as she and the baby took turns stacking discarded end pieces like play blocks—two-by-fours and four-by-fours that Dillon had indeed cut up and saved with just such a thought in mind. Had he heard her right? He listened closely for another slip, but it was only "sweetie" this and "big boy" that.

Suddenly the baby grabbed the woman's blouse and gave a mighty tug.

"Uh-oh. You're hungry, huh? You're still nursing? I'm sorry, honey, but I'm not…" Head down, watching, she did nothing to stop the tugging, nothing to back up her feeble protests. "I can't. I wish I could, but it's not…my faucet doesn't work anymore."

No surprise, Dillon thought. He'd had her pegged all along for a young mother. He didn't want to think about what might have happened to her child. She'd had some trouble, no doubt about that. Again he started to declare his presence, but the baby's actions tied a quick knot in his tongue. It was little Nicky, all right—the one who saw his mother's blouse as a refrigerator door. He'd drawn a bead on a tit and wasn't taking no for an answer.

"I hate to disappoint you," she whispered, but she wasn't resisting. Her shoulders, arms, hands, molded into a soft shell around the baby, cradling him against her as though they did this together every day. She tipped her head back, eyes closed, and chanted, "I really, really hate to…I'm sorry, Joey. I'm so sorry…so sorry…so…"

The baby didn't seem sorry.

But Dillon was. He couldn't take his eyes off the amazing sight, couldn't speak, couldn't forgive himself for not speaking. If he had any manners, he would duck. Now.

Too late. He was looking straight into a tearful pair of blue eyes, and all he could think was, *Nick would kill me if he walked in right now.*

He couldn't tell what the woman was thinking. At first she only stared; nothing moving but the tears silently slipping down her cheeks. But then her shoulders began to tremble, and she shook her head slowly, methodically, a strange spark igniting her eyes.

"You're not taking him."

"Okay," Dillon said quietly. He'd seen that look. He'd heard those words. He knew that state of mind. More like chaos of mind. Without losing eye contact, he found the top of the ladder and quickly made his way from sleeping platform to main floor on stockinged feet.

"You can't take him away," she said, voice on the

rise, arms clutching for dear life. But it wasn't this baby's dear life. It was someone else, somewhere else.

This woman was someone else. And Dillon, for just a moment, was somewhere else, trying to talk another wretched soul into letting go. He closed his eyes and shook off the memory as he knelt beside her.

"He needs me" came the raspy claim, and from the sound of enthusiastic sucking, on that count she wasn't too far off.

"Joey, it's okay. Nobody's taking anybody." A juicy smack signaled the release of suction. Dillon glanced down at two big brown eyes and one distended pink tit. He wasn't asking, and the baby wasn't telling. He averted his own crazy-curious eyes, but he managed to sound pretty calm. "Look. He's all finished. Looks like he enjoyed himself, too." *The little scrounger.* "Didn't you, Nicky? His mom named him after Nick. Kinda looks like his uncle Nick, doesn't he?"

"Nick?"

"Yeah, Nick." The name seemed to bring the woman to her senses, her eyes into focus. Dillon craned his neck and scanned window to window. "You don't want him to see you like this, do you?"

"Nicky?"

"Baby Nicky. Nick's little nephew. He's a cutie, huh?"

"He is." Still clutching the boy close, she took a swipe at her tears with her free hand. "He really is. We were just playing."

"I know. I didn't mean to…" He pointed to the

loft. "I was up there sleeping. That's where I sleep whenever…"

"Because it's quiet here." She gave a tight-lipped nod. The baby was beginning to squirm. "I'm sorry. I didn't think there was anyone…"

The sound of voices outside startled them both.

"It's Nick. Please don't—"

"It's okay." Dillon gave her a pointed look. "Better button up."

"Joey?"

Dillon stood quickly and stepped between the woman on the floor and the search party. He knew damn well he was wearing guilt on his face like tomato paste, and for what? Being out of his…boots?

Nobody moved while Nick took visual account of every detail before assuming the jealous lover's tone.

"What's going on?"

"Nothing," Dillon said calmly. "They just came in here to play. Joey thought the place was empty."

"I'm sorry I woke you up," said the woman on the floor behind him.

Wordlessly, Bernadette stepped in and reached for her baby. For a moment, Dillon wasn't sure the woman who called herself Joey would give him up. Her breasts were covered, but her tears were unmistakable.

"Now look what you did," Bernadette crooned to her boy, who was vacating a dark wet patch of denim in Joey's lap. "This lady's a trainer, and you are sooo not trained, little Nicky. I'm sorry about that."

"I should have seen it coming," Joey whispered. Dillon turned to offer her a hand, but Nick was there first. She looked up at him, all sad-eyed and wounded, and Dillon didn't know what to think.

Bubbles broke the silence. "I told you he was leaky."

"We'll be getting along now," Bernadette said. "It was nice meeting you. You want me to take those jeans and throw them in the wash? I know these guys don't have a washing machine on the place."

"I still have chores to do today. A little diaper leakage only adds spice to the mix." Joey drew a deep breath, now studiously avoiding both men's eyes. "And since I'm on my way back to the barn, I'll walk out with you. We hardly got a chance to talk. Did you kids have a good ride? What did you think of True Colors?"

She had pulled herself together with amazing ease. In his stockinged feet, Dillon was unable to do the thing he most wanted, which was follow the crowd. And he knew Nick wasn't going anywhere. When the women and children were gone, Dillon was going to have to face up to the Man. And he hadn't even done anything.

"What happened?"

Dillon stared at the door, shaking his head. "I'm not sure."

"What do you mean, you're not sure? Why was she crying?"

"Nick, I'm tellin' you, that woman's got..." Dillon gestured—door, Nick, door again. "You don't wanna get yourself...she's seriously..."

Nick was still waiting.

"I didn't do nothin' to her, if that's what you're thinkin'." Dillon sighed. What was he supposed to say? "She came in here with the baby, didn't know I was…" *Draw him a diagram.* "I was up there sleeping. She was down here playing with the baby. That's it. That's…I swear to God."

"I'm not accusing you of anything." But Nick stared long enough to extract a confession if there was one to be made. Finally he lifted one shoulder. "I figured you must've said something to her."

"Like what?"

"Like maybe you don't like the idea of her staying here. Maybe you accused her of something, made her feel bad."

"I don't know anything about her, Nick." The roar of a car engine drew their notice, and they exchanged glances. *Women.* Dillon raised his brow as the tell-tailpipe beat its raucous retreat. "Except her name sure ain't Joey."

"I don't care what her name is."

"Me, neither," Dillon said quickly. "Names don't mean much. Especially white people's names. Smith, Anderson, Jones—you run into a hundred of 'em, same name, none of 'em related."

"You forgot about *Black*."

Dillon chuckled. "My great-grandfather's name was Black Bear Runs Him. I'm thinking of claimin' the whole thing back again. Maybe in Lakota."

Nick wandered over to the window nearest the driveway, halting several feet away with a scrape of his boot heel. She couldn't see him, but they could both see her headed for the trailer house and not the barn.

"Why won't she tell me her name?"

"In the old days, everyone had a secret name. It was between you and *Tunkasila*. If you told it around, the name lost its power." Although Dillon didn't think this was true for women, it sounded good. He was reaching, but what was a partner for? "She came to you with little to show for herself except a big fear and a big loss."

"She knows I won't hurt her."

"She needs to keep some kind of power to herself right now. They say knowledge is power. Maybe just knowing who she is might be too much power for her to give away. It might be all she's got."

Nick turned away from the window, maybe taking some kind of comfort from Dillon's words, or at least his presence. He gave half a smile. "You scare me sometimes."

"When?"

"Times when you talk like that and it starts to make sense." He shook his head. "I don't have a secret name. How 'bout you?

"Hell, all my best secrets became scandals a long time ago."

"They did? Where was I?"

"You had my back, just like always." Dillon nodded toward the trailer house. "Now you've got hers."

Nick folded his arms and stared out the window again, this time at the barn. "How would you feel about racing True Colors?"

"Me?"

"Us."

Horse racing? *Nick?*

"He's your horse."

"You're my partner. It's not gonna happen unless we both agree."

Dillon grinned. "What's the one thing that sets a man apart from a dumb beast? It's the courage—"

"—to take a chance," Nick recited. It was a maxim they'd used on each other more times than either could count.

But horse racing? Dillon had thought *he* was supposed to be the dreamer in this outfit.

He clapped a hand on Nick's broad shoulder. "Welcome to the dark side, man."

11

Nick found his mysterious guest sitting on the floor beneath the wall phone, hugging her knees, the John Deere cap dangling from her fingers. Like a big-eyed child wary of a scolding, she watched him every step of the way as he crossed the warped brown linoleum from back door to boxy kitchen. He washed his hands, drank some water from a coffee mug, peered through the unadorned window at an unclouded sky, all the while trying to come up with something to say. It was no good asking. That much he knew.

He'd begun to worry that at some point she might decide to give him the answers he no longer really wanted. All too often, truth was a bitch. Whatever it was in this case, sooner or later truth would take her away—which would have been fine just a few days ago. How long had she been with him now? Less than a week, and he'd let himself get all tied up inside over something that made no sense. But the reason it made no sense was because he was tied up over it. The truth about Joey was none of his business.

Believe it, he told himself, *and keep it simple on your end. The only truth is what you see for yourself, what you do and the way you do it. That's it. The rest is only talk.*

When he turned to her again, she stood slowly, as though he'd summoned her. "I was just about to…" She made a futile gesture toward the phone.

"Go ahead. I'll leave you alone if you want."

"I don't. It's the stupidest thing I could do right now." She took a step closer. "I don't know what happened to me, Nick. You must think I'm crazy. Dillon must think—"

"He's okay with racing True Colors," he said quickly. He noticed the change in her expression right away, the vacancy beginning to fill. "I mean, trying him out. Says he'll go with my decision, but if he's got real *cante*—you know, heart—seems like we oughta give it a shot with you here." He lifted one shoulder. "As long as you're gonna be here, anyway."

"Give me a few days with him. That plowed field is a pretty good place to work him, but if there's a track close by, I'd like to run him against a stopwatch." Her passion swelling as the plan grew, she touched his arm. "I won't waste your money."

"What do you charge?"

"Not me, but all the other fees that have to be considered. You can easily afford me, Nick. I don't eat much."

He wasn't worried so much about his bank account as about the fact that sooner or later she would make that call, and he wasn't sure what he would do when the sonuvabitch showed up at his door, looking to take her back. He'd seen it before, good women like his sister letting love get the best of them, suck them dry, then leave them feeling ugly and ashamed. Louise was doing fine on her own, but there had been a time when she'd needed more convincing than Nick could stomach. She'd gone to the phone, gone to the door, offered the friggin' parasite more chances.

Okay, so he *did* know what he would do. He'd done it before. *The only truth is what you see, what you do and the way you do it.* And he would do it again.

"Did Nicky tear out a chunk of your hair or something?" He wanted to brush a stray lock back from her face, just for an excuse to touch her. He tried a smile instead. "Last time they brought that little rascal over, I gave him a ride on my shoulders, and he got two little handfuls off me. I didn't cry, but I came damn close." She glanced away. He knew he'd hit a nerve. "You okay?"

She shook her head in a way that said it hurt to move. "Could you just hold me for a minute?"

He drew her into his arms, held her against his chest

and imagined her being his to keep. Anybody came for her right now, he knew exactly what he would do. When the door opened, he turned his head and gave his unsuspecting partner a look that left no doubt.

Dillon nodded, backed out and closed the door without saying a word.

Far be it from him to interfere unless he wanted to sacrifice a few body parts, Dillon thought. Which he did not. Better to get a cold drink from the garden hose than try ribbing or ragging his way into the kitchen past *that* thoroughly astounding little scene. It had been too long since Nick had let a woman into his life, and he was guarding this one like a pit bull. It was no use warning him about the boatload of baggage she was carrying. As far as Nick was concerned, all she had to her fictitious name were the clothes on her back.

She also had a kid somewhere, a detail Dillon would happily file under *none of my concern* if he didn't foresee this thing biting his partner squarely in the ass very soon. Any other detail but a matter of the heart. Any other heart but Nick's. He wished he didn't have to know so damn much, but everybody had their gifts. Dillon knew women, and the look on that woman's face had been unmistakable. She was no wet nurse. She'd had a baby, and she'd lost it somehow. Death was the obvious guess, but Dillon wasn't ready to place any bets.

He headed for the barn, where the water from the pump would be cold, if nothing else. He still had time to ride out to the south pasture and fix the leak on that stock tank before he got ready for work. Leave Nick alone with the woman for a while, he thought. Maybe he was getting something out of her.

She would have Dillon's full sympathy along with Nick's—if it was just her. But suddenly Nick was doing the unthinkable, dropping vital bits of his hard-earned body armor at her feet. What would stop her from reaching into his chest and tearing the man's heart out? Once exposed, Nick wasn't much of a defensive player. Dillon knew Nick, and the signs were clear. His partner was one lovesick puppy.

Yup, Dillon wished he didn't have to know so damn much.

He wished he didn't have to remember any of what all his damn knowledge had cost him. And the people he loved…

The army had prepared Nick for the kind of work that was left to be had in the Western oil fields. The boom in the late seventies and early eighties had long been busted. The drop in foreign oil prices had put the cap on countless wells, but with enough activity left and a few new friends, Nick had found work with a drilling contractor when his hitch was up. And because jobs at home were tight, Dillon had laid claim to Nick's shirttail. But when Nick's little brother,

Johnny, decided that his time had come, Dillon had his doubts. Not that he didn't think of John as a brother, too, but Nick hadn't been around for a while, and Dillon had.

Johnny Red Shield was twenty going on twelve. He was the kid who would perform an Olympic-caliber swan dive off a tree branch without checking the depth of the water first. On one occasion Dillon had fished him out of the river and later teased him about the gallons of water and the number of minnows he'd coughed up. Nobody ever faulted Johnny for the way any escapade turned out. He was too damn lovable. Johnny was the kid you never left behind when you went on a party, even though you knew you would have to carry him home. He was the one who got the girls. He was the one who had the bottle rockets or the weed or the keys to somebody's car.

But Nick hardly knew the twenty-year-old Johnny. He remembered the kid brother who was everybody's pet, back when calling John a roughneck was all in fun. The three of them had shared some good times when Nick was home on leave, but those times were like holidays. To really appreciate the day-to-day Johnny… well, you had to be there. Nick had been there until he wasn't. His parents were still around back then, and they'd expected Nick back in the fold. Time in the military was for going, doing and bringing home the tales. Nick had kept order in the household before, and he would surely return to restore it.

But Nick had other ideas. He couldn't help his family without making a life for himself—a job that required, well, a job. Starting out as a roughneck, he soon picked up more specialized rig-crew skills, a truck driver's license, considerable respect and connections with operators and contractors throughout the area. He'd saved Dillon's newlywed bacon by setting him up with the contractor, but he hadn't known what he was in for when he'd said, *Come on out, Johnny-boy. I'll train you myself.*

If John was the family favorite, Nick was the hero. If anyone could provide, decide, protect, redeem or rescue, it was Nick. Roughnecking was hard and often dangerous work, but jobs of any kind were tough to find on the reservation. You get one shot on my say-so, he'd told Dillon. Learn your job, do it well, and you can support a family. He'd given John the same advice. One shot, he'd said. No screwing around.

What Nick didn't understand was that screwing around was Johnny's stock in trade. Dillon's misgivings about John strained his relationship with Nick. Give the kid a break, Nick would say, even though he never took any breaks for himself. He brought his sister out to Montana close on John's heels, put her in school, then enrolled in a class on his day off. But John was allowed to "work into a routine." One shot became three and then five. The slack was never cut; it was stretched thin and made light. Too easy, Dillon had said, and he'd been wrong about that. Dead wrong. He would never forget his last quarrel with John.

Nick will always be the brother you want and the one I've got.

Maybe he was right. God knew Dillon had enough problems of his own without worrying about what was going on next door. His strong-minded wife was threatening to "move back to civilization," where she could deliver what would have been their second child "by a doctor who knew the difference between a woman and a ewe." Nick was trying to drive a truck part-time, attend college part-time, work in the field full-time and keep two female housemates—his sister and his girlfriend—from killing each other at any given time. Johnny was barely hanging on to his job, sleeping on Nick's sofa and enjoying life when he wasn't hungover.

Nobody ever talked about John's condition the night of the fire. According to Bernadette, John had claimed to be sick, said he wasn't going to work. He wasn't staying home, Nick had told him. He was getting in the truck. John's sofa time was over. Nick would take him to work or the bus station.

John was in no mood to go Greyhound.

Monica was due any day, and she was miserable. Dillon was trying to get home early when John showed up for his shift on the same rig. Nick wasn't scheduled to work that night, but he'd offered to finish out Dillon's shift. Or at least Dillon chose to recall it as an offer, but maybe he'd asked. Or hinted, or complained about what was going on at home. He remembered feeling slightly queasy when Nick had clocked in. Johnny was hanging back looking sulky and green around the gills. Nick was pissed. The vibes were bad all around. It was no time for Dillon to press his momentary edge over Johnny to squeeze out a favor, but he'd done it. No question now. John would pull his shift because Nick would see to it. And Dillon was outta there.

He'd tried to breathe easy after leaving the field. Hell, Nick was the one who'd brought the kids out there. Dillon was a family man. He was making his own way. He was highway- and homeward-bound when he heard the explosion. John's face flashed in his mind like a slide projected on a screen. Something told him Johnny was a dead man.

Fire and smoke filled the night sky. The stench of oil aflame seared Dillon's nose and sickened his stomach. His pulse skated on the screams of a dozen different sirens, and there was no real thought given to what he would find or what he could do. It was all Nick, Johnny, drive and run.

Heat, smoke and flame consumed the night. Soot-covered men dashed around like ants. Directions meant little in all the noise and confusion. Questions meant less.

"Which rig is it?" Dillon shouted into one face. "Have you seen Nick Red Shield?" he spat into another. He grabbed an arm. "John? Johnny Red Shield?"

He found them at the core of a knot of paramedics who were trying to pry John's body from his brother's intractable embrace. Both men were tattered and charred. John flopped like a rag doll draped in the arms of a would-be animator, while there was monster life in Nick's eyes and ungodly voice in his throat. With the whole world on fire, Nick's rage ruled. His own pain was unthinkable, his injuries so hideous even trained eyes betrayed their shock. But he stood tall and kept them all at bay in that horrible splinter of eternity that eventually became, simply, the night Johnny died.

Dillon doubted Nick remembered much of it. But he had no way of knowing for sure beyond his personal belief in a merciful God.

It was hard enough for Dillon to live with the memory. Monica had lost the baby. Nick had lost a big chunk of his life. Years later, Dillon had lost Monica and everything that went with her, including the two children—their daughter and the son they'd made while they were trying to hang on to their life together. Some people tried too hard; some didn't try hard enough. Either way, *trying* didn't seem to count for much in the final tally. The only way to get by was to adopt a life-goes-on philosophy and maybe convince the kids to get an education. "Nobody loves a roughneck," Dillon would say to them. He was pretty sure they had no idea what he was talking about, but they always humored him. "Yeah, Dad, we know."

But Nick had gone too quiet. He had spent too much time alone. He never turned family away, but he seldom sought anyone out. He had been the only survivor from the five-man rig crew, and he never talked about it. Never mentioned luck, bad or good, his or Dillon's. Never said he regretted surviving, but Dillon wondered sometimes, the way he kept it all in. He was present, but he was untouchable.

Nick will always be the brother you want and the one I've got.

So what? Dillon wanted the answer now as much as he had then. They treated each other like brothers. Always had, according to Dillon's way of thinking. The doing mattered more than the being, but since John no longer *was* and could, therefore, no longer do, Dillon often wondered which brother the boy had carried to his grave—the one Dillon wanted or the one John had?

And how much of Nick had survived *the night John died*?

"You're playin' in the water again."

Dillon turned to find Nick peering at him through the barn door, halter and lead looped in his gloved hand. Always doing something, that guy.

"Tank was low."

"I just filled it this morning," Nick said.

"*My* tank."

With a quick slice of his hand, Dillon sent a sheet of water toward a crow dropping in for a landing on the tank rim. The bird flapped, squawked and sent him away from his stock-tank reflections with a wistful smile. "We should get one of those automatic horse waterers. Kinda like a drinking fountain."

"We can work with what we've got." Good ol' straight-answer Nick. "I was thinkin' we'd take the stud out to the rodeo grounds and let Joey try him out on the track. You wanna go?" He offered the invitation quietly, without looking up from the project he was making of reversing a twist in the nylon lead. "If you have some time."

What? Dillon was about to be included? Sure, they'd had a little talk. Not exactly a heart-to-heart, and no indication that Nick believed he hadn't done something to make her cry or act crazy. The new limitations on Dillon's welcome were pretty clear, especially around the woman.

"When were you thinking?" More touched by the gesture than he wanted to be, Dillon opted for sarcasm. "I can't make any promises until I check my calendar, but I can sure pencil you guys in." He scribbled a couple of loops in the air and added a punctuation mark. "You gave this Missouri woman full access, and haven't even let me touch him yet, man."

"The stud? Hell, I just barely got him home. Nobody's stopping you from trying him out, especially now that Joey's already started—"

"See, that's what I'm talkin' about. You're all about *Joey* all of sudden. Take it easy, man." Dillon laid a hand on Nick's shoulder. "It isn't like you to go stickin' your neck out like this."

"I've been saying all along, if we're going to make it in this business, we need a stud that's a proven winner."

"I'm not talking about taking a chance on the horse." Dillon took a step back, and his hand fell away. "Okay, what do I know? I know what you're thinkin', man. I married a woman who came from another planet, and look what happened. She hopped the next space shuttle, back to where she came from. But she never tried to pass herself off as anything but an alien. This one you're mixed up with, Nick, I'm just sayin'…"

Nick snorted. "Man, you're worse than my sisters."

"I'm just sayin', it's one thing to pick up a stray cat, but this ain't no animal somebody left on the road. This is a pretty mysterious woman. Pretty and mysterious. You're thinkin', kinda makes her interesting. I'm thinkin', kinda makes her dangerous. Because you don't know who she is, and you don't know where she's been or who her people are. I'm just sayin'…"

"Say it and get it over with." Head down, hat brim tipped low, Nick thought he was hiding his amusement. But the corners of his damn mouth were twitching.

Dillon sighed. What could he say? His whole life, Nick had been out of control exactly once. Who else did he know who could say that? Not that it was something Nick would say, but Dillon was the talker.

"Hell, I'm just talkin'. Figured I was on a roll." Dillon grinned. Getting Nick to smile had that effect on him. "Louise never misses *America's Most Wanted*, so if Missouri Woman turns up on the show, you're covered. Otherwise, I suggest you keep the family jewels in a safe place."

"I'm covered there, too, D. Any more advice before we see what kind of a quarter-mile True Colors has in him?"

Dillon shrugged, feeling more than a little foolish for preaching safety to Nick, who handed him the halter. Wordless instructions. Nick would hook up the two-horse trailer while Dillon collected the horse.

"Hey," Nick called out to him before he reached the door at the far end of the barn. Dillon swung around. "Her name's still Joey."

It wasn't much of a track by any horseman's standards, but Joey pronounced it fit for her purpose. Situated at the edge of town, the track circumscribed an arena that played host to outdoor events in the summer, including the Fourth of July rodeo, various forms of entertainment involving monster trucks and crashing cars, and the occasional western-style horse race. Mobridge was a cowboy and Indian town—owned by cowboys and frequented by Indians.

With a feed store and a veterinary clinic conveniently located nearby, Nick was able to fill Joey's initial shopping order for hot feed, supplements, wraps, Absorbine and, most important, a stopwatch.

In the process of talking the vet out of a load of sympathy over her "crazy freak accident" and into loaning her a stethoscope for gauging stamina, Joey piqued the young man's curiosity and soon had him examining True Colors and fairly swooning over the horse's excellent physical condition. No charge.

Nick wasn't sure what to expect at the track, and he felt funny about taking Joey's instructions, considering what a messed-up little mouse she'd been until the moment he'd lifted her into True Colors' saddle. Instant authority. Now she had him and Dillon both stepping off yardage and swinging gates for her. Dillon got his chance to try the horse during the warm-up, but he was clearly not the same horse under Dillon's adept but merely human hand as he was for Joey. How many hours had she spent with the stallion? Judging by the fit the two of them already had going for them, those hours defined the cliché *quality time*.

What Nick had seen the first time she'd ridden the flashy stud had been a pale prelude to the display they put on for their audience of two in the early evening shadows behind the crow's nest of the Sitting Bull Stampede arena. Even without a proper racing saddle, she somehow adjusted herself and her gear into a sleek, seamless package, a natural fifth appendage. There was no starting gate, whistle or gun, only some imperceptible signal that ignited an explosion of equine energy and jolted human heart rates. Bent low over the horse's outstretched neck, Joey fairly floated in the saddle, her arms pumping like pistons precisely tuned to push the horse's nose through time and space.

It was over in little more than half a minute. Nick glanced at Dillon, who shook his head in disbelief even before he managed to uncurl his fingers to reveal the face of the stopwatch. Speechless, they turned to watch horse and rider take a pace-easing turn at the far end of the track. Joey had risen taller, knees still bent, weight in her calves, yellow-gold hair fluttering like a major-league pennant.

"Was that as fast as I think it was?"

"I don't know," Dillon said, dazed. "My thumb might have been slow on the uptake. But I'm thinkin' that is one fast Paint horse."

"That's not a horse, man, that's a cheetah. Told you I could pick 'em." Nick punched his partner's shoulder, a parting shot before he scaled the fence. He hadn't felt this giddy in…

He had *never* felt this giddy.

Dillon scrambled up beside him and grabbed him by the arm. "She really knows what she's doing."

It sounded oddly like a warning. Nick chuckled. "No shit."

"That's no lady, Nick. That's a jock." Dillon's pointed look was vaguely disturbing. Accusatory.

Nick shook off his partner's hand. "She helped her father out when she was growing up. I told you about that, didn't I? Or she told you."

"I'll bet you any money, that woman's a professional jockey."

Any other time, Nick would have won the staredown, but the sound of trotting hoofbeats and the feel of Joey's approach pressed him for attention. "You got it," he said as he dropped to the ground on the track side.

"How much?"

"You name it," Nick called over his shoulder as Joey rode up to him, her mount prancing like a stakes winner.

Joey dismounted with catlike grace before Nick had a chance to offer her a hand. Her fireball mount lowered his head like a docile pup to enjoy the reward of a vigorous neck scratching. She flipped the reins over his ears and favored Nick with a new kind of smile—one that said *yes!*

"Name what?" she asked.

"The first baby," Dillon said, catching up. "If it's a girl, I vote for Joey. If it's a boy, I still vote for Joey. You're a hell of a jockey."

"He means True Colors' first baby." Nick patted the horse's mottled shoulder, impressed with the animal's relative calm on the heels of delivering his burst of speed. "We're already making bets."

"What did you get for a time?" she asked, exhilarated, her face flushed and glowing. She spared Dillon's proudly proffered stopwatch a glance as she loosened the cinch.

But the arch of her brow wasn't the response the

men expected. *Hell, she could have won a race with that time, easy.*

"Like I said, I probably added a second on either end," Dillon said. "If I'd'a blinked, I coulda missed the whole thing. You wanna go again?"

"That was a good run," she said as they fell into step with her, heading for the horse trailer. "Let's not push it. He's in fine fettle, as my dad would say. And look at him, so cool and collected. He's such a sweetie. But what's really sweet is the way he moves," she enthused as she parked the horse for loading.

Nick pulled the saddle, while the stallion, in response to some private signal, lowered his big head into Joey's small hands to be relieved of the bridle.

Her tone mellowed. "So steady and smooth, every joint oiled," she murmured, as though she were pouring a lover's praise into the horse's long black velvet ear. "Every muscle tuned perfectly to the bone, and all that momentum flowing from his body…"

Saddle in hand, Nick stared, waiting breathlessly on the finish.

She glanced at him, looking startled, as though she'd caught him standing outside a window eavesdropping on her.

"We've got ourselves the makings of a racehorse here," Joey said, going immediately back to her chirping. "It's all there. All he needs is careful feeding and the right workout regimen."

"They start racing this month in Pierre, next

month in Aberdeen," Dillon said, and Nick reminded himself that his partner had a talent for going from skeptic to believer in no time flat. "You got one track in Iowa, one in Minnesota, a bunch in Nebraska. I don't know how many allow Paints to race against Quarter Horses, but I can find out."

Nick handed Joey a halter in exchange for the bridle. "You sure you wanna do this?"

"For you? Yes. Absolutely."

"How much racing have you done?" Dillon asked. "You can't tell me you're not a jockey."

"Not now, but I was." She offered Nick an apologetic glance. "I started out with my father, but it was more than that. I had a good run myself."

Dillon persisted. "How long ago did you quit?"

"I've been out of it for a couple of years. I was ready for something else."

Ask her, Dillon. You're doing fine so far.

But whatever she was ready for and the choice she'd made were only pieces of history that didn't interest Nick's partner. And Nick decided he didn't need to know. The woman was here for now, staying at his place, eating his groceries. She might as well be useful.

"Hank Two Dog still has that bay gelding he raced last year," Dillon said. "Did pretty good his first time out but didn't bring much *toniga* to the table after that. I bet we could run this one against him, kinda like a tryout."

"Let's see where we are with him in a week," Joey said. "What's *tonega*?"

"Guts," Dillon said. He grinned. "The edible kind."

"That's not the right kind of saddle." Nick eyed the two saddles on the trailer racks—the heavy western style he was comfortable with and the one he'd just stored that struck him as a hybrid, neither fish nor fowl, Western nor eastern. He shut the curved door on the front of his old two-horse and snapped the padlock. Damned if he wasn't thinking about hunting her up a saddle.

"It'll do for now," she said as True Colors loaded readily for her.

They stopped at the last gas station east of the river, which gave Nick's passengers an excuse to disappear. Dillon had to run across the street to Gibson's to "check the magazine rack" for God knew what. Whenever a new interest came crashing down on him, Dillon loaded up on papers and magazines. Nick filled both the pickup's gas tanks, paid the bill and asked for change for the pop machine. Then he stood there, feeling like a jackass. Dillon was just doing his usual, but Joey…

It'll do for now.

If she was playing with him, at least she had the decency to make do with what he had. He was pretty sure she wouldn't be around much longer. Nick knew where the pay phone was in this place. He didn't need to walk around the corner to the side of the building to know who was using it.

Getting her shit together while you wait.

And wasn't that exactly the way he wanted it?

12

Over the next few days, Nick tried to pay attention to the work he had to do, while Joey threw herself into the work she'd made for herself. What he wanted to do was go his own way, meet up with her in the kitchen for supper and then go off to bed without too much talk. When she was ready to leave, he wanted to be ready to take her to the airport without asking any questions.

But nothing was working the way he wanted it to.

For one thing, he wanted to get the dirty jobs done around the place before he had to take off on his next hauling run. He prided himself on well-maintained pens and a barn that smelled more or less clean. More saddle soap and horse hide, less hay dust and horse manure. To that end, he was forever pushing the front end loader on his faded blue 2N Ford tractor around the yard or shoveling, forking and hosing the crap out of the barn, especially after a long winter. He didn't keep any wrecks around unless he could keep them running, no cast-offs except the few four-leggeds he couldn't exactly turn away and no ramshackle buildings except for the one Dillon had been inspired to drag home because God had let it go for a song. He'd never had a trainer working for him—likely never would again—and he wanted her to look back on her time at Wolf Trail Ranch and remember him as the big Indian who ran that neat little horse operation.

Okay, he wanted to make an impression, but it wasn't like he was going out of his way. His way was to walk the walk, do the work, spend his free time wheeling barrows full of manure out to the compost pile. Watching was also his way, and the training of True Colors gave him something well worth watching while he worked. The painted beauty of considerable stature willingly danced for the pale beauty whose size was immaterial. Separately each had turned Nick's head, but when they worked as a team, he was hard-pressed to look away.

But getting blinded, hooked or outright had was not his way, either.

One more thing Nick wanted was for the vision of his flashy Paint horse galloping ahead of the pack toward the finish line to die on the vine. He'd been hanging around Dillon too long. The smoke from his partner's damn pipe dreams was finally getting to him. He couldn't seem to keep his mind on building up the manure pile when his first and undoubtedly last female house guest was tearing down his mental resistance to anything involving smoke, dreams or her kind of woman.

In case anyone asked, Nick was no expert, but he had a few ideas about what *her kind* was. A guy had to be careful around the kind of woman who made canned soup taste like homemade simply by putting it into two bowls—one for him, and one for her. Or the kind that disappeared behind the bathroom door smelling like horse sweat and came out distinctly damp and drifting on a scent that had definitely fallen from the night sky rather than his showerhead. Or the kind who kept on going throughout the day, tending to the task she'd assigned herself, staying a step ahead of her steadfast melancholy until it finally caught up with her when she took it to bed at night. She was the kind who could break a man's heart without trying.

On the other hand, there was always *his* kind— the kind he carried on his back. He hadn't met a woman yet who could stand up to the Dragon Lady, who was itching to take on the newcomer. After hours of shoveling and considerable sweating, he'd used up what was left of the hot water trying to settle the Lady down. The shower soothed her some, but her kind had no sweet scent. He sometimes wished she'd been grafted onto some other part of his body, where he could easily reach her with some of that cream they'd used on him in rehab. He'd dreaded being touched, but after a while he'd learned to enjoy his massage therapy. Nowadays he tried to tell himself the itching was all in his head, but in her younger days, the Dragon Lady had been a great one for plastic surgery, and to this day she couldn't stand a chill. His body was literally too thin-skinned in some places to handle any direct cold.

He slid into a clean pair of jeans and reached for the long-sleeved shirt he'd hung on the hook on the back of the door. But getting dressed to walk across the hall in the dark suddenly seemed pretty stupid. Why bother? Joey had retired to his room, his bed. He was headed for the other room, the spare. Hell, he acted like an old boarding school nun sometimes. He left the shirt on the hook, left the bathroom light on, left his door open to remind his guest that she wasn't alone in the dark. She was a big chicken, she'd said.

And he was chickenshit.

He stood at the window and watched his beautiful Paint pace the fence in the blue-white moonlight. The stallion knew that his females were out there somewhere, and he didn't care that it was too early in the season for him to breed them. Another month, Nick wanted to assure him. But what consolation would a man's assurance be for a hungry, healthy stud?

Especially coming from a man feeling the hunger but missing out on the health.

Yeah, he knew it was all in his head. Ugliness had a way of messing with a man's mind. True Colors wouldn't know anything about that. The mottled pattern on his hide only added to his beauty. His colors didn't repulse the females. It would probably even draw them to him.

The moment his mind showed him female drawn to male, he felt a hand touch his back. It took the form of a small shape, a cool contact, and the only thing that kept him from flinching was the knowledge that he'd developed a powerful imagination. When he thought about something hard enough, he could almost make it happen. He could banish physical pain, and with it he could set a whole host of feelings aside—loneliness, guilt, anger, desire. He could put all of it on the run.

He waited, but the feel of the hand would not go away. On a deep breath he caught her scent, and he thought Dillon might have been right. He had gone over to the dark side, where people lived in dreams. The hand stirred slightly, lightly, moving over his taut and terrible skin.

An unholy hand, or that of an angel?

"It's your turn," he ventured. "Tell me what you see."

Her hand nearly left him, all but the tips of her fingers tracing a long, hard, puckered ridge of tissue that could not be called skin. More like the "proud flesh" on a horse with a poorly healed wire cut. Some of his own raised scars had been removed, but there was dense testimony still scribbled on his skin, and she seemed intent on reading him with her fingers. He lacked the will to stop her.

Finally she said, "You left the door open."

"I thought you were asleep."

"That's the first lie you've told me since we met, Nick." She pressed her hands flat, fingers splayed over his shoulder blades. "Tell me what you wanted me to see."

"That I'd left the door open," he confessed quietly, tempted to warn her about leaving permanent prints. "That you could come in if you wanted to. Or have a look and then walk away."

"This is a test?"

"A setup, maybe. If I'd wanted you to see the whole truth, I would have turned more lights on."

"What I saw through the door you left open was a sexy, sexy man. Tall, broad shoulders, strong back tapering into a pair of—" shivers trickled down his back, chasing the slide of her hands, pooling at the base of his spine "—soft jeans that fit him just right."

He sucked in his breath as her fingertips slipped beneath the waistband. He told himself to turn around, but *himself* shot back, *Don't spoil this.* He braced his hands on either side of the small window as she laid her cool forehead against the middle of his back.

"I see the truth," she said, her breath a delicate

caress. "I can't imagine what you must have gone through. Is it tender at all?"

"I feel cold a lot. Your hands…"

"Hurt?"

The word had no meaning in the company of wet lips and tongue tip skating in and out of live-nerve territory, tracing tiny circles on his back. No sound, he told himself. No movement, no scaring her away. *Any noise you could make now would sound pitiful, anyway*, himself warned.

"Tell me if I hurt you," she whispered. "Tell me if I do something I shouldn't."

"I'm not…" He started to turn to her, but she pressed her thinly clad body against his back and slid her arms around him. Her hands, tucked in his waistband, came together on his belly.

"Not so fast, mister. This is what you get for turning your back on me." She unbuttoned his jeans. "Is this okay?" she whispered as her unholy hand went for the zipper, intent on lowering it tooth by saw-blade tooth.

He sucked it up, said a quick prayer, told himself there was no going back now. Himself said *amen*. And the free-wheeling hand of an angel slipped nimbly between biting zipper and tender flesh, barely touching him. *Barely* bearable. Nick drew a quick breath. Losing his precious control was not an option. Mentally he jammed his cock into the zipper.

"It would seem so," she said, sliding her hands over his hips and peeling the jeans off his cowboy ass.

"Yes, ma'am." He kicked them away as he turned and took hold of her waist. "That works fine."

"How fine?"

He chuckled. "I'm willing to let you be the judge."

Her hands went to his shoulders, and he lifted her, met cotton-covered breasts with nose and lips and tongue as she wrapped arms and legs around him, doing her damnedest to impale herself even though her panties and his resistance stood in the way.

Mount him and crack the whip on him, would she? There was no way in hell he would cross the line before she'd been there and back a time or three. Convinced she was riding high, she had placed her butt in his sling and given his hand easy access—over, under, around and through—ah, so slick and easy the way she'd spread her legs around him and left herself wide open for a stealthy finger foray, barely touching, tenderly obliging her physical pleas for more.

It was her turn to catch her breath in surprise as he laid her on the bed, stripping her, kissing her, touching her, tasting her. With measured patience, he coaxed her to come fully and safely and with complete impunity, making it too good to be anything but a leg-up. And up. And up.

But the full ride would require one more bit of tack. Closer to crazy than he realized, he tore into a packet and tore a hole in the damn condom.

"Smooth move," he grumbled, and she moaned. "Hold that thought, honey."

"No, it's okay." She dug her nails into his buttocks. "I want…I *want* you to."

"Don't worry. Got a whole damn…" He fumbled for the box, leaving him only one hand for her, while her two for him were going for the goal without a fumble.

"I'm not worried, Nick," she whispered as she took him inside her. "I'm not worried, I'm not worried, I'm not…not worried."

Worry was nothing. The finish line was all.

He held her close, cherishing the weight of her head on his arm and the feel of her heartbeat mixing with his. She wasn't asleep. She was tucked against him like a contented cat, one moment still, the next stretching and stirring one limb or another, exploring him with foot or fingers. No discovery had thus far turned her away. Maybe his body was more distinctive than it was disfigured.

And maybe a little pipe smoke floating around the mirrors in a guy's head wasn't such a bad thing, as long as he didn't get hooked.

"I'm leaving day after tomorrow for a four-day run," he told her. He'd mentioned it earlier, but that was *before*. "I'll be heading east this time, south and east. Making a circle through Minnesota, Wisconsin, Illinois, Iowa, back to Minnesota and then home again." *And?* "I could make a swing into Missouri if need be."

For a moment she said nothing. Finally, "What need would there be?"

"Whatever need it is you can't tell me about."

"Are you thinking of putting me back where you found me?"

"Not anymore." He was thinking about keeping her as long as he could. Right now, that was all he was thinking. "Are you on the pill?"

The breath from her small laugh prickled his skin. *Of course she was.*

"Dumb question, huh? I don't mind using a condom. I mean, I use 'em. Always have."

"I got a little carried away. I wanted…"

"I did, too." He leaned away, seeking her eyes in the shadows. "I don't want you to go, Joey, but I know the time's gonna come. Okay? I'm not a fool."

"I don't want you to go, either. Four days is a long time." She smiled, her hand absently traveling over the highs and lows of his hip. "You're going to be surprised how much I can do with True Colors in four days."

"You've been long on surprises, but tonight you outdid yourself."

"That explosion on the oil rig," she began tentatively. "The one that killed your brother. It almost killed you, too, didn't it?"

"Damn near."

"What caused it?"

"Drill stem hit a pocket of natural gas while we were making a connection. Gas came rushing through the stem, covered the rig floor. All it took was a spark and it was great balls of fire, baby." He glanced down at her. "That's what they told me, anyway. Truth is, I don't remember too many details. Don't much want to." He touched her hair, tucked a bit of it behind her ear. "So don't ask, okay?"

"Okay." She kissed his shoulder, touched the image of fingers that had once clawed his neck. "It's like a tattoo."

"Battle scars. It's always seemed easier to keep the bad times to myself." He caressed her hip. Pale moonlight revealed the dappled bruise, but no colors. And no story behind the colors. "How about your map of Florida? I tried to be careful."

"It doesn't hurt anymore, but you'd never know from the way it looks."

"It'll be gone soon, and it'll stop hurting inside, too. You won't forget, but you'll put it away somewhere safe. You'll go on to something else."

"Like you?"

"Like a different state, maybe. A different town, different friends, a different kind of—"

"No, I mean, like you putting the hurt away and going on to something else. I don't think you've done that." She rubbed his cheek with the backs of her fingers. "You'd be a wonderful father, Nick."

He snorted. "And you can tell that just by looking at me?"

"I could tell by watching you with your sister's children, by listening to you talk about them. I can tell by the way you treat me."

"If I've been treatin' you like a kid, I guess that phase of whatever we've got goin' is officially over. Even though…" He gave a humorless chuckle. "I'm way too old and too beat up for a girl like you."

"I have news for you. Between the ages of fifteen and fifty, a woman doesn't appreciate being called a girl."

"I hear them calling one another *girl* all the time."

"That's different. I think. I've never really had any women friends. Or girlfriends, either. Well, one. Amy. She worked on the backstretch for a summer job when I was apprenticing. She said she was coming back to her job the next year, but she worked for a veterinarian instead. Which was a good plan, you know? She was in college, getting all kinds of good experience. We lost touch, but I'm sure she stayed in school and became a vet. She knew what she wanted."

"And what did you want back then?"

"I wanted to ride."

"Among other things," he said, echoing her tone from an earlier remark. "You said you quit because you were ready for something else."

"Clearly I was wrong. The first time I rode him, True Colors showed me just how wrong." She propped herself on one arm, her confidence in the moment displacing memories. "Everyone dreams of finding a horse like that, Nick. A Seabiscuit or a Seattle Slew. When a horse from a big-name farm becomes a winner, big deal. No surprise. He belongs to some oil-rich sheik or Texan or some, you know, *business*man. Who cares?

"But when a real horse lover discovers that one-in-a-million horse, and you know it's heart-to-heart, one heart finding the other in the dark—" she touched his chest, pointing out the place of discovery or punctuating her point, he wasn't sure which "—that's a dream come true. From the jockey to the trainer to the little old lady in line with her two-dollar bet, who wouldn't want to be a part of something like that?"

"I don't know. Maybe the big Indian who just wanted a great stud for his mares?"

He liked the part about one heart finding another in the dark, but the image it brought to mind wasn't so much about horses' hearts or human hearts as it was about one tender piece of a clueless whole casting around in some big, empty space on the off chance of bumping into its destiny.

And if he had any sense, he would be worrying about all this image-conjuring he'd been doing.

"Well, you got him," she said.

"But we're not talkin' Seattle Slew here," he reminded her. And himself. "If you get him in shape, we're just talking about trying him out on a couple of South Dakota tracks."

"I can almost guarantee you won't want to stop there."

"Dillon's the one you won't be able to stop. Me, I'm the cautious kind. One step at a time."

"Does it scare you?" She tilted her head. "Taking chances?"

"What have I got to lose? Like you said, I've got the stud. If this thing doesn't work out, hell, I wasn't looking for a racehorse."

"How about taking a chance on me? Does that scare you?"

"I think you know what you're doing." He laughed. "Kinda wish *I* knew what you were doing, though. Yeah, that part scares me a little bit." He touched her chin. "Tell you what I'm not afraid of, and that's your boyfriend."

"My boyfriend?"

"Whoever left you the way he did. I've been through fire, Joey. A lot of guys claim they're tough, but I wear proof. Whatever it is I don't know about him, it don't mean shit. I know all I need to know."

"Good," she firmly pronounced as she laid her head back down in the pocket of his shoulder.

"Except his name and where he lives."

"And what he does."

"I see what he does. He beats up on women."

"He rarely does that kind of dirty work himself." She popped up again. "No, Nick, listen to me. The kind of man who does something like that himself is bad enough. But someone who pays other people to do it for him…we're talking a whole different league."

"Sounds like something out of a gangster movie." He looped his arm around her tense shoulders and drew her back down. *You're safe if you stick with me.* He chuckled. "I like westerns, myself. One on one."

"What a myth that is. If it had been one on one—one cowboy, one Indian—I have a feeling we'd be looking at some different faces on Mount Rushmore."

"You sure as hell wouldn't be lookin' at human faces. You'd be lookin' at Paha Sapa the way it was when Iktomi brought the first man through a cave to the upper world."

"It was a *man*, was it?"

"So they say. A Lakota man. You never hear about women falling for Iktomi's tricks. It's always men. They say it was warm and safe inside the earth, but Iktomi, the old spider, he talked the first people into being born through the mouth of that cave—Wind Cave in the Black Hills. Once they got out, they couldn't get back in." He slid her a glance. "Not for lack of tryin'."

"Back to the womb, where it's warm and safe," she reflected. "Is that what getting inside a woman is all about?"

"It is if it works for you. Sounds better than the truth. Something like, *You want me to act like a man? I'll stop being a baby if you'll let me get in there and make one.*"

"And if I don't?"

"I'll howl at the moon."

"We can't have that." After a pause, she asked seriously, "Why don't you have children, Nick?"

"I'm gettin' too old to have kids."

"No, you're not."

"I'm not married, for starters. I know some people

don't think that's important, but I do. I'm gone a lot. When I'm home, I don't go out much. I live in a trailer house on a post-Custer, pre-casino Indian reservation, which means you gotta drive half the day to get to a shopping mall." He gave her something close to a smile. "These are not preferences you're gonna find listed in the lookin'-for-love ads."

"They're not deal-breakers, either."

He tucked chin to chest for closer scrutiny. "You lookin' for another job?"

"Maybe I'm looking for a place that's warm and safe, and a man who isn't afraid to take a chance on me." The kiss she planted on his chest instantly hardened his nipples. "Somebody who doesn't care what my name is and doesn't scare easily."

He didn't scare easily, but none of whatever this was came easily. And she scared him more with every minute they shared.

A clap of thunder rattled the trailer from skirting to shingles, rousing Lauren from secure sleep to abrupt panic. Nick stirred, shifted, and settled quietly. She wanted to crawl inside him and hide, but a lightning flash sent her stealing from the bed. She had groomed and fed and cleaned and restored, but she couldn't remember whether she had left Nick's clever system of gates in overnight order. A glance out the window told her that she'd already fallen down on the job. True Colors could only be standing in the rain because he couldn't get into the barn. Off the floor and over her head went the nightgown that had once been Nick's T-shirt.

Quiet. Quiet as a mouse in Alice's mouth.

Near darkness, rumbling night. Within the small front closet no slicker came to her fumbling hand, but she felt flannel. Shirt jacket over T-shirt, bare feet in new boots—*don't think, just dash, do it, dash back.*

Where was a flashlight when you needed one?

Never mind. Do what needs doing and be done, lickety-split.

The wind ripped the trailer door from her hand. She fought to recover the handle, and *bam*! Another gust smashed the door shut with Lauren pasted on the outside like a postage stamp. She was soaked to the skin by the time she made the halfway point—the leeward side of Nick's truck. She slid her back along the driver's side door until her butt hit the rubberized running board.

Another bolt of lightning shattered the night sky. A dash back to the trailer would have been her next move but for a distress call from True Colors. Tamping down her fear in response to his, she pushed off from the running board and ran headlong until she tripped, landing on hands and knees on muddy gravel.

Thunder danced circles around her.

She was facedown in the road again. Bare legs, bare hands, bedeviled by gravel and mud beneath and death overhead. A sob tore at her throat, but she didn't let it out until the steel cable of an arm looped around her waist, plucked her out of the mud and hauled her to the barn like a sack of feed. With a one-handed shove, her blessed rescuer opened the barn door just wide enough to roll them both inside.

She huddled against his bare chest, struggling for breath. Finally he moved away from the door.

"You okay?"

"I left True Colors…locked out."

Wordlessly he sat her down on a feed box and tended to her oversight. All it took was the release of a bolt on the bottom of a Dutch door, and the agitated horse was admitted to shelter. Nick's words of comfort reached Lauren's terrorized head and soon stayed her trembling.

She found the switch for the tack-area light, gathered some of the paraphernalia she'd put away earlier, and made her amends to the horse with a soothing rubdown. Nick took up the cause on the opposite flank, and the three of them recovered in tandem.

"I'm sorry," Lauren said finally, wiping her liniment-drenched hands on a horse-hide-treated towel.

"I must be gettin' old." Nick clapped his hand over the left side of his smooth chest. "You gotta stop scarin' me six ways from Sunday, woman."

"I'm sorry. When I heard that thunder, it hit me right away. You showed me how to secure those gates so he could go in and out at night, and I woke up—"

"Why didn't you wake me up?"

"You needed your sleep. You have a long day ahead of you tomorrow. And I didn't expect that wind."

"Out here, you expect wind and you respect lightning. Look at you."

She followed his orders from the ground up. Boots, bare legs, skinned knees, wet T-shirt that would win her no contests, droopy flannel shirt, all of them smeared with South Dakota clay. Her eyes finally met his, caught them smiling.

Rain hammered the metal roofing. More thunder brought a pitiable complaint from the mighty stallion on the other side of the wall. Two whining, wet dogs slunk through the narrow opening he'd left in the barn door, and Alice the cat's glowing eyes peered down from a stack of square bales.

"What a crew." Nick shook his head, chuckling. "We should all say good night and go back to our corners."

"Our separate corners?"

"Tomorrow the sun'll rise and give us back our self-respect."

Two claps of thunder collided just beyond the walls. Lauren ducked under Nick's arm.

"Well, all right, tomorrow's still a ways off."

"You'll be gone tomorrow."

"Back in four days," he promised, rubbing her back. "You're quivering like you're plugged into a live socket. We need to get you dry."

"I'm the live socket." She looked up and smiled. Strands of wet black hair framed his angular face like a boyish mop. "You're the plug-in."

Ka-boom!

It was his turn to tighten his hold. "Damn, that was close."

"Too close. What have you got out here for blankets?"

"Out here? They're mostly covered with horse-hair." He raised his brow. "Wait."

The small single light bulb over the tack stall cast garish shadows on his back as he walked away, affording her a view of the spiderwebbing and Rorschach-like blotches that covered his skin. The taste of ash and tears burned in her throat.

"Got a couple stored up in my footlocker," he was saying as he opened the box and began rifling through its contents. "Gifts, too nice to use." He pulled out two thick horse blankets. "Louise made these. And this." It was a star quilt, carefully wrapped in plastic. "We're big on blankets. I put some cedar in here, and some sage." With the plastic peeled back, he took a sniff. "Not too bad." He started to hand them to her.

And froze in the act. The look in his eyes reflected the tears standing in hers. She hadn't felt them coming. He challenged her without saying a word. But he didn't have to. He had already predicted that she would judge, and he was ready for judgment. But not pity.

"Have I told you that…you're the kindest, gentlest man I've ever…"

He nodded once.

"And that's what I see. That's really all I see, Nick."

"Bullshit," he said softly as he laid the blankets in her hands. "And I mean that in the kindest, gentlest way."

"I mean, I...I see what happened. I can almost see you on...on fire, almost. And I want to..."

"Feel my pain?"

Throat burning, she stared until she blinked, unintentionally shaking a tear loose.

Damn his eyes. *They were smiling.*

She dropped the blankets and stumbled over them getting to him, getting her arms around him, scolding him. "Yes. Yes, but don't you dare laugh at me, don't you dare, because I really just want to..."

"Want to what?"

"Take you inside me where nothing bad can touch you."

He kissed the damp streak on her cheek, smoothed her wet hair and made a soft claim on her lips. "You should've held that thought until I finished making your bed."

"Don't worry," she promised. "It's not going anywhere."

He lifted her hay-bale seat by its twine bindings, heaved it into the corner next to True Colors' stall and fished a jackknife from his pocket.

"We'll be like camping out." Clutching their bedding, she watched him cut the twine and then took the hint to break up several straw bales and make their nest. "Is it dangerous being in a metal building during a thunderstorm?"

"In case you didn't notice, I live in a metal building." He broke open another bale near the barn door. "This is for you two. Here." He whistled, pointed, called the dogs by name. "Lie down."

He turned off the light. "Now you," he said as he took Lauren's hand and led her to their two-bale pallet topped with horse blankets. "Come here."

"Don't I get a whistle?"

"No, but you get to lose the boots." He pushed the flannel shirt off her shoulders. "And this thing smells like Dillon."

"The one underneath smells like you."

"No, it doesn't, 'cause I wash mine."

"To me it smells wonderful, like you. And it feels soft, like you've worn it a hundred times, and last night when I put it on, I…" She laid her hands on her chest and rubbed the loose shirt over her nipples. "And it made me dream about you."

"What did you dream?"

"That I'd gotten under your skin."

"That was no dream," he whispered as he whisked the wet T-shirt over her head. "But I wasn't gonna tell you."

She asked, "Why not?" Not because she didn't know or need to know, but because a naked woman crawling into a haystack had to keep up conversational appearances.

And because he understood, he kept up his end, putting them on par appearance-wise by shucking his jeans and conversation-wise by confessing, "I was afraid you wouldn't like it there."

He shook the folds from the quilt, swung it around his shoulders and gave her his body for her blanket. Storm-chilled and rainwater soft, skin welcomed the feel of skin, warmed to the task of warming and burned with the freedom for loving. She tried to keep up with him, kiss for kiss and caress for caress, but she fell behind about the time gentle hands gave over to sucking lips and teasing tongue traveling over and down and deep inside, giving her fits and preparing easy entrance to the place where nothing bad could happen to him.

Dillon loved the morning-after smell of a prairie thunderstorm. It was the smell of cool water and quick greening and life teeming in the grass. He parked his pickup near his bargain sanctuary, got out and had himself a full body stretch, making a lazy grab for one of the morning sky's scarlet streaks. It had been a long night, with enough gamblers trapped by the storm and enough cash in the ATM to make it interesting.

Almost as interesting as Nick's barn door left standing open. Dillon chuckled as he struck out across the yard. Later he would have to razz ol' Nick about leaving his barn door open, see if he could trick him into checking his fly. It was only a matter of inches, but anything Nick left out of place begged notice. Handle in hand, Dillon started to tug.

Then he stopped, his jaw gone slack.

Curled together in a pile of hay near the door, the

two dogs lifted noses in his direction. But they'd clearly been ordered to stay, and stay they did. In a darker corner far from the door lay a bigger pile of hay, a longer bed, but this one had blankets. The mop of black hair at one end explained half the mystery.

Could be trouble, Dillon thought. A sick horse. An orphan calf.

Or…could be a guy in the doghouse. Could be funnier'n hell.

Dillon's gaze traveled to the other end of the blanket roll, where a helix of legs and the sweet embrace of an unmatched pair of feet had escaped the covers. He backed away, grinning, as the sun popped up between two buttes like a golden bubble. He would have to make the man he considered his brother a victory song, but a pesky nursery rhyme threatened to spoil his composition.

Big bad Nick, never blows his horn,
But the dogs in the doghouse were all forlorn.
Where's the big man who found Little Bo Peep?
Shackin' in the haystack, fast asleep.

Full of himself and jazzed for his partner, Dillon sprinted around the corner of the old church, punched his fist in the air and leaped for an imaginary lay-up in the hoop he would put up over the door someday.

13

Lauren's arm was cocked and set to throw a stick for Mama and Buzz when the porch light came on and Dillon appeared on the trailer steps. He called her name and made the universal hand sign for telephone call.

Her pulse rate's giddyup told her it couldn't be anyone but Nick. She pitched the stick and jogged across the driveway.

"Is it Nick?"

"Deep voice, man of two words. 'Joey there?'" Dillon reported as she sidled past him at the door. "That would be—"

She grabbed the phone. "Nick?"

"Hi."

She grinned like a teenager with a severe crush. "Hi."

"She wasn't, but she is now," Dillon teased, loudly enough for Nick to hear.

"Tell him to go outside for a while," Nick said. "Yours is the only voice I wanna hear right now."

Still smiling, she glanced at Dillon.

"Stop talkin' dirty to her, Nick," Dillon shouted. "She's blushing."

"Isn't he late for work?" Nick grumbled in her ear.

"He has the night off. He made the best chicken and dumplings for supper, and he even cleaned up while I went back outside and fed the horses. I was just…" She turned her back on Dillon, leaned her shoulder against the wall and imagined Nick's face. "How was your drive today?"

"Long. Lonesome."

How could two words hit home so hard from so far away?

"I notice Alice is gone." She also noticed the quiet click of the trailer door closing behind her.

"The cat was the only rider I had waiting for me this morning. I was kinda surprised. Half expected you to come running out the door at the last minute."

"Will you be half surprised if I'm still here when you get back? Don't answer that," she said quickly. "Because then I'll have to wonder whether you'll take me for granted if I don't keep you guessing, and you'll have to figure out which half of the surprise you really prefer, and I don't think we want to go there right now, do you?"

"Right now, let's keep it real simple."

"Perfect," she said, thinking only of Nick, and fixing on *simple* and *perfect* and *right now*. "True Colors had a good workout today."

"That doesn't surprise me. You're good for each other."

"You sound tired."

"Thought I'd fall asleep soon as my head hit the pillow."

"You're in bed?"

"With the lights out, fresh air coming through the window, trucks out on the highway whooshing past in the night. Usually all I need after a long drive. Didn't do it for me this time." He sounded unusually edgy. "Talk to me, Joey."

"Buzz isn't shy around me anymore. I was playing with him and Mama when you called. He likes to fetch. She doesn't. She'll let him get the stick, and then she'll try to take it away."

He gave a deep chuckle. "That bitch."

"Do you mind if I let them in the house?"

"I don't keep animals in the house." Pause. "But, uh, you can if you want."

"I wish you had a phone beside the bed. We could be like teenagers and talk until we fall asleep."

"I didn't have a phone when I was a teenager. I don't even like talking on the phone. Usually."

"You have the nicest telephone voice, Nick. I wish I could take it to bed with me. The phone, I mean, with your voice coming through it, into my ear." She closed her eyes and rested her head against the wall. "But Alice has you all to herself now."

"Like she gives a rat's ass."

She smiled. "In her case, a rat's ass would be a lot to ask. I'm sure she'd give a fig."

He would have laughed, she thought, but he was tired. She would have laughed, at least a little, but being utterly alone for the first night in a very long time was no laughing matter.

"You gonna be all right tonight?"

"I wish you were here. Right now. I'd make it perfect for you. I'd keep it simple."

"I'm as close as the phone, Joey. I'll give you the number here, so you can just pick up the phone. And don't worry about waking me up. Is Dillon around?"

"He went out."

"Tell him to stay—"

"I'm not going to tell anyone to do anything. I'm fine. I'll be fine. It's just so good to hear your voice. Could we talk a little more?"

"As much as you want."

"Could *you* talk a little more?"

He laughed.

"That's good, too. Laughing. You have a nice telephone laugh. Voice, laugh—what else can you do over the phone? Breathe?" She listened, but there was nothing. "Can you sigh for me, Nick? Can you make me believe you've just kissed me and you hated to pull away?"

"How about I just made love to you and hated to pull out? Would you like to hear that one?"

"Not now," she whispered. "I don't want to hear that one except for up close and in person."

"And I don't wanna play guessing games," he said. "Will you be there when I get back?"

"I should be there with you now," she said. "So much can happen when someone goes away."

Nick had clearly been drifting off when Lauren finally let him off the hook—or laid him down gently on the hook. She would have to be content that one of them could sleep and hope that canine companionship would turn off her worries for the night. She peered out the window into the twilight, where a man wearing a cowboy hat, a denim jacket and jeans bent to tousle an attentive shepherd's ruff. Clothes didn't make the man, but they were a reminder.

She glanced over her shoulder. Plenty of quiet books. She could turn a switch for sound. TV or radio—she could have her pick. Or she could turn to Dillon, who pulled no punches. She went to the front closet and reached for a windbreaker with sleeves so long it had to be Nick's. She pressed it to her nose and smiled. Sweet leather and spicy Nick. He hadn't washed himself out of everything.

Dillon dropped a glowing cigarette underfoot and crunched it in the gravel as she approached. He shoved his hands into his jacket pockets. "How's the man?"

"The man is tired." Lauren chuckled as she boosted herself onto the open tailgate of Dillon's pickup truck. "He said I could take the dogs in the house overnight."

"After you told him I had the night off?"

"Of course not. I mean, it's not about you. It's about me being scared at night. It's about me and my paranoia, which is crazy. Of course. Paranoia. Crazy. Right? But nobody's going to find me here." She scooted to one side, making room for him to join her. "Do you think?"

"I try, but it helps if I have something to go on." The tailgate rattled as he levered himself up. "Like, who's looking?"

"Nobody." She lowered her voice. "I'm supposed to be dead."

"Dead?" He was genuinely surprised. "Hit and run?"

"Something like that. It's complicated."

"More complicated than your boyfriend being an asshole," he surmised.

"Isn't that what an asshole does? Complicate things? Speaking of which, do you know whether…" She paused. She wasn't sure she should ask. But one of the things she was learning to appreciate about the two men she'd been imposing on was their generosity with the benefit of the enormous doubt she must have stirred up for them. "When you use one of those prepaid telephone cards at a pay phone, do you know whether the calls can be traced? It's too late—I've already done it—but what would it take to trace a call like that? I mean, I'm sure they can find the phone, but can they find out who bought the card?"

"Who's *they*?"

"Say, the police. Or the FBI."

"You got me there. The FBI hasn't solved a case on this reservation since Columbus, but nowadays, I think they can find out anything they want to. Especially about people who aren't out to break any laws." He eyed her. "You're not, are you?"

"Not at the moment."

He gave a fair-enough nod. "Breakin' that man's heart, that would be a crime."

"He won't let that happen."

"He won't let it show." Dillon adjusted his cowboy hat as though he were using the sweatband to scratch his head. "I guess there's no point in me asking who you're talkin' about calling."

"It isn't a boyfriend or an ex-boyfriend, but it is someone who was involved with…the incident."

"The one that left you stranded on the road," he assumed.

"Mainly I'm just trying to make sure I'm not putting anyone else at risk. I'm not a criminal, but…"

"You have criminal friends?"

"Acquaintances," she acknowledged. "Associations."

"An association of criminals? You mean, like *real* dealers?"

"I don't know exactly what they deal in. I've generally chosen not to ask too many questions. Even what I knew, I chose not to know."

"And it caught up to you."

"It caught up to me." It was a relief to admit it, especially to this man. It was almost like talking to Nick, but safer. Dillon willingly served as the buffer Nick wouldn't want to know he had.

"What about…? Did they do something to your—"

"Please don't ask me to talk about that part of it, Dillon. It's like that oil rig fire Nick doesn't want to talk about. Or the time you burned your house down."

"He told you about that?"

"That's all he said. After your family left, you burned your house down."

"Aw, Nick." Dillon gave a wry chuckle. "I don't mind talkin' about it. I was a nutcase. What do you wanna know? What kind of fuel? Gas, siphoned out of Nick's pickup, because mine was empty. In those days it was always empty. Everything was empty. Was I drunk? Very." He made a presentational gesture. "Your turn."

"How long ago?"

"Six—seven years ago. Lucky seven. Statute of limitations on guilt is officially up. And it was your turn for tellin' me something, not asking."

"Give me seven years."

"If I quit askin', that doesn't mean I'm gonna step

aside for anybody who tries to ride roughshod over my partner." He grinned. "If you're gonna ride him, you do it barefoot."

"Is that Indian humor?"

"We're talkin' humor with some teeth to it." He leaned closer, confiding, "Like, 'If Dillon has the night off while I'm gone, you might wanna keep the dogs in the house overnight.'"

"It wasn't like that. In fact, he said…" He was laughing at her, silent but sure. "You're kidding, right? Between the two of you, I never know who's putting me on. But I do know that there's absolutely no problem with you staying wherever you want to."

"If he comes home and smells dog in the house, you won't be able to quit cleaning until he can't smell it anymore."

"He's *so* sensitive to the way things smell."

"Yes, he is." He went quiet for a moment. "Have you ever smelled burning flesh, Joey? I'm talkin' living human flesh that's actually on fire." She hadn't, but he wasn't really asking. "I can't say I have, either. I got there too late. They were already burned and blackened, like roasted meat. John was…" He shook his head. "The only way I could tell it was him was by Nick holding on to him the way he did. Nick was the one brought him out. Nick was the one. He smelled flesh on fire—his own and his brother's."

"It must have been horrible," she said softly.

"Words don't cut it sometimes. There's no way to

know what he lived through that night, no way to describe what he went through afterward, month after month. You've seen the scars?"

She nodded. "Battle scars, he said."

"It was a long, hard battle. It helped him, being with people who know what that means. His military service qualified him for treatment in a VA hospital. He battled the pain, and then he battled the pain medication." He sighed. "Damn, I know I'm talkin' too much."

"I won't tell him."

"He's a private man. But just so you know, he's already done his time in hell. Just so you know."

She gave a nod. As Dillon had already pointed out, words were inadequate. Nick trusted her. Clearly Dillon didn't, but he credited her with having a conscience, which was more than she probably deserved. She wasn't sure she trusted herself *or* her conscience anymore. The rhyme from a children's game echoed in her mind: *Heavy, heavy hangs over her head…*

"I made some calls today," Dillon was saying. "Got the scoop on racing True Colors down in Pierre and then after that in Aberdeen. If you want to take a break sometime tomorrow, maybe we could take a ride down to the casino where I work. Some people I want you to meet."

"I'm really not—"

"We could even, like my ex-wife says, *do lunch*. The next time you get to the Cities, we'll *do lunch*, she says. Like a grilled cheese sandwich is some big event."

"No thanks, Dillon, really. I'm steering clear of introductions and social events at the moment."

"One of them is Hank Two Dog. He still has that racehorse I told you about. He thinks he's gonna make a ropin' horse out of him, but that's another story. He's willing to let us use him if you need a training partner for True Colors. Plus, Hank's seriously into this stuff. He knows a lot about the races they run around here. Only two tracks in the state, but he's ventured out-of-state some, too. He's got his doubts about racing Paints, of course. He's a Quarter Horse man."

"He can keep his doubts," she said. And then, against her better judgment on the one hand, but in the interest of her best judgment on the other, she submitted. "But I guess I wouldn't mind borrowing his horse."

"It's a date, then."

Lunch was done on Hank Two Dog's lunch break. Hank was someone Lauren had known in many guises. His job at the casino paid the bills, while his be-all and his end-all were tied up in horseflesh and steeped in horse lore. He let Dillon carry the conversation while he consumed a pile of food that had started out on the buffet table as separate dishes. He nodded, put in a word or two between forkloads, nodded some more.

When the last of the meat-cheese-mayonnaise gravy had been wiped from the plate and consumed with half a dinner roll, Hank turn to Lauren. "Dillon says your father trains racehorses."

Lauren stared, her brain slow to shift gears. She'd almost forgotten where she was and what she was supposed to be doing there. When had her father been mentioned?

"I've been around the tracks for a long time," Hank went on. "Maybe I know him."

"My father's been out of it for a long time. He died eight years ago."

"*Ohan*," Hank said. "Where you from?"

"Nebraska, originally, but I've lived a lot of places," she recited by rote. But she added the rare tidbit, "A lot of trailers, a lot of backstretches."

"Feels like I've seen you somewhere." Oddly, he wasn't looking at her, and she didn't think he really had been.

"I was around the tracks for a long time, too. Who knows?" *Besides CNN?* she thought. This meeting was a mistake. Or a wake-up call. Her face had been banged up but not rearranged. If she started hanging around horse racing people, eventually someone would recognize her.

"You wanna use my horse for a workout, you'll need another rider," Hank said. "My son Ben's your man for that. We built a stretch of railed track we use for practice, nice and wide. You can bring your Paint over to my place. I wouldn't mind getting in on it myself."

"Early morning is best," she said, turning to Dillon. "Whenever you have the time."

"Ben goes out and messes with the horses a little bit before he catches the bus most mornings," Hank said.

"Tomorrow?" Dillon suggested. "Or do you wanna wait for Nick?"

"Tomorrow. The maiden race is always a crapshoot. But we'll be ahead of the game if we give him some practice against experienced competition."

"Nick showed me the breeding on that colt he picked out, and I told him the papers looked impressive. I'm surprised he didn't say nothin' to me about racing him." Hank turned to Dillon. "Have you read the stories they've been runnin' in *Indian Country Today* about this offtrack rebate business some of the Indian casinos are getting into?"

"Heard some guys talkin' about that on the floor the other night. What's the deal? We're cutting into the bookie trade?"

"Times are changing. You got your Internet betting, your simulcasting sites in places like North Dakota, where they don't have a track but they have a racing commission. We're living in times of virtual reality, man."

"And I was just getting adjusted to *real* reality," Dillon said with a smile. "Sounds like a rebate is some kind of a kickback to people betting big money on the ponies through these offtrack sites. Are we getting into that here?"

"Not so far. But it's big money, and a couple of the tribes that are into it, sounds like they might be rubbin' shoulders with the bad guys. That's what the Indian casino critics always want to see coming. You'll be getting yourselves mixed up with the Mafia, they like to say. 'You'll have to start packin', and you know what happens then.'"

"You'll shoot your eye out, kid," Dillon aped, and the two men harmonized in a belly laugh.

"Which mafia?"

The men looked as if they've just remembered her presence.

"Aren't there a bunch of them now?" Lauren asked innocently. "The old godfathers seem pretty tame next to the Colombians and the Russian—" She glanced from one attentive face to the other and shrugged. "I don't know. Are they all called mafias, or is that reserved for the Italian brand? Maybe not all of them are into gambling."

"The horse racing industry has been trying to clean up its image, but lately it's been one thing after another," Hank said. "Mostly it's stuff they say goes on all the time with Thoroughbreds. You know, doping, fixing races. I always say you just can't go wrong with Quarter Horses."

"Paints are racing alongside Quarter Horses," Dillon pointed out. "Paints are squeaky clean."

"And too pretty to win a race," Hank argued. "We don't care about color. You start worryin' about color, you lose track of what counts. You take that kind of thinking to the track and you lose. I mean, that's—" Hank checked his watch. "Shit, I'm late. Let me know when you're coming out to the place," he said as he pushed his round belly away from the edge of the table. "I'll have my horse and my boy ready to show you the difference between a Quarter Horse and a Paint."

Dillon turned to Lauren. "Ready?"

"Oh, yeah." She smiled at Hank Two Dog's retreating back. This would be fun. "I'll be with you in a minute, Dillon. After I make a quick pit stop."

"Wrong racetrack, Joey. What should we call a pit stop in our sport?"

"I'll let you figure that one out. Shall I meet you back here?"

Dillon decided to check his work schedule and suggested meeting at his truck. Lauren's trip to the restroom took a detour as soon as they parted ways. She called Jack's cell phone.

"Can you talk?"

"Yeah, but make it quick. I'm sitting out here in the car, waitin' on this damn woman."

"I thought you were looking after Joey."

"The woman they got taking care of him, she had to bring him over here to play with her sister's kid. Hell, it's not like Little Joe plays with kids yet. She just wanted to see her sister."

"You don't like the nanny?"

"I don't like being her chauffeur. But she'll be gone

pretty soon. He wants a real professional, he says. Not somebody who looks like Robin Williams in drag. What's up?"

"My baby's okay?"

"Looks fine to me. I don't think you have to worry. I mean, about him getting everything a kid needs."

"I want to see for myself, Jack." Lauren closed her eyes, fighting the nausea that consumed her every time she thought about the prospect of someone else caring for her son. "I don't know how I'm going to do it, but I have to find a way to see my baby. Just to hold him for a few minutes and watch him eat his food, change his diaper, teach him to say a new word. Just one more word, Jack. Does he still say *mama*?"

"He's doin' okay. You gotta believe that," Jack said quietly. She heard the sympathy in his gruff voice, recognized it for the real deal. Rare, but real. "How about you?" he asked. "You found someplace to stay?"

"I'm with the man who found me."

"Nice guy, is he?"

"Yes." She covered her eyes with an unsteady hand. "He's a lifesaver."

"That's all I wanna know about him," Jack said. "You get on with your life, okay? This life you had, you put that out of your mind."

"You know me better than that, Jack. I'm not a loser."

"You're not a corpse, put it that way."

"No. I'm not a loser, and I haven't lost my son. Jack,

what do you know about using Indian casinos as rebate shops for—"

"People do it. It's legal."

"Is Raymond involved with any of that?"

"I wouldn't know, and I wouldn't be askin'. You were always pretty smart like that. What do you wanna—"

"I'm going to ride again, Jack. I'm working for someone who has a horse that could really go places, and I could take him there. I think Raymond might be interested. Can I tell you why?"

"Hell no. You're fuckin' crazy."

"Maybe. And I used to be smart like *what*? Like what I didn't know wouldn't hurt me? That didn't pan out, Jack. So now maybe I'm crazy like I've got nothing to lose. Can't be a loser if I don't have anything to lose."

"Little Joe," he reminded her.

"You're saying he's still mine to lose?"

"I'm sayin' you could get us all killed. You, me, the man who saved your life—all of us."

"Aren't you the one who's supposed to do the killing? What if you weren't his man anymore? What if they gave a war and nobody came?"

Jack snorted. "This ain't the sixties, little girl, and you ain't no Hanoi Jane. You need to get real. "

"I guess Hanoi Jane took a pretty big chance, didn't she?"

"Damn straight. I'd'a shot her myself when she pulled that publicity stunt, except I was sittin' in some mud hole south of the DMZ while she was sittin' on an antiaircraft gun havin' her shits and giggles with an NVA gun crew up north. Take my word for it, little girl. When they have a war, people always show up. One way or another, the guys in charge get other guys to carry the guns. It never pays very well, but what're you gonna do?"

"I didn't know you were in Vietnam."

"I was supposed to do the killing there, too. And I did. You get them before they get you. That's just how it works in this life, little girl." He sighed. "But I'm getting old, and I'm getting real tired. So, yeah, you play with fire, you could get a few people killed. Maybe not much of a loss. Guess it depends on how you look at it." Then, urgently, "I gotta go. The woman just came out of the house. Man, her sister's uglier'n she is."

"Joey?"

"He's wearin' that little baseball cap with the chin strap. He's gonna be a Cubs fan. Good man." Finally, solemnly, he repeated, "He's gonna be a good man."

Lauren eased the telephone receiver into its cradle and rested her forehead against the top of the phone. Raymond Vargas would never raise a child to be a good man. It would never happen.

14

Nick's original plan called for him to be home by midnight, but pushing every stop but one put him back in the Wolf Trail driveway by what he hoped was suppertime. He'd been eating fast food in the pickup for four days. The ache in his chest had to be heart-burn. But no sooner had he parked near the barn and dragged his stiff body out of the driver's seat than the ache was gone. Chased away by a voice on either side making music in his ears.

"We were trying to decide between frozen pizza and mac and cheese. You're just in time to break the tie," his partner reported loudly.

"You should've called, Nick," his woman said softly. "We would have made you a nice homecoming supper."

He started to close the door, then remembered to reach back inside and let the cat out of the duffel bag he'd left sitting open for her on the passenger side. Rudely awakened, Alice emerged with her cat eyelids at half mast, and took a look and then a leap, knocking Nick's cowboy hat askew on her way over his back, down to the ground and off to her own races. All the while, the two he'd left behind were catching him up.

"We've got True Colors entered for his first race down at Pierre," said Dillon.

"I rode him against Hank Two Dog's gelding, and he ate it up, Nick. The ground, the competition, the second hand on the stopwatch, the admiration of your friend Hank."

"Yeah, ol' Hank didn't have much to say about his damn foundation Quarter Horse breeding after True Colors smoked his Peppy Two Jacks Three Bars in His One Good Eye, or whatever the hell his name is."

Nick chuckled. Dillon had hit just about every name in the Quarter Horse stud book.

"We didn't *smoke* him," Joey said. "We could've, with all the gas True Colors had left in his tank. But we didn't."

"Seriously smoked," Dillon begged to differ. "Gave Hank's horse a new name. Smoked Pepper Jacks Jerky."

"We did what we needed to do without making a show. I wanted him to come from behind, because he probably won't get a good start the first time out." She finally looked up at Nick, took a breath and smiled. "How was your trip?"

"Who, me?" Nick adjusted his hat. "Not too bad. I'm still back there on choices for supper."

"We could go have supper at the casino, say hello to ol' Hank," Dillon suggested. "I have to work later tonight, but—"

Nick clapped a hand on Dillon's shoulder. "I am not goin' anywhere, partner. You guys go on ahead. Just curious—how long has that pizza been gathering frost?"

"I can do better than that if you can wait a little longer," Joey said. "What time do you have to go to work, Dillon?"

"Tell you what, the more I think about my suggestion, the more I like it." Dillon slipped Nick what he probably thought was a subtle wink. "It's prime rib night. If I leave now, I can beat the crowd."

"Before you go, let's see what you think of this," Nick said, leading the way to the tack room in the front of the big horse trailer. "Hauled some Thoroughbred colts to a guy in Wisconsin, and we got to talkin' about saddles. Ended up hangin' out a little longer than I should have." He pulled his surprise off the bottom peg on the saddle rack. "He sold me this one. Says it's top-of-the-line, and it's almost new. He said his jockey was too heavy for it. I told him mine was a featherweight." He turned to Dillon. "Makes that Aussie saddle look like it was made for a knight in full-dress armor, doesn't it?"

Joey laid her hands on the poorest excuse for a saddle Nick had ever run across. The thing didn't weigh more than five pounds and looked like a leather Band-Aid. Black with a white seat, the colors matching his horse, it had caught Nick's fancy when he first saw it, but now that he'd brought it out for Joey, he was seeing less True Colors and more *two* colors, one more than he should have dared.

It probably didn't show, but when her eyes met his, he felt like he was blushing.

"Did I do okay?"

"It's perfect, Nick, but you didn't have to buy a saddle. Hank offered to loan me one."

"You're riding my horse, you won't be sittin' in Hank Two Dog's saddle. This guy threw in a bunch of other stuff, including an old jockey shirt that my sister Louise will be using for a pattern. Don't worry. You're not wearing anybody else's sweat-stained silks."

"Why can't I make my own? You don't think I can sew?" She laughed. "Okay, you're right. I can't. And you're the sweetest man."

Dillon groaned. "Gettin' a little deep around the ankles here. Time for these boots to be walkin'." He tapped Nick's arm. "Nice touch, man."

Dillon earned major points for knowing exactly how and when to walk off into the sunset. He was getting so good at making himself scarce that Nick made a silent vow to start contributing to his church.

They checked in with True Colors, and then Nick

helped Joey turn macaroni and cheese into a meal fit for a traveling man's homecoming. But he was less interested in the food sitting on the table than he was in the woman sitting on the other side. Intent on reporting every bit of progress she'd made with his horse, she supplied most of the table talk. And he was grateful. It was good to be home, good to be able to hear her voice and watch her lips move at the same time. But the few times he glanced at her eyes in time to catch her gaze, she rejected the contact in favor of a change of direction, subject, tone, whatever it took to escape him. Something was going on behind those blue eyes that she didn't want him to see.

Fair enough, he said to himself. You're the same way. You've got plenty of private problems. It doesn't mean you're hiding anything that makes a damn bit of difference to anyone else. Bitter tastes, bad odors, hard feelings—some things a person didn't need to be spreading around. He could plainly see that she was healing on the outside. On the inside, that was her business. Hers to suffer, hers to share. He could go either way.

But her problem had nothing to do with the fact that he was back and dying to take up where they'd left off. She quietly made that clear when she joined him in the shower stall that he would never again curse for being too small. She made it even clearer when she rubbed lotion into his road-weary back, from his nape to his knees. Clearer still when she lay with him, thrilled to his touch, took him to the only place where a man dared to tap the source of a woman's primal power. He loved that she became monstrous and insatiable, that she held him and demanded of him, claimed all he had, and when he was spent, she held him still. But now she was back to being a small, soft thing, quiet and content in his embrace. She made him part of something beautiful, something he had never been, and it humbled him.

Moving carefully, he reached for the covers they'd kicked aside. She stirred to help bring the sheet to their shoulders, letting him know she was still awake.

"You like the saddle?" he asked. "You'd tell me if it was a bad idea, right?"

"It's beautiful." She caressed his chest, applying the word there, too.

"It won't hurt my feelings or anything if you don't use it. Is Hank's better? I mean, better for you or the horse or…" He sighed. "I probably came off sounding like some bigheaded…"

"Not at all." She scooted like a caterpillar, using his body as support until they were face-to-face on his pillow. "I was looking for some way to take care of some of the extra stuff myself. When we win a purse, I won't feel so bad about the expenses, but until then, this whole thing was my idea."

"You're just trying to cop all the credit in advance." He smiled into her big looking-glass eyes. In the space of no space and the time of no time, she had gone from hot mama to eager-to-please girl. "I like to drag my feet until I've got no heels left on my boots, but once I'm in, I'm in all the way."

"I noticed."

"Yeah." He kissed her forehead, for better or worse, blessing or curse. "I want you to have all you need, but you have to clue me in."

She smiled and messed with his hair. "You did fine."

"I got an earful from the guy who sold me the saddle. He says if we do well, it can really add to the value of the horses we raise. I told him about you, and he says a good trainer and the right jockey can make—"

She went still. "Told him what about me?"

"That you've had a lot of experience."

"Is that all?"

"Joey." He took hold of her hand and pressed her fingertips to his lips. "That's about all I know."

"I guess it's a good thing. It's more than I want anyone else to know."

"All they have to do is watch you ride." He braced himself, head in hand. "Joey, I want to know why you quit."

"I was ready to move on. It's a sport, Nick. A game. After a while, you move on."

"Did something happen that I should know about?" No response. Against his strongest nature, he persisted. "Joey, if you had an accident, if you got hurt in any way, that's something I should know about."

"You can't be a jockey and not get hurt. It's more

dangerous than…" She tried to reassure him with an upswing in her voice. "I took my spills over the years, but nothing serious. If you were a more discerning lover, you might have noticed that I have one or two little souvenirs from the racetrack."

"This finger." Of the four he had just kissed, he singled out the center finger, center knuckle, rubbing it between his own thumb and fingers. "Broken?"

"Three times. Once by a horse and twice by doctors trying to fix it."

"This leg," he said, feeling for the surgical scar he'd noticed below her knee. "Broken?"

"A three-horse pileup when I was eighteen. You can't see the other breaks very well. Here." She drew his hand to her collarbone. "Feel that little bump? And a chipped tailbone. That was the one that hurt the worst."

"All at once?"

"Oh, no. The finger and the tailbone were part of the same incident. I didn't notice the finger at first because of the other." She pulled his arm around her back. "If you've ever *really* fallen on your ass, you don't joke about it."

"And what's this?" He kissed the scar at the base of her neck.

"Okay, so you *are* discerning. That's from a trach tube. Little windpipe dysfunction. Part of the collarbone accident."

"You've had enough," he said gruffly. "No wonder you quit. I'm not letting you do this."

"This stuff happened early on, Nick, before I had all that experience you were bragging about."

"Finish that statement you made a minute ago. More dangerous than what?"

"I don't know. What's not dangerous these days? I only told you because you asked, and I have to be honest. Right? You wanted an honest answer. Yes, I've had a few hard knocks. But I'd almost forgotten the flip side, which is the part you live for, and that's finding a horse like True Colors. Finding him and having the chance to develop him and ride him. I've never really done that before. Not on my own."

"I don't want you getting hurt."

"I don't, either, which is why I'm going to be careful. True Colors is in good condition. I'm in good condition. We're going to be fine." She hooked her leg over his. "But there's one more thing I need."

"What's that?"

"A new identity." Her moonlit eyes sought his. "I need a name."

"Joey's pretty new for you, isn't it? I don't know where it came from, but I'm pretty sure it's a new handle."

She acknowledged the truth of his presumption with a tip of her head. "But I don't have a last name." She was struggling to get where she was going, and taking the long way around didn't help. "I was thinking maybe Red Shield."

"You don't look much like a Red Shield." He

wasn't going to make it any easier. Sooner or later she was going to have him turned fully inside out, but she was going to have to work for it.

"What about a *Mrs.* Red Shield?" she said.

"You want to pose as my wife?"

"If posing is my only option."

"You're…proposing?" He couldn't believe she would go that far. "Marriage." He said it only because somebody had to. Somebody had to stop the dance and say the word so that somebody else could back off. "Is that what you're suggesting?"

"Yes."

"For how long? You're thinkin', one of those perfect days we talked about would be easy enough. As long as everybody's cool and things are goin' right."

"And you've thought, one of these days, maybe I'll get married. Haven't you? I'm suggesting we make it a perfect day for me, one of these days for you."

"Why?"

"I can't be who I was anymore. I need to be somebody else, and I want to be Mrs. Nicholas Red Shield."

Are you satisfied? You've pushed for it, and now you have it. A desperate woman's desperate lie.

He drew a deep breath. "What's your name? Really?"

"It's Lauren."

"Who's Joey? Your boyfriend?"

"No. Joey is not and never has been my boyfriend, and that's another honest answer." She tucked her face against his neck, her nose taunting Dragon Lady's claws. "It was just a thought. Maybe one of these days, hmm? You think about it."

Think about it?

Thanks a lot, woman. Like I have a choice.

"That's not the way it's done, Joey. Or Lauren, or—" Exasperated, he slid his hand over the side of his neck—protection for or from Dragon Lady, he couldn't say which.

"Joey," she said. "It's better if you call me Joey. It's the name you know me by."

"Hell, it's not done that way no matter who you are. I get to propose, and *you* get to think about it." He slid his hand into her hair. "You're killin' me, Joey."

"That's the last thing I want to do. I promise you, Nick. No matter what, I won't see you harmed by my crazy…by getting involved with me."

Running his own horse in a legitimate horse race was almost exciting enough to overturn the woman's latest attempt to mess with his mind. Nick had done some bronc riding as a kid, but he was out of his element at Fort Pierre Racetrack. It had to be small potatoes for Joey, but he felt like a boy pulling in for his first day of school. Even Dillon, for all his usual cool, was noticeably wide-eyed.

It was Joey's time to shine. Pierre was only a hundred miles away, but they stayed overnight so that horse and rider would be fresh on race day. Joey was up at the

crack of dawn for a light workout on the track. She
pronounced True Colors to be the perfect racehorse—
eager, energetic, sharp and sound. There was, she said,
no match for him anywhere on the premises. Nick
wasn't going to say anything, but it wasn't True Colors
who gave him concern. Just like driving down the
road, it was the crazy drivers with their bald tires and
bad brakes that a guy had to watch out for.

Nick played owner, trainer and groom, while
Dillon claimed the scout's role. He wasn't a big
gambler, but he'd been to the races. No matter what
the occasion, event or attraction, Dillon was always
curious about its flip-, back- or underside. He had no
qualms about snooping around until somebody chased
him off. The practice, he claimed, was called *getting
the lay of the land*, and for once Nick was willing to
call it *good work*. Dillon's scouting report was replete
with rumors about which jockeys were likely to ride
dirty, or herd, box in or bully the competition. The
horses in True Colors' maiden race were all inexpe-
rienced, but there were fears that this one might drift
or that one might sag, and fears were often muttered
on the backstretch.

To boot, Dillon returned with the day's track
program. He opened the folded paper underneath
Nick's nose, pointed to the fourth race and ran his
forefinger beneath a line of print starting with True
Colors' name. *Owner, Wolf Trail Ranch, Trainer Nick Red
Shield, Jockey Joey Red Shield.*

· "How did this come about?" Nick asked.

"I just did what I was told. She said it wouldn't look good for the jockey and trainer to be the same person." Dillon cocked an eyebrow. "Real disappointed I missed the wedding."

"You and me both."

"Congratulate me, fellas. I made weight without tossing my cookies," Joey announced as she approached her team—two men and a horse. "Just kidding. Not having to worry about my weight is one of two major advantages I have over the guys. The other is that horses just naturally like me better. I'm convinced they prefer women."

This was not the time to quibble over names or roles or preferences of any kind. It was post time. The black-and-white stallion was the standout in a field of two sorrels, three bays—one with flashy white socks—a brown-and-white Paint, and True Colors himself.

Nick wasn't holding his breath. From the flipping gates to the flailing hooves to the rocketing finish, he simply didn't need to breathe. It looked more like sailing than running, and the running took less time than registering the win.

It hit Dillon first, and Dillon hit Nick with a solid backslap that further curtailed his next breath. He had to gasp for air as he grabbed his partner's shoulder with one hand and the fence rail with the other.

Dillon was pointing to the scoreboard, but Nick's

gaze followed horse and rider. His magnificent prancing horse, *his* gloriously elevated rider.

"They did it," he marveled quietly, wary of believing and broadcasting the claim too soon.

"Come on," Dillon enthused. "We're her entourage."

And because he was familiar with "the lay of the land," Dillon took charge of leading True Colors, rider still aboard, and parting the small gathering at the winners' circle to take center stage. Long-odds bettors wanted to show their appreciation. Joey fumbled with her goggles, while some anonymous camera digitized her smile, minus her distinctive blue eyes. It was a brief moment, but not brief enough for Nick, who couldn't wait to put himself between his jockey and the handful of people representing *the public*. She was flushed with the victory, uneasy with the attention.

Dillon actually had to remind Nick that the winning owner had a purse coming.

The drive home took a little over two hours. Piping up from the backseat, Dillon said he wanted to treat everyone—especially Hank Two Dog—to a celebratory supper. But Nick was having none of it.

"It was a helluva lot of fun, and we sure proved our point, but it's been a long day. Taking first takes a lot out of a guy." Nick glanced toward the passenger seat. "You wanna back me up on that, *Mrs. Red Shield*?"

"Yeah, what's that about?" Dillon asked. "I was countin' on being Nick's best man someday."

"I decided *wife* might not be credible," Joey said, flashing him a coy smile. "I went for *daughter*."

"Waahn," Dillon teased in typical Lakota fashion.

"Credible to who?"

"Anyone who might be asking, which is nobody," she said, adding, *"Yet."*

"Like I said, we proved our point. If we don't want anybody askin', maybe we oughta quit while we're at the top of our game."

"The Fort Pierre Racetrack is hardly the top of my game."

"This is really gettin' good," Dillon said with a chuckle.

"It'll be a while before anyone notices us, Nick. Today we ran a maiden horse, first time out, and we had beginners' luck."

"We did? But you keep saying—"

"That's what *they're* saying—anyone who's talking about the fourth race at Fort Pierre, all maiden horses, all small-time owners and unknown jockeys. We're a little backyard, family operation. Hobbyists. We're mentioned at the bottom of the sports page in a newspaper too small to have sections."

"Indians with backyards and hobbies?" Nick chuckled. "Now, that's news. Careful with the details if you don't want anyone making a story of it. We might all look alike, but there aren't many of us left, remember. And you still don't look like a Red Shield."

"But, hell, Indians with a first-place finish, that's—"

"That's what you want," Joey insisted, cutting across Dillon. "You're on your way to making a name for your stud. His own name, not just the names a generation or two back. You'll have something you can take to the bank."

"Not to mention the prize money that covers—"

"That covers expenses for this race and one, maybe two, more," Nick said. "Beginners' luck ends when?"

"Since he won, he can't run against maidens anymore. But the next win will still be considered a fluke. The third..." Joey slid her hand across the seat in his direction. "We might not win every time. Are you going to quit if we only place?"

"How soon before my horse risks getting claimed?" He'd entered True Colors in an allowance race as a horse that was not available for purchase, but unless or until he reached the level of stakes racing, the claims races that were available to him would eventually require him to set a price on his horse.

"We'll cross that bridge when we come to it. It's not an issue at this level."

"You're sure?"

"I'm sure. I know what I'm doing. My father made his living at this." She gave a perfunctory smile. "It wasn't a great living, but it kept pancakes on the table."

"It isn't how I want to make my living."

"You're not feelin' the fever yet, partner?" Dillon

chuckled. "You got a fever, all right, but it ain't horse fever." He started whistling the tune to "Jackson."

"Look what you've done," Nick grumbled, slipping Joey a sideways glance.

"You *could* make an honest woman of me."

"I doubt it."

"What's the special tonight at the casino, Dillon?" Joey asked, turning to the back-seat troublemaker. "Mrs. Red Shield would love to celebrate *taking first* with something besides glorified macaroni and cheese."

The very last thing Lauren wanted to do was hurt Nick in any way. In her whole life she'd only perfected one salable skill, and that was riding a fast horse to finish ahead of the pack. If he wanted nothing else from her, he could at least accept this much without misgiving. Not that he had any way of knowing how much this was, since he didn't know who she was, but surely he could see that she was no bug jockey, no amateur, certainly no hack. If she put his horse in a position to be claimed, it would not be without doubling, *tripling,* his investment. And only if such a move turned out to be the one that would save Joey.

But Nick was hurt. From where she stood outside the glass confines of the casino restaurant waiting to take another stab at calling Jack, she could see Nick's lack of interest in the conversation he and Dillon were supposed to be having with Hank Two Dog and the manager of the casino, for whom she had vacated her

seat at the table. Nick had agreed to the dinner suggestion after they took True Colors home. He would have preferred to stay with the horse, but she and Dillon had tag-teamed him. And so there he was, looking impatient, even angry. The truth was, he had good reason. More than he could imagine.

The idea of marriage had popped into her head one minute and rolled off her tongue the next. Her impulses had a way of showing up half baked, half dressed, and already half realized. *I love you. Let's do it.* Of course, she'd wisely left out the *I love you* part. Talk about total exposure… Put those three words together and you had full lunacy. But saying them might have made all the difference. Had she told Nick she loved him, the name she'd signed at the racetrack might not have been a lie.

And then what?

And then another half-baked idea she was trying to cook up could be moving closer to fully baked and possibly accomplished without turning her into a thief. If she could use Nick's horse to get Vargas to expose himself somehow, there was no question. She would do it. She would do anything to get her baby back.

And so, from where she stood outside the restaurant, she could clearly see that Nick's struggle mirrored her own. They had nothing going for them—no trust, no truth, no time—and yet, for her part at least, she could say the words right now and mean them. *I love you, Nick.* But he would never know.

Her third try finally yielded pay dirt.

"Jack, I've been calling—"

"You gotta stop this. I'm tellin' you, the boy's fine."

"Does he have a new nanny or the same one you don't like?"

"No changes yet. Look, I know where you're calling from."

"How do you know? You can't—"

"Some Indian reservation in South Dakota. Am I right?" She swallowed hard. "You see? I *can*. And so can he. There's only one secret that's keeping you alive, and that's a secret I'd like to keep between us. But you're makin' it real tough."

"Jack, I was thinking. Why couldn't you *disappear* Joey the same way you disappeared me? You could disappear, too, Jack. We could all—"

"It doesn't work that way. That baby is his son, and he's the one who calls the shots. I'm the doer, and *I did not do her*. You get what I'm sayin'? That's…that's the kiss of death. And you're nothing, little girl. You've gotta get it through your head. *You. Are. Dead.*"

He cleared his throat. "Listen to me now. I don't know why you asked about betting rebate shops, but take my advice and keep your nose out. I don't know what you think you're gettin' into, but it's no game. You hear me? No horse racing, no casinos and no cops. Because nobody's gonna connect him with any of that. He's real careful that way. But if you or anyone who looks like you starts showing up at the tracks, he'll know. And he'll connect you with a bullet. You and me both. You get what I'm tellin' you?"

"Yes," she said softly.

"What's that?

"Yes, Jack, I understand."

"You're nobody now, but you used to be somebody. A little somebody, but a somebody. You were all over the news, right? You know that."

"I only saw one—"

"Yeah, well, pretty face, mob connections, horse racing and all like that, it's news. You get back into race riding, you don't think somebody's gonna recognize you?"

"I'm not exactly hanging around the backstretch at Santa Anita. This isn't even a Thoroughbred."

"What isn't a Thoroughbred? You gotta stay away from any kind of horse racing. I'm tellin' you, little girl, you've had your reprieve. You're smart, you'll make a whole new life. Hook up with a nice guy, have yourself a couple kids. I'll look after Little Joe. I swear to you, that boy—"

"Now *you're* the one who doesn't understand." She pressed her back against the wall in the telephone alcove, closed her eyes and remembered her baby wearing the baseball cap she'd bought for him a few short weeks ago. It was an image she had to hold fast in her mind. She had nothing, not even a picture of him. "You can't cut me off, Jack. You have to let me call. At least give me that much."

290

KATHLEEN EAGLE

"The night I let you off, that's the only time I ever done anything like that. The only time I went soft. Fuckin' stupid. I don't know what I was thinkin'." Silence came cold and hard. But then, in a voice too small for Jumbo Jack, "I'll take your calls when I can. Just…just you be careful, little girl."

"Thank you, Jack."

But the line had gone dead.

15

Nick had taken a far-corner seat in Louise's living room and buried his nose in a newspaper, feigning a lack of interest in the "costume" fitting that was going on a few feet away. He was an old-fashioned Lakota male, which meant he had his standards. As a rule, he couldn't be hanging around when the girls had their hands busy with their creations and their mouths going with the stories females everywhere traded among themselves.

But no self-respecting Lakota male permitted somebody in his charge to participate in a public doings without the best garb he could provide. Joey had worn used silks in her first race, and he would not have her wear the shirt a second time. It was probably pretty obvious that anything to do with Joey interested him, but beyond that, there were certain appearances people tacitly agreed to keep up and respect. A good event costume was important.

Louise was the seamstress in the Red Shield clan, but Bernadette was on hand to offer her opinion. With most of the children in school, she had at least one hand free to fetch and pin and iron, while Louise made use of the sewing machine that occupied its usual place at the kitchen table. A master quilter, Louise had pieced Nick's selection of fabrics into a tapered red blouse with an inset V-shaped black bib, the canvas for the appliqué she had fashioned incorporating the initials Joey had re-quested—RS. On the sleeves Nick had suggested a smattering of stars.

"I like these colors." Bernadette held out an open pin for Louise, who was fussing around Joey, eyeballing and setting pins where the final seams would be.

"Red for Nick and black for Dillon." Arms out-stretched like a scarecrow, Joey caught his eye from across the room and smiled. "We should make a logo for the Wolf Trail."

"We have a brand. What would we do with a logo?"

"We'd put it on a sign, put it up where you turn off the highway. On the Web site, too." She glanced down at the front of the shirt and risked getting pricked as she touched the red letters with an admiring hand while Louise worked under the opposite arm. "You could incorporate the colors and letters, maybe. What are the stars for?"

"The Wolf Trail is the Milky Way. It's a bridge between this world and the spirit world," he told her as he leaned over to give little Nicky a hand in getting a rubber ball out from under his chair. "There you go, baby."

"Do the spirits wander back and forth?"

"I hope not," he said. "I see them winging, not wandering. I see them racing one another on beautiful spirit ponies, gliding from star to star. A freewheeling ride on a good horse must be about as close as we can get to touching heaven. What do you think, Bernadette?"

"I think our brother Nick went away so this Romeo could come. E'en it, Lou?"

The girls were giggling as Joey smiled innocently. "It certainly works for me," she said. "We won't need heavy boots or helmets, but we'll wear silks like this. This is beautiful, Louise."

"I don't see why they call them silks when they're made of nylon," Bernadette said.

"They can't call them *nylons*. Those are stockings." Louise reached for a bit of black cloth strewn with appliquéd red stars. "Is this the way you wanted the helmet cover? I made it to match. You'll wear stars on your head."

"I love everything about it, Louise. You do such beautiful work."

"Nick says he has to be hauling horses the next time you race," Louise said.

"Dillon's going to take me. It's in Aberdeen."

"Would it be all right if I go and watch?"

"Of course. We'll be coming back the same day, so lots of driving for a very brief show, but it would be fun to have another woman along."

"I don't mind the drive. I just want to see how this shirt looks in the horse race. They have a printed program, don't they? With all the names? I want one of those."

Joey exchanged glances with Nick. "I'm riding under the name Joey Red Shield," she confided.

"Ee'n it?" Louise stretched out the all-purpose idiom in amazement as she turned on Nick. "Did you get married without telling us?"

"'Splain your way out of this one, Lucy," he muttered as he went down for the lost ball again and rolled it across the floor to the baby.

"The truth is, I asked him, but he turned me down." She flashed him a so-there smile. "It's just that I don't want to use my real name. There was this man who…" She made a self-conscious gesture toward her face and the injuries that were hardly noticeable anymore. "He might try to find me, and he could be dangerous. He's totally psycho."

"I know what you mean, but don't worry. My brother enjoys kickin' that particular brand of psycho ass."

"You know what, girls? Kickin' ass is one thing. Takin' names is something else." He heaved himself out of the saggy-bottomed chair, much to the relief of its whiny springs. "I'll be waiting in the pickup."

Nick was headed for a pickup in Sioux Falls. He'd left home on a head of steam hot enough to fuel his whole trip, but a few hours on the road had a way of settling a guy down. He felt bad about taking off the way he had, a day early. He couldn't believe Joey had brought up the bit about asking him to marry her. Busting his balls was bad enough, but getting a guy's sisters in on it was downright indecent. What people said about him was probably true: he couldn't tell a joke, and he couldn't take one. He was too damn touchy.

This was a typical run, covering a lot of his usual territory. Melting snow and greening grass were good for his business. People bought and sold a lot of horses in the spring. It was a time to ride and rope and race, and soon it would be time to breed. He was looking forward to putting his new horse to work on the job he'd been chosen for in the first place. June 1 was the target date. By then his life would surely be back to normal. Publicly he would be talking up the plans for the crop of fillies and colts in the making. Privately he would be counting the advantages of the lone-wolf lifestyle. If he was down to counting them on one hand, he would never tell.

And the Wolf Trail partners would already be reminiscing about their days as racehorse owners. Dillon would make it out to be a brush with racetrack immortality. *This close* to the record books, Dillon would say, and Nick wouldn't counter with any reality checks. He wouldn't want to become a character in one of Dillon's updated Indian myths. *Romancing the Jockey*. A twenty-first century Iktomi tale. Haunted by the image of a lonely wolf succumbing to the wiles of the trickster, Nick held out against calling home. He tried to get Alice to pretend she enjoyed his company, but she didn't seem to like his attitude. After a good thirty-six hour sulk, he didn't, either. So he called home, got no answer, left a curt message and went back to sulking. He sulked from Nebraska to Colorado to Wyoming and back to South Dakota, where his mood finally started to improve.

There was no way he could make it back in time to attend the race, but as the drive time wore on, he realized he was actually thinking about it. He'd lost all touch with reality. He was coming in from the southwest, marking the familiar sights that usually signified *almost there, almost home*, but his heart and mind were skipping past the end of the trail and tagging another hundred miles on to his journey. Didn't seem to matter that this race would be starting right about the time he pulled in at the Wolf Trail. He was one pure-D pathetic cowboy. He would saddle up old Rusty, take a ride down to the river and clear his head just as soon as he parked his outfit and unloaded his

gear. Maybe he would call the track at the Brown
County Fairgrounds, too, just to make sure his horse
had made it through the race without any mishaps.

And his jockey.

He'd barely gotten in the house and shut the door
behind him when he had to change his plans. He had
company. He didn't recognize the car or the two men
who emerged wearing white shirts and pants with
ironed-in creases. They were either missionaries or
cops, both equally unwelcome at the moment. Since
they weren't smiling like car salesmen, he was betting
against anyone proposing to show him the light today.

Which left him looking at another encounter with
the dark side.

The guy with the receding hairline and the bushy
red mustache led the way. He would be the talker. The
sidekick was probably Indian, at least part. Presumably
he was the token. But Nick never discounted the de-
ceptive nature of looks. Best reason a guy ever had for
getting a handle on the situation by employing the
senses over the tongue. He met the men outside,
choosing the shade of a small cottonwood, the only
tree in the trailer house yard.

The talker pulled out FBI identification and intro-
duced himself as a special agent. "And this is Michael
Dacotah, with the NIGC. We're looking for—"

"Where are you from?" Nick's question was for
Dacotah.

"He's with the National Indian Gaming Commission," the talker supplied. "Our agencies are working together on a broad investigation involving some offtrack betting activity and a possible tie-in with—"

"Back up," Nick said quietly. He lifted his chin. "I'm askin' *him*."

"I'm from Cheyenne River."

"Charlie Dacotah?"

"He's my father's brother. I've been gone for a while. Went to school in Kansas and then out East. I'm working out of the field office in Tulsa."

Satisfied with the sidekick, Nick turned to the talker. "What did you say your name was?"

"Special Agent Thomas Bowker."

"I just pulled in from a long haul. Haven't hardly gotten in the house yet." But he gave a nod toward the front steps. The talker was all name, rank and agency, but the sidekick had roots. It wasn't much, but enough to get them through the door. "You guys want some coffee?"

Nick offered coffee and chairs at the kitchen table. Bowker declined the first offer, which left only the chair, and he turned that down, too. It was only after Nick made it clear that there wouldn't be much talk until the coffee was on the table that the agent finally gave up on the idea of a drive-by snooping.

Bowker started off with questions about what kind of traveling Nick had been doing and how long he'd been gone. Nick knew he didn't have to answer—this being billed as a "friendly visit"—but questions seemed to pass for small talk with this guy, so Nick gave small answers. He'd been out west for a few days. On business. Horse business. Other people's horses.

Michael Dacotah didn't speak until he had shown due respect for Nick's coffee by drinking more than half a cup. Then he explained what had led the two men to Nick's door.

"My concern is Indian gaming," Dacotah said. "Tom's focus is organized crime. Lately some of our Indian casinos have added what they call a race book to their business, and it's brought in a whole new crowd of players with a different set of connections. Between Tom's agency and mine, we've got our eye on one individual in particular, and we're trying to track a few leads back to the source, which we think might be our man."

"You're talkin' to the wrong guy," Nick said, feeling strangely relieved. "My partner's the one who works at the casino."

"We know that." Bowker braced an arm on the table and leaned in. "We also know that you own a racehorse, and that you recently ran first in a race at Fort Pierre."

"Bought the horse to use as a stud. He's a Paint, but he's bred for speed. Thought I'd let him prove himself." Nick glanced at Bowker and then turned to Dacotah. "I don't have any kind of connections. That was a maiden race for both of us."

"But not for your jockey," the sidekick said.

"We just had a conversation with some people over here at your casino. Everyone's talking about a woman calling herself Joey who rode your horse against one of the locals. What was his name?" Bowker looked to Dacotah for help in the native department.

"Hank Two Dog. And it's not everybody talking," Dacotah said. "It's mostly Hank Two Dog."

"He says the woman rides like she might be a professional jockey. We're wondering how long you've known her, Mr. Red Shield."

"Awhile," Nick said. Relief had given way to defensiveness at the mention of his jockey. "You accusing me of something?"

"Not at all, no." Bowker leaned back in his chair, eyeing Nick as though he were trying to decide which card to trump him with. "We're looking for a jockey named Lauren Davis."

The talker had thrown down his ace.

"No reason to be mysterious about it," Bowker claimed. "Her disappearance has been reported in the news. Disappeared in Illinois, car turned up in Missouri, no driver, no body, no explanation. It's a long shot, but you got a female jockey disappearing there, one turns up here, you gotta check it out, right? There aren't that many of 'em."

"Did you check the race card?"

"The what?" Bowker sat up straight. "I said *female*, not—"

"He's talking about the *horse* race," Dacotah said,

subtly arching an eyebrow for Nick's benefit. *Trying job, this translating.*

"You mean down in Fort Pierre?" Bowker was asking. "Didn't have to. Your first place win is big news around here."

"Guess Hank must be our big news announcer." Nick chuckled. "Check the race card. My jockey's name is Joey Red Shield. She's my wife."

Bowker glanced at Dacotah. *Did we know this?*

Dacotah shrugged.

"How long have you been married?" Bowker persisted.

"Long enough for me to know she's not the woman you're looking for. What did this woman do?"

"She's likely dead," Dacotah said.

Then let her rest in peace.

Lauren Davis. Nick had been turning the name over in his mind, trying to figure out what to do with it, and now he knew. Bury it. Put it on one of those accident fatality markers, find that fateful spot on the road to Mexico, Missouri, and pound the damn thing deep into the ground.

"Her boyfriend is a man named Raymond Vargas," Dacotah continued. "He's been under investigation in a case that involves some members of one of our better-known crime families in an offtrack betting ring that's used the services of certain tribal casino race books. They're also suspected of money laundering, tax evasion and fixing races. It's a big case, and Ms. Davis might be able to help us if she's still alive."

"And we might be able to help her," Bowker put in. "We don't know why Vargas would want her dead. But we do know that people associated with him have been known to disappear, commit suicide…"

"Die in horrible accidents and like that."

"The stuff movies are made of," Nick reflected. But he was busy filing away another name. Raymond Vargas. He pictured it carved on a stone marking a real grave and a real corpse. *Here lies the boyfriend. May God damn his soul.*

"Yeah, the next *Scarface*," Bowker predicted. "Only this guy's never been touched. Good friends, good looks, good taste in clothes, which are all made of Teflon. A few years back they almost had him for fixing a race—doping a long shot that beat the favorite by something crazy like a dozen lengths. Vargas owned the favorite. Turned out Vargas and his associates won a shitload of money by losing. They might've nailed him if the jockey hadn't committed suicide."

"He's part of the mafia?"

"Not exactly, but we think he's connected," Bowker said. "He's a gambler who's gotten by with some lucrative racetrack schemes. We think Vargas and his associates are setting something up through some of the rebate shops that your tribal casinos have been opening up lately."

"Which is legal in a lot of states," Dacotah explained. "High rollers get rebates on their action. Kinda like when you buy a car? You get a deal for doing business with the shop. The money comes from fees they would be charged if they were betting at the track."

"What kind of fees?" Nick asked. The more he learned about horse racing, the less, he realized, he really knew. And the less comfortable he was participating.

"The track fees that make pari-mutuel betting possible. You need the fees for purses, taxes, stuff like that. But offtrack betting over the phone or on the Internet is a way to get around those fees. Kinda like bookies, only it's legal. In *some* states."

"For the moment," Bowker hastened to add.

"But it's becoming big business, with plenty of potential for moving large amounts of cash from pocket to pocket," Dacotah said. "Very attractive to the kind of people we're talking about. And our tribal gaming businesses are particularly vulnerable."

"Okay, you've convinced me. Joey and me, we're done with horse racing." Nick pointed a finger skyward and recited dramatically, "From where the sun now stands."

Dacotah laughed. "It's all right, Chief Joseph, nobody's suggesting you surrender your horses. These small racetracks aren't dealing with the kind of money we're talking about. We heard about your jockey, and we thought she might be our boy's missing girlfriend."

"If she's hiding out, what better place than an Indian reservation?" Bowker suggested.

"You kidding?" Nick protested. "Word gets around by moccasin telegraph faster than the Internet."

"Only if you're hooked up." Dacotah finished his coffee, signaling that he would be leaving now.

"Is that the right time?" Bowker was checking his watch against the clock on the wall.

Louise had made the horse-head clock from a kit and given it to Nick for his fortieth birthday. It was the only clock in the house. Good clock, dead batteries, Nick would have said if he'd thought the man was really asking.

But Bowker was giving his kind of signal. He knew the time.

"We won't make it back before five, Mike. May I use your phone, Mr. Red Shield? My cell never wants to work out here."

"Sure." Nick pointed the way.

"He's got the wrong service," Dacotah said. And then, with a smile, "Can't tell *him* that, though."

"Gotta have those moccasins."

"I heard about your broodmares. You got a hold of some of that Badlands bunch, supposed to be descended from Sitting Bull's horses." The man from Cheyenne River glanced out the window, searching the horizon. "You believe it?"

"Why not? They went missing. If they couldn't get to an Indian reservation, what better place than the

Badlands?" Nick said, recalling Bowker's earlier comment. "Wilderness is the only safe place for a fragile creature."

"*Ohan.*" Dacotah passed him a card within a handshake. "Good luck with your horses."

His visitors gone, Nick sat staring at the card. National Indian Gaming Commission, working with the FBI. Interesting. Like most Indians, he was pretty skeptical about the FBI. They were supposed to investigate any serious felonies committed on the reservation, but their track record was dubious, at best. Nobody had trusted them since the heyday of the American Indian Movement, back in the seventies. But with all the talk of connections, Nick was beginning to think he might need some of his own.

Pocketing Michael Dacotah's card, he glanced at the horse-head clock and smiled. Louise would never say anything about it, but it would please her if he remembered to replace those batteries. Built into his brain was a reliable timepiece. He didn't need a clock to remind him that a hundred miles away, his horse had already run his race. He could probably get the results with a phone call, but they wouldn't be able to tell him whether Dillon had come up with any dirt on the competition. Or how Louise had felt seeing her red-and-black handiwork come flying out of the starting gate. Or whether Joey had glimpsed heaven through her goggles, even for a split second.

Or whether anyone had gone to the fairgrounds looking for a woman named Lauren Davis.

A call that couldn't yield the important answers wasn't worth making. Let them tell him all the news themselves. They would be home safe soon, and tonight they would either be celebrating or commiserating as they replayed the race. Either way was okay by him, as long as there was no disagreement over the plan he was formulating for tomorrow.

16

Rarely had Nick given as much thought to what he would say as he did while he was keeping watch for Dillon's pickup. It seemed strange enough to be watching for people—he'd stopped minding anyone else's comings and goings long ago—but thanks to a visiting FBI agent and his sidekick, he found himself looking for a different someone in the coming than she had been in the going. It was no laughing matter, but it sure was funny. Whoever the hell she was, he could hardly wait to see her face.

Sighting a dust wake on the approach from the highway, Nick determined his own approach and headed outside to mind his family's comings. *His family.* His sister, his business partner and a woman he'd taken in off the highway. Watching them pile out of the truck looking all drained and defeated, he was beset by the urge to gather them in and tell them how little the loss of a horse race mattered to him. But he resisted. He would show them what was important to him by lightening their load. He headed straight for the back doors of the two-horse trailer.

But he was cornered before he could even start the chore.

There was shy Louise, taking the trailer doors right out of his hands. There was Dillon, suppressing a grin while he pulled out the ramp. And Joey, still dressed in her silks, was wearing all new hair, which was more noticeable but less important than the twinkle in her eye, the twitch at the corners of her mouth and the sassy swagger that could not help undoing any show they had planned for him. His family had brought home another victory. Anything else on his mind would have to wait while he gave their surprise its due.

"Guess what?" Without waiting for the obligatory *what?* Joey jumped him, legs around his waist like a kid on a stick pony. She was lucky his reflexes functioned well and he caught her. "We won."

"Another first place?"

"Your horse so completely outclasses and outper-forms all his competition, it is just... You won, Nick!"

What could he do but hug her and laugh with her and say fool things like, "You little monkey, you're just full of surprises."

"Which is a surprise in itself, because you thought I was full of shit." Her big smile and bright eyes captured his fancy as she dug her fingers into his shoulders and hung on. "Didn't you? Come on, admit it."

"No way," he said, grinning. "The horse maybe, but not—"

"You should've seen her ride, man," Dillon enthused as he emerged from the trailer at the front end of a backing horse. Joey slid off her mount with a proud smile. "She flies like this little Red Baron, gunnin' it down the track, dive-bombing the finish line."

"I should've been there. We gotta get a movie camera." Feeling strangely discomfited, Nick adjusted his hat. "I like your hair." The truth was, he didn't know what to think of the sorrel color and the mop-chop cut, but he figured he was supposed to say something.

She plunged her fingers in and fluffed. "You do?"

"You almost look like a different person."

"Like a whole new identity?"

"It's a start."

"Here's the real man of the hour." She turned to the big Paint and claimed the lead from Dillon. "Tell your boy what you think of him."

"You kinda like this game, huh, True?" Nick rubbed the horse's black-velvet muzzle and then checked his legs, one white stocking and ivory hoof at a time. "Got you runnin' your socks off? Looks like he threw a shoe."

"It was on when we loaded him, so it must be in the trailer."

"I'll take care of him. You guys go on in the house and get yourselves—" He took the lead rope from Joey's hand, took another long, gratified look at her face. "You look so different."

"Pretty sure I'm still me," she claimed quietly, but she looked down at her hand as if to check and make sure. "I didn't throw a shoe, but I think I broke a—"

He had planted a doubt that needed removal. In spite of all the witnesses, Nick hooked his arm around Joey's neck and kissed her, first hard and quick for her achievement, and then soft and slow, purely for his pleasure. And the witnesses made themselves scarce.

But Dillon found his way to the barn soon enough after Joey had gone inside. With True Colors cross-tied in the aisle, Nick had already bent his back to his horse-shoeing chore, the animal's pastern braced against his knee, hoof upturned to receive Nick's full physical attention while Dillon filled his ear with who was doing what in the house. Showering, making coffee, putting sandwiches together—generally settling in, being back home.

"We'll get something to eat, and then I'll take Louise home," Dillon said. "She really enjoyed herself. I'm glad she went."

"I am, too." Nick tapped in the first nail.

"You know, you've been gone the better part of a week." Considerable pause. "And you didn't call."

"Yeah, I did." Nick lopped off the nail head. "Couldn't seem to catch anyone in."

"Anyone waitin' to talk to you was in every night from dusk to dawn." Dillon squatted, sitting on his boot heels with his arms braced on his knees. "I know, cuz. I've had plenty of doubts about her, and I still do. But I know one thing—she's not doing any of this for herself."

"She wants to earn her oats while she's here. You gotta respect that." Nick dug into his jacket pocket for another nail. "It's a good way to be."

"You must've made good time today. Didn't expect you to beat us back."

"Got back a couple of hours ago."

"You had visitors, did you?" Nick spared him a glance, and Dillon added, "Two coffee cups."

"I did." Nick lined the nail up with the hole in the shoe. *Tap, tap, tap.*

"I did, too. Last night at the casino."

"Bowker and Dacotah?" Nick sensed his partner's reluctant assent. "What did you tell them?"

"I didn't tell them anything. Dacotah's been around before, checking out who's into what around the casinos. Bowker's FBI out of Minneapolis by way of Aberdeen. I knew the name. They started asking about your new horse and this professional jockey they'd heard about. I just played the big Indian. Told 'em they'd have to talk to you. But I spoke with Hank after they left. He said they asked him about some guys he knows down in Oklahoma, where one of the tribes has some kind of affiliation with a pretty big racetrack. Anyway, he let slip that he was impressed with your new horse, and this woman you had training and riding him."

"Did you tell Joey any of this?"

"Thought I'd tell you first."

"Did you tell them anything about her?"

"Nothing. I told 'em she was your business, and that you were away. Said you might be back today." Dillon's knees cracked as he stood, giving a sigh. "Hell, man, I didn't even refer to her by name."

"I told them she was my wife." Nick set the hoof down. The horseshoe clicked against the cement. His knee ached, and his brain buzzed. "By tomorrow she will be."

Nick waved to his sister as Dillon turned his pickup around and got ready to taxi down the Wolf Trail runway. Joey was still inside the house, but he knew that she would come to find him, and he kept busy while he waited for her. He had things to say, and the trailer was no place for him to say them. The warm spring had dressed the prairie to host his proposal. The soft evening sunlight, the long slant of its shadows, the easy breeze and the tweedling grass-nesters would accent whatever plain words he managed to string together.

He rode his stallion bareback around the corral with only a hackamore, just to see what the horse was like skin to skin, or nearly so. He was impressed. Joey had put such a sweet handle on him, the horse could probably be ridden Indian-style—a length of rawhide looped over the lower jaw and a blanket on his back. Back on the ground, he went over the horse's painted hide with a bristle brush and discussed the secrets of putting females at their ease before you approached them with your studly proposition.

Warm as the air was, Nick shivered inside when Joey walked up behind him in the corral. She said nothing. She simply laid her hand on his back and moved it back and forth. It felt like encouragement.

"Let's take a ride on True Colors," he suggested as he turned to her.

"Both of us?"

"We're not going far."

He put her up first and then mounted behind her. With Joey resting against his chest like the proverbial nesting spoons, he turned his back to the sinking sun and pointed the stallion's nose in the direction of the river. Not for the first time, Joey's slight weight and small frame struck him as an unlikely mate for his body, but the fit was perfect. She could find full refuge from the sun in his shadow, complete protection from the wind under his arm. He gave her the reins and slipped his arms around her.

"Did Dillon tell you how much money we won?" she asked after a long easy silence.

"He gave me the check. I'll take out some gas money for him, and the rest is all yours."

"No way. I'm earning my keep, remember?"

"We're past that. You should have something for yourself." He pointed toward a grassy ridge. "We're going up that hill, but go around. There's an easy approach on the south side. "

"Hold on," she said. "Let me show you what True can do."

She urged the horse through a smooth trot and into a rocking-horse canter, signaled and controlled by her seat. "And that's bareback with a hackamore," she said proudly as they reached the top of the ridge.

"And two passengers."

He lowered her to the ground and then followed. Pretty smooth, he thought, even with the hard landing on his weak knee. She was already admiring the scenery, exactly as he'd intended. He took a seat in the grass, and she followed suit. He liked this spot because no buildings or roads were visible, but they could see the river and the rolling hills and the buttes at the edge of the sky.

"It's beautiful out here, Nick. You're so right. It's the perfect place for horses."

"It's the perfect place for anything that eats grass or anything *that eats anything* that eats grass. Some trees cling to the riverbanks and the creeks, but nothing else really wants to grow here." He plucked a stem near the patch of new grass True Colors had quickly set to work on. "This grass—buffalo grass, it's called—the roots go down so far into the earth, you gotta work hard to kill it. And when you take those roots away and plant something with little feet, like corn or wheat, the earth misses those sturdy roots so bad, she just dries up and blows away.

"But you see how she's lovin' up the grass with just that one rain we had? Because ten, twenty feet down, that's where the roots tickle her womb. That's where she's always moist and fertile, even if she's gone without water up here on the surface for season after season. So this is the perfect place if you can thrive on what it has to offer."

"Or you're willing to adapt?"

"Sure. The Lakota people took a long time to get here, but the grass and the grass-eaters suited us, and we suited them, so here we are." He lifted one shoulder. "People don't like Indians and buffalo, you'd think they'd go somewhere else. They don't like the way the river flows and the grass grows, and they're not here to adapt. They want to kill what's here so they can replace it with something else."

"But they failed," she said decidedly. "The grass is coming back for another season, and I saw some buffalo when we went to Louise's house. You've survived, Nick. And thanks to you, so have I."

"You live to fight another day," he said, thinking, yes, they had something in common. "Somebody else would've come along and helped you."

"Or not. Who knows what would have happened to me?"

"The important thing is, what happens now?" He

nodded toward the northeast, where the backwater made its fingerling forays into the river channel. "That direction, our land goes all the way to the river. I have a quarter section across the road, and there's almost a section on this side that I own with my sisters. Dillon owns a little land, too, and we lease another section south of the house. I run a few cows, but the horses are my life. I make a pretty good living. I'm not a big talker or spender or dreamer, but I'm nobody's fool." He eyed her speculatively. "I don't make any promises I don't mean to keep. I'll keep you safe for as long as you want to stay with me. I want you to marry me."

From the look in her eyes, she hadn't seen it coming.

He swallowed. Big speeches sure required a lot of spit.

"Will you do that?" he persisted in the softest voice he could find.

"As long as you're willing just to *call* me your wife, that's probably—"

"Not enough. It has to be real. You need an identity, and it has to be real. But you're not stealin' my name. You have to let me give it to you."

She smiled as the breeze carried a lock of her hair across her eye. "You really want to?"

"I really want to." He lifted the hair from her face. "But I need a straight answer."

"Yes," she whispered. Then, in a stronger voice, "My straight answer is yes."

"I can line up a tribal judge tomorrow. Dillon's uncle…" He'd surprised her again. "What? Too soon?"

"The sooner the better. Is there time to find me something to wear? A dress would be nice. I could probably…" She reached for his left hand, rubbed her small thumb over his knuckles. "Would you wear a ring? Maybe I *will* take some of that money, just this once."

He took a white box from the breast pocket of his denim jacket, opened it and showed her the two gold bands he'd ordered on his way out of town and picked up after his unexpected visitors had left. He'd thought to get her one, just for show, but the guy at the store had given him a deal on the set, and he'd thought, *What the hell?* "I can always take these back if they're not right, get something else."

"When did you decide?"

"You told me to think about it," he reminded her. "I haven't been able to think about much else. Somewhere along the way, it started making sense."

"Sense?"

"Yeah," he said. "Which means it's what I want, so I thought up a bunch of reasons for doing it. The rings were…" He took the small one from the box. "When something makes this much sense, I like to be prepared. You wanna try?"

"You try," she said, offering her hand. "For practice." He slid the ring over her knuckle, and she looked up at him with a smile. "How did you know?"

"My hands remember things. As for the dress—"

"I can use the one I came in. I'll bet Louise can fix it up just fine. This is the important part." She stretched her arm for a long-distance view of the ring on her hand. "How does yours look?"

"Haven't tried it. The guy measured. It should fit. I thought you should be first to put it on. But not for practice."

"No, for real." She snatched her ring off and quickly put it in the slot inside the velvet-lined box. But she took a moment to admire the pair. "Mine looks so small next to yours."

"I bought you a dress, too. I went into the store for…" She was looking at him again like he was turning weird before her very eyes. "I don't even know why I went into that store. I was on the road, stopped at a café, and there were these dresses in the window next door. And this one was…well, I could see you wearing it." He smiled, glad for the evening breeze cooling his face. "Like I said, I haven't been able to think about much else. If a guy's determined to make a fool of himself, he might as well do it in a big way."

"You said you'd keep me safe as long as we're together."

"Or die tryin'," he said, only half kidding.

"That's not funny." She closed the lid of the ring box and tucked it back into his pocket. "I don't want to bring any trouble here. I really hope I don't. But you have to know that you're taking a risk."

"Like I've never done *that* before." He chuckled and tugged on True Colors, who had reached the end of his tether. "There's a character in Lakota tradition—

a god, I guess you'd say, but more like a force of nature. His name is Yum, the Whirlwind, and he's the spirit of chance, risk, games—those are things we've always prized. To hear Dillon tell it, casinos fit right in with Lakota tradition. And horse racing? In the old days, a good Lakota would bet the farm on a fast horse. Or the equivalent of the farm. Everything he had."

"The tipi, maybe?"

"Never the tipi. That belonged to his wife. No risk involved. That would be sure calamity, betting the tipi."

"Chance, risk and games," she echoed. "A whirl-wind of excitement, all your basic amusement park rides. Tightrope-walking, free-falling, flying around a track on four legs or four wheels…"

"Playing with fire," he added ruefully. "Chance, risk, games…wasn't there a fourth?" He smiled. "Oh, yeah. Yum was also the source of love. Interesting mix, don't you think?"

"The ultimate gamble," she acknowledged.

"Compared to all that, standing between you and your badass boyfriend seems pretty low on the risk scale."

"Badass *ex*-boyfriend."

It was not an outfit Lauren would have chosen for herself, but the choices she'd made in another life didn't fit anymore. Amazingly, the soft blue dress with its slightly flared skirt and tailored jacket fit her per-fectly and didn't look half bad with her new hair. It matched her eyes, Nick said, and she felt prettier than she had in a very long time. Nick wore a blue shirt and a bolo tie with a tan jacket that looked new, even though he said he'd bought it many years ago. He thought he'd worn it maybe twice. Tapered, with a western cut, the jacket enhanced his long, lean torso. So different from her badass ex-boyfriend's GQ style.

So blessedly different.

Dillon, Bernadette and Louise met them at the judge's chambers in Fort Yates, home of the Standing Rock tribal offices. The paperwork was completed first, declaring Nicholas Red Shield and Lauren Davis to be husband and wife. Dillon's uncle performed the wedding ceremony, and Dillon played a haunting song on a carved wooden flute. Then he announced that the best man would treat the wedding party and all their kids to dinner at the casino.

"No way am I taking kids," Bernadette said. "I have a babysitter for the rest of the day and a date with a slot machine tonight."

Nick took his share of teasing at dinner. Louise's remarks were gentle and sparing, but Bernadette was merciless. Her brother, the mighty oak, had fallen hard and fast. But watch out when he made up his mind, she warned her new sister. "He doesn't fool around. Much."

A live band played country music. Lauren managed to coax her new husband out on the floor for a wedding dance, which stretched to two and three, as long as the music was slow and easy. The downbeat of a rock song prompted their retreat from the floor.

But he promised her a surprise in return for letting him off the dance hook.

Their retreat was stymied at the edge of the parquet floor.

"Hey, Nick." An attractive man with an eager smile offered a handshake. "Mike Dacotah."

"I remember." Handshake accepted, Nick slipped his free arm around Lauren's shoulders. "You work for the BIA. Or, no, you're Indian gaming…something or other."

"Some government acronym. Hard to keep them straight. This must be your wife."

"Joey, this is Michael Dacotah. My wife, Joey."

"Hank Two Dog says you're quite the jockey," the man recounted as he offered his hand. The gesture, she was learning, was typically neither firm grip nor pump-handle, but rather the easy touch of one hand to another.

"Nick bought a fabulous stud, terrific breeding," Lauren said. "When we realized how fast he was, we just had to try him out. I did some race riding when I was a teenager."

"Not that long ago, I'm guessing. How long have you two been—"

"Awhile," Nick said. "But I think we've already had this conversation. Joey and I are celebrating another first-place win, and we don't get the chance to do this very often." Nick made a move to shoulder past the man, asking quietly, "Not tonight, okay?"

"You know how to get in touch with me." Oddly,

the man took Lauren's hand again. "Pleasure meeting you. Hope your luck holds." He smiled. "Sounds like you've got yourself quite a horse."

"What was that about?" Lauren asked as Nick hustled her past a row of flashing, ding-dinging slot machines.

"He thinks I know something about some case he's investigating for whatever department he works for. I've owned a racehorse for all of, what, a month?" He nodded toward a pair of elevators. "Let's go upstairs before somebody else wants an introduction."

"Upstairs?"

"We have the bridal suite tonight." He pushed the call button and grinned. "Yeah, there's really a bridal suite."

There were also spring flowers, a bottle of sparkling wine chilling in a bucket, thick white robes lying at the foot of a king-size bed and an oversize whirlpool bathtub. Nick found some music on the radio. Lauren left him to deal with opening the wine, took one of the robes into the bathroom and filled the tub. When she returned, she found him stretched out on the bed, arms tucked behind his head. He sat up quickly, as though an alarm had gone off.

"Are you done already?"

"With what?"

"Your bath."

"That's *our* bath, silly." She offered a sassy smile as she cinched the belt of her robe. "Have you poured our wine?"

He nodded toward the two glasses he'd poured

two-thirds full and carefully arranged beside the bottle in its silver bucket, the vase of tulips and lily-of-the-valley and an array of votive candles on the table next to the window.

"Louise brought the flowers and candles," he said. "I think the champagne came from the hotel." He reached for her hand. "Come look at the sky."

Beyond the window, rose-blue dusk provided a setting for the stars appearing by turns, winking at the newlyweds.

"You've turned out to be quite a wedding planner." She held her wineglass with one hand, flipped open his belt buckle with the other. "But I hope you don't think you're going to be wearing the pants in the family all the time."

"You gonna fight me for them?"

With a flick of her wrist she unthreaded his belt from his pants, dropped it on the floor and began unbuttoning his shirt. "Are *you*?" she asked.

"Not if all I get when I win is my own damn pants."

"*If* you win," she said as she pushed his dress shirt off his broad shoulders, "you get *your* pants *and* mine."

"What would I do with *your* pants?"

"Wear them on your head."

Laughing, he swept her up in his arms and carried her to the bathroom. "Game over. Hey, this tub really is big enough for both of us."

"I'll go get the wine while you test the water. And then I want you to make yourself comfortable."

With the party transferred to the bathroom, Lauren turned out all the lights except for the candles, whose reflections danced in the expansive mirror. She felt incredibly sexy as she peeled back her robe, let it drop to the floor and stepped into the water, all for her husband's viewing pleasure. He made room for her between his long legs, and she lay back in his arms and enjoyed the love of his hands until her need for him drove her to turn and take him for the first night's ride.

In the aftermath, the whirlpool jets mixing with languid satisfaction felt glorious. They added more hot water and determined to become water creatures.

"I could get used to this."

"More wine?" Lauren started to rise, but he stopped her and retrieved his glass from the floor.

"Take mine. I don't drink much, and I'm not ready to let you move." He wrapped his arms around her. "Tell me about the race in Aberdeen."

"We won by three lengths," she said after a long drink. "And he's really only been breezing so far. He's got a lot more in him. We should start thinking about more competitive tracks."

Nick was quiet for a moment. "I'm thinking about retiring him to stud."

"He can get in plenty of sex between races. I mean, I know his jockey's a married woman now, but she's not exactly—"

"Ready to be a broodmare?" Beneath the water, he rubbed her belly. "Don't worry. Your horse and your ol' man are two different kinds of stud. I need him to produce."

"He can do so much more, Nick."

"It's too damn risky. Nobody's looking for Joey Red Shield. That's who you need to be right now. You signed Lauren Davis away this afternoon."

"It was just a name. I'm still…" She set the wine down and turned to face him. "I'm still good at it, Nick."

"You said you gave it up long before you met me."

"But now I'm back into it. This horse is such a—"

"Joey, listen to me." He laid his hands on her shoulders. "Like they say in the movies, you gotta lay low for a while."

She giggled. "This is your imitation of—"

"Take your pick. It's been a while since I've seen a movie. You changed your name and your hair. Now you need a new profession. You want excitement? How about—"

"I'm not talking about big tracks, Nick. We could go to Canterbury in Minnesota. We could go to Nebraska, Oklahoma. I would never be recognized there."

"You could be recognized right here." She tried to shake the notion off, but he wasn't buying. "Lauren Davis is missing, and they haven't found her body. If somebody was paid to kill you, either he wasn't very good at it, or he doesn't know the difference. Either way—"

"Either way, he's not a threat. If his little slip-up is discovered, he's dead, and he knows it."

"It's your health I care about, not some hit man's. I said I'd keep you safe, and since I don't know much about your enemies, I don't trust anybody." His hands slid away with a *plunk*. "I can't even trust my friends."

"You mean Hank Two Dog? He said I could ride. So what? A lot of people can ride." She smiled. His hair framed his face in spiky wet tendrils. Her husband was adorable. She offered him the odd assurance of "Lauren Davis is dead."

"*Presumed* dead. The trouble is, she hasn't been buried. I don't know about anyone else, but the feds are looking for her. I know that for a fact."

"They have to, don't they? But that'll be over soon. They say if they don't find a missing person within the first few days…" It occurred to her that he wasn't talking about some routine investigation going on in a world outside theirs. "How do you know that?"

"Look, I'm not a particular fan of the FBI. Nobody around here is. But you're, you know…white. Yeah, it makes a difference. Maybe it wouldn't be such a bad idea to clue them—"

"You haven't, have you?"

"No, I haven't, but they're asking around, and they're gettin' close."

"How could they be…here?"

"Hank told somebody you rode like a pro. The guy downstairs? He's with some federal Indian gaming commission, but he's already paid me one visit in the company of an FBI agent. And they've questioned Dillon, too. I doubt there's more than one female jockey gone missing lately." He sighed. "Like I said, I'll keep you safe or die trying, and I don't know much about your enemies. I'm trying to protect you from anyone who looks at you sideways."

"Oh, God." She stared at him. For all his lovely brawn and all his harrowing experience, his innocence shone like a beacon. "You *would* die trying, wouldn't you?"

"I don't plan on it."

"No, but I know you," she claimed, leaning closer.

"Right."

"I do. Your heroism is legendary."

"Right. You know what, it's our wedding night, and I'd rather…"

She smiled, kissed him, slipped her hand between their bellies, found his penis and turned it rock hard with a deft caress.

"Oh, you're talkin' about *that* hero. You might have something there."

"I certainly do have something here." Something more, and now more, and still more.

"You get him on the case, he will definitely—" he groaned and whispered "—die tryin'."

"How do I get him on my case?" She sank into the water until her chin touched the warm surface, scanned her husband's smooth chest, met his eyes and smiled. "I think I'll have a little talk with him."

The underwater tête-à-tête lasted until she had to come up for air. "He's interested in my—"

"—in your case, *inside* your case." He pulled her over him, and she wrapped her legs around him— nightwings enfolding starfire, taking in and holding on and praying that the gods would make it work, just this night, one perfect night. "Inside my wife…my wife…"

"My sweet, sweet husband."

17

Nick lifted his face from the pillow, grabbed the receiver in advance of a second shrill offense and gruffly responded, "Red Shield."

"How's married life?"

"Damn you, Dillon, what—"

"I wouldn't be asking, but I had a feeling you were either asleep, tied up or dead."

"What are you talking about?" He rolled to his back, reached across the bed and had his answer. He jackknifed and surveyed the empty room.

"If you hurry, you can catch her," Dillon was saying in his ear. "The airport shuttle leaves in about two minutes, and she's planning to be on it."

"Stop her."

★ ★ ★

The paunchy security guard was all business. He wanted to know who she was, what room she had stayed in and what she was carrying in her canvas tote bag. She didn't need this. Sneaking away from her bridal bed had been difficult enough, and then she'd had to slip out to the pickup after she'd asked the desk clerk about transportation to the airport. Leaving Nick was not something she could achieve without bearing down, blinkers on, full attention to the road ahead.

"I don't have anything," she insisted as he claimed the bag. "I didn't even—" She glanced toward the front desk, the lobby, the elevators, the alcove with… *Oh, God, here comes trouble.* "Dillon, please tell this man I'm not a thief. I'm taking the shuttle to Bismarck so that I can surprise Nick with—"

"You've surprised him, all right, Joey. He's on his way down." Dillon turned to the desk clerk. "Tell Nick Red Shield to meet us at Security."

"Please let me go," Lauren said quietly, grabbing his arm. "It's for his own good."

"What are you gonna do with this, Mrs. Red Shield?" The guard's discovery in her tote bag turned all heads.

"Isn't that Nick's gun?" Dillon demanded. "The one he keeps in—"

"The pickup," Nick said, turning all heads in another direction. "Joey, where do you think you're going with that gun?"

The security guard elbowed Dillon. "Isn't that a song?"

"Close, Artie, but this ain't the time."

"Am I under arrest or something?" Lauren asked, studiously avoiding Nick's eyes.

"You could be," the guard said. "Or your husband could be. Depends on your story."

"There's no story," Nick said. "A misunderstanding, maybe."

"Will she be taking the shuttle?" the desk clerk asked. "They're ready to head out."

"Tell them to go on."

"I've decided to go home, Nick." A fleeting glance was all she dared spare him. "My flight leaves in—"

"You don't have any ID."

"Yes, I do. Trust me."

"Never trust a woman who says *trust me*." He laid his hand at the base of her neck. "We're going back up to the room."

"You can't make me," she protested, spinning away from the warmth of his hand. "He can't make me go back up there with him, can he?"

"Jesus, Joey…"

She turned on him. "I made a terrible, terrible mistake. You're not the man I thought you were, and I'm certainly not the woman you thought—"

"Artie, could we…" Nick nodded toward the security office door. "I need to speak with my wife."

"I'll be right outside." Artie hefted the pistol Nick

had greeted Lauren with the night they met. "I'll just take this with me."

"It's not loaded. Not unless she found the loaded clip in the console. The one in the gun is empty." He glanced at her pointedly. "I don't know how she thought she was gonna get it on a plane," he said as he ushered her into the office and closed the door.

"I was going to check it. And I was going to pay you back."

"For what?"

"Everything." She folded her arms, making her stand in the middle of the small box of a room. "Including the money I took from your wallet."

"That first night we were together, I didn't get any sleep for the noise you made with all your cryin'. But you're sure quiet when you're sneakin' off."

"You sure sleep soundly after..." She waved her hand, as if she might actually wipe the precious hours away. "Oh, Nick, you could've saved us both a lot of trouble if you'd kept quiet and just let me go."

"You think I wouldn't have gone after you?"

"Where? You don't know where I'm going."

"I'd find you. For a small woman, you have a way of cutting a wide swath."

"I guess it's a good thing you stopped me, then. You knew I wasn't going to be around forever. No promises, you said, and I thought, *this man gets it*. You never said anything about going after me."

"Why did you marry me? What good is the name without—"

"That was just another one of my stupid ideas." He pulled an incredulous frown, and she quickly added, "I'm sorry, but it was. I'm sure you can go back to the tribal court and just have the whole thing erased."

"Erased? It's a legitimate court. You don't just erase…" He raised his chin, eyeing her speculatively. "Come to think of it, you can divorce me in tribal court, but I don't think I can divorce you. They have no jurisdiction over you."

"Then how can they marry us?"

"They didn't. We did. The judge is recognized by the state as a justice of the peace, but we're the ones who got married. You took me, and I took you."

"I *took* you, all right," she claimed, turning her shoulder to him. "I had a plan, Nick. I was going to try to use your horse to get to the man who tried to kill me. I might have been able to lure him into doing something that would…" She searched the ceiling for help. None found, she sighed. "I was going to let him claim your horse."

"Why?"

"What does it matter? I'm in trouble, and I'll do whatever I have to do."

"I don't see what good it would do to—"

"I didn't say it was a *good* plan. It was just a plan. But if the FBI knows about me, then…then that's not going to work." She pointed a finger. "Which means you're no good to me, Nick. And this place isn't exactly out of sight and out of reach anymore, is it?"

"Then what was last night all about?"

"It was all about—" she glanced away and back again "—sex. Good sex. It was good, wasn't it?" He nodded. "I really did try to earn my keep. And I thought…" She gestured toward the door. "I just thought this way would be easier. You know? I can't stay now."

"Are you sure you don't want to talk to the authorities?"

"The authorities," she said, and she couldn't help smiling. "That's funny, Nick. Like, the coppers. And the gangsters. Maybe you haven't been to the movies lately, but you've sure seen a lot of old ones."

He lifted one shoulder. "Whatever you want to call them, the police might be able to help you."

"Maybe I'm not quite as white as you think. As in lily white." She gave a humorless laugh. "I really don't want you to know what I've done or where I'm going or who I've been involved with. I want to be Joey for you. Okay? Can we just leave it at that?"

"Sure," he said, his eyes devoid of feeling. "But now that your getaway plan failed, there's no rush, is there? You might as well come home with me and pick up your stuff."

"I really don't have any stuff."

"And then I'll take you to the airport, bus station, friend's house, wherever you wanna go. Just like I've always said I would."

"Nick…" She turned away from him. "I have to—"

He grabbed her arm, spun her around and kissed her so suddenly that she had to kiss him back. Without thinking, she rose up on her toes to meet him, to artlessly, fully open herself to him.

He came away from the kiss with eyes alight.

"You're good at a lot of things, but lyin' ain't one of 'em. I know what last night was about. The sad thing is, I'm not the only one you're lyin' to."

She shook her head, desperate to recover her resolve.

But he was relentless. "I don't care what you've done, Joey. I don't care if the devil himself wants you dead. He'd have to get past me."

"I don't want that."

"What, then? I'd walk through hellfire for you, and you know I'd—" He grabbed her shoulder when she tried to back away. "Look at me, Joey. Tell me you don't love me."

Pressing her lips together to keep them from trembling, she wound up and slapped him as hard as she could. Her hand, heart, eyes ablaze, she stood firm.

"You can't make me stay."

"I could." His hand came away slowly from her shoulder, finger by finger. "But one time, and one time only, I made somebody I cared about do something against his will. I live with the consequences."

She turned quickly, opened the door and strode past the security guard, who sat outside the office door.

"Artie, give me the gun," Nick said.

The guard released the magazine, glanced at the couple and then shoved it back into the butt of the pistol. He handed it to its owner without checking for rounds Nick had already said weren't there.

Nick handed the weapon to his wife. "Take it. I use it for rattlesnakes mostly. I keep the spare clip loaded and handy, but this one's empty. When you get there, first thing you do, you get a box of bullets and you load the damn thing. I hope you don't mind shooting the sonuvabitch the next time he decides you've been around long enough." He paused. "You change your mind, Joey, you know where to find me."

She could not look him in the eye. Nor could she change her mind.

Dillon returned from his errand feeling like the bad-luck best man. Driving the runaway bride to the airport the day after the wedding wasn't supposed to be on the list of his duties. But it was Nick's call. If the situation were reversed—and in some ways it had been—Nick would do the same for him without jawing over the details. It was a long drive up to Bismarck and an even longer drive home, where he found Nick's pickup parked next to the barn. The man would want a report. Maybe even an ear.

He was currying True Colors. Dillon had watched Joey perform the same chore standing on a cinder block, and he'd knocked together a wooden step for her so she could reach the horse's back. She was no slacker. That much he could say for the woman. A cold bitch? Maybe. But Nick had seen fit to do what he did, and he had his reasons. If he'd made a bad call, if there was a price to pay, so be it. They both knew the drill.

"You got her to the airport okay?" Nick asked without looking up. He was generously applying the elbow grease, kicking up puffs of dust and horse hair.

"Yep." Dillon wished he could say what Nick wanted to hear—that she'd changed her mind and was waiting for him back at the house.

"Got her some more cash?"

"Yep."

"Did she say anything?"

"She said thank you. And I didn't say shit. You know how hard that was?"

"Next to impossible." Nick dropped the currycomb into a rubber bucket and unhooked the cross ties. "I'm thinking I'll put him out with the mares this week."

Dillon patted the horse's flank. "Give 'em our best, big guy."

Nick opened the Dutch door and turned the horse loose in the corral. "Thanks for standing up with me yesterday and helping me out today." He laid a hand on Dillon's shoulder. "You're still workin' graveyard, huh? You must be tired."

Dillon had to ask. "It's none of my business, man, but was it because of her kid?"

Nick scowled. "What kid?"

"*What kid?* Nick, she has a kid somewhere, or *had*. I'm guessin' a real young kid."

Nick's hand slid away. "She told you this?"

"Not in so many words."

"Yeah, well, you're dreamin' again." Nick gave a mirthless chuckle. "Something like that, she would've told me."

His tone said no skeptical commentary invited.

"She's like you, keeping the bad stuff to herself." Dillon tapped his partner's chest with the back of his hand. "Nick, the day she was playing with Bernadette's baby and I was asleep up in the loft? She didn't know I was there, and it was kinda one of those deals, you're caught between hoping they'll go away and coming out to—"

"What happened, Dillon?"

"You know what that baby's like. No ears, that one. She tried to tell him no, but he tore into her blouse and latched onto her tit. Thing is, once he started, she kinda gave him a little help. Plus, she called him *Joey*."

"So, you…"

"Well, the choice to stay out of sight was already gone by the wayside. You saw her that day, she was…I mean, I can't believe you didn't—"

Nick's patience thinned to the see-through point. "Did she tell you *what happened to her kid, Dillon?*"

"No, but I told her I knew what it was like to lose

your kids, and she just looked sad. I figure her baby died, or he got—"

"—taken from her. She wouldn't go back there otherwise. We're talkin' some serious evil where she's headed."

"She's obviously been workin' on *something* for a while."

"Whatever she thinks she's doing now, it isn't what she planned. She got scared." He glanced out the open door. "I'm going after her. They've already tried to kill her once."

"That plane already flew."

"I have to find her, and I'm gonna need some help. There's no time to backtrack and go searching under every rock."

"I'm with you, man. Whatever you need."

"I'm not sure what that'll be. Joey was gonna let this guy Vargas claim True Colors. Why, I don't know. According to those two agents, Vargas is into high-stakes gambling and all kinds of criminal crap, which… Hell, he tried to *kill* her."

Dillon nodded. It all sounded pretty dramatic, but if Nick started painting his face for war, Dillon would take on his share of the charcoal.

"I'm gonna give Michael Dacotah a call. Jesus, I hope I can trust him." Nick shrugged, shook his head. "I got no choice."

Michael Dacotah was more than happy to stop at the Wolf Trail the next morning on his way back to the area office in Aberdeen. Nick had a feeling the man was expecting his call but not necessarily his news.

"My wife took off on me," he told the man soon after he arrived. No coffee offered, no chair. Simply a handshake and the reason for the meeting.

"You think she went back to—"

"I don't know where she went," Nick said. "Where this Vargas holes up. If you can tell me what you know, maybe we can help each other out."

"That's not the way this works, my friend. We trade information, and you're the one who goes first."

"You're gonna be sorely disappointed. I picked her up off the side of the road down in Missouri. She'd been left for dead. I didn't even know her name until—"

"So she's not really your wife."

"We're married. That much is legitimate. She wouldn't say much about what happened to her. Said she needed to disappear, forget the whole mess, because the guy responsible was some badass sonuvabitch. But there was one detail she couldn't leave behind, and I don't know why I didn't see it."

"Her son."

"Joey," Nick said. Dacotah nodded. It had to be true, then. "How old is he?"

"Little guy. A year, maybe." Dacotah shook his head and did Nick the courtesy of staring off toward the highway. "She was hiding out with you, and you had this horse and she's a top-rated jockey, so you decided to get into horse racing? Not the best way to keep her identity a secret."

"I don't know what was up with that." *Are you sure you don't want to talk to the authorities?* he'd said, and she'd laughed at him. He couldn't blame her. He wasn't one to talk, period, and here he was, running off at the mouth. "She wouldn't tell me much at first, which was fine by me. I offered to drop her off somewhere, but she said she had no place to go. She told me she'd ridden her dad's racehorses when she was a kid. Other than what you've told me, I don't know anything about this Vargas she was hooked up with."

"Raymond Vargas is slick, and he's deadly. A small businessman and a big gambler, although nobody's been able to pin down just how big. He keeps a legitimate profile in the horse-racing business. He's owned some winning horses, mostly when he had Lauren Davis riding them, but she's been out of it for at least a couple of years."

"She had a baby."

"Right. By the way, they were never married."

"I know." Certain things, a guy just knew. "What's his connection with Indian gaming?"

"We don't know for sure what they're trying to set up, but Bowker is working a case in New York involving a gambling ring that's handling sports betting all over the world. Offtrack betting. Some of our Indian casinos—especially the ones that are too isolated to get a lot of foot traffic—they're looking for

Internet traffic. Frankly, they're getting some shaky advice. Especially when the tribal leaders aren't as involved as maybe they could be and they've got management companies working deals for them."

"Is Standing Rock into this Internet stuff?"

"Not so far, but this kind of stuff can start out looking perfectly legal. They just busted a guy in Fargo for doing illegal wire transfers. But his business was hooked up with UND in an offtrack betting service that was legit. You see the offtrack handle jumping from ten million to more than two hundred million in a single year, you start to wonder."

"Is this guy connected to Vargas?"

"Jigsaw puzzle. That's the name of the game," Dacotah said with a smile. "You pick up a piece here and a piece there, you try to fit them together. We know that Vargas and his associates are interested in doing business through conduits like the kind we're talking about. Charitable gambling, Indian gaming— they must look like the new frontier to these guys. They could launder all kinds of money, not just gambling proceeds. The more cash you run through, the harder it is to account for it. Any criminal activity you can name—and I mean the big stuff, from drugs to terrorism—you follow the money."

"This is getting way too 007," Nick said. "I just want my wife back."

"Bowker thinks we can connect Vargas and his associates to charges big enough to put them away indefinitely. We want to head off any plans they might have for turning Indian casino race books into channels for dirty money. The New York Racing Association has already canceled contracts with some of the casino rebate shops. They want full disclosure, and we're urging casinos to comply voluntarily. We're the ones who noticed this possible connection between the FBI's case and our race books. We want to help them get these guys."

"You get Vargas…"

"You get your wife."

"If he doesn't get her first." Nick shook his head. "Why in hell would he be interested in claiming my horse? Joey says…" He gave an apologetic smile. "Lauren. My wife. She says the horse is capable of competing at a much higher level. But surely these guys are into big-stakes races, Thoroughbreds. My horse is a Paint. She was talking about taking him to bigger tracks, but we were talking Minnesota, Nebraska, Oklahoma, not—"

"Oklahoma," Dacotah said, fairly pouncing on the word. "We had some reports out of Oklahoma. There's an Indian casino has a race book with one of the tracks down there, and some contacts…" He made the wobble-hand sign for *shaky*. "Could be some movement afoot. I can tell you where Vargas lives, but I'm interested in what he's up to. Which probably has nothing to do with your wife, but maybe it could. How much do you think she knows?"

"Nothing. She went after her baby."

"Do you know where she went?"

"No. She took a plane out of Bismarck. She didn't have anything when I found her, so I don't know where she came up with ID or what name she's using."

"She must have some connections of her own. Nick, this woman could be using you."

He accepted the notion with a shrug. "I'm all she's got."

"You don't know that. You don't know how far she'll go."

"She'll go as far as she has to. And so will I."

"We can track the flight and check phone records, but we don't want Vargas to get wind of this investigation. If we can find Lauren Davis…"

"Joey Red Shield. Maybe Lauren Red Shield."

"All of the above," Dacotah decided. "I think she's got something with this idea of using your horse as bait. How much are you willing to risk, Nick?"

"Everything I have."

18

Lauren "Joey" Davis Red Shield was flying the way she rode a good racehorse—by heart, instinct and keeping the saddle just barely in contact with the seat of her pants. She'd never been good at making plans, and this day was no exception. In her last contact with Jack she had arranged the fake driver's license she'd needed to build a new identity, which had come in handy for boarding the plane. She had detected unusual urgency in Jack's voice when he told her to *be* this new person now. No going back, he'd said. Things had changed, and she might not be able to count on him much longer.

Her escape had done a number on two men. Nick deserved better. Maybe Jack did, too. But right now

there was only one man, one number—enemy
number one. In movie terms, Vargas's number was
up. Lauren smiled as she approached a bank of
phones at the Springfield airport. She decided
against calling Jack in favor of taking a cab all the way
to the farm and using the drive time to consider what
she might face and how she would deal with it so
she could leave Nick to his horses and Jack to his...to
whatever Jack had in his life besides his boss. It was
up to her to get her child back. No matter what
identity she assumed, she was, first and foremost,
Joey's mother.

She remembered the security code, along with the
general idea of how to use the gun packed in the small
bag she'd bought at the Bismarck airport so she could
get it onboard in checked luggage. Following Nick's
advice, she made one stop on her way west from
Springfield. Your basic big-box store—one-stop
shopping for bullets, a bagel sandwich and baby toys.
She'd grabbed a toy pickup truck on the way to the
sporting goods aisle. A big blue one, like Nick's. Her
husband, Nick, the man she'd slapped silly because he
didn't deserve to die for her sins.

She looked at her right palm—where she could still
feel the sting every time she thought about it—and
the back of her left hand, where Nick's ring glim-
mered in the early evening light. He had given his "big
Indian" heart, which her heart, for all her little white
lies, would not allow her to turn away. He would have

given her the ride, the horse, the shirt off his scarred back, and she would have taken it all for Joey's sake.

But not his life. She couldn't go that far.

The life of Raymond Vargas was another matter. She was going to kill a rattlesnake with Nick's rattlesnake gun. If he hadn't changed the security code, and if he went into the library for his usual nightcap after everyone else in the house was in bed, she knew exactly where and how she would do it. She could even take out the new girlfriend if need be. Do the woman a favor. Lauren sat back in the cab, smiled, and thought about Nick and his old movies. She was on her way to carry out a hit, and she was smiling.

Lauren entered the house through a quiet patio entrance and found the place dark and apparently deserted. She checked the garage and discovered that Raymond's Porsche was gone but the Escalade was there. Raymond was out. Jack must have taken Joey and the nanny somewhere, since they clearly weren't on the premises. She couldn't have planned it better.

Please, God, bring Raymond home first, so I can kill him.

Not the most reverent prayer, but she could ask forgiveness later.

Raymond's "library," where the books were for show and the bar was for real, was a perfect room for a murder. The bar was visible from the foyer, and the double doors, which always stood open, gave her a place for both easy cover and access.

Mrs. Red Shield, in the library, with the gun.

But she would leave no clue.

Approaching headlights shone through the sheers on the library's floor-to-ceiling windows. Lauren's heartbeat tripped into overdrive. She took her place and waited, ears attuned to every sound. The door from the garage admitted him to the house. Footsteps on the wood floor. The clicking of the light in the bar cabinet. Cocktail glass, decanter stopper, glass-on-glass clink. Now was the time. Lauren came out from behind the door, concentrating on the heft of the gun, the need for two hands, straight arms, gun pointed toward the light. She was unsteady, and she rushed her shot, but she took it. It was all noise. Quick thunderclap, shattering glass.

And then she realized that she hadn't shot Raymond Vargas. It was Jumbo Jack, who was still standing, slowly turning, with a pistol in one hand and a glass in the other.

She was a dead woman.

But he drained the glass, set it down on the bar and inspected the new hole in the shoulder of his sport coat. Then he looked up at her and laughed.

Laughed.

"You shot the wrong guy, little girl. The man you really wanna see dead has gone to the races."

"Oh, Jack," she gasped. She looked down at the strange, heavy thing she was holding, suddenly confused about what it was doing in her hand and how to safely separate the two. She looked up. Jack, still standing. Herself, not dead yet. Table. *Phone.* "I'll get you some help."

"What are you doing?"

She traded the gun for the telephone receiver. "I'm calling 911."

"Put the phone down. This is nothing. I've got a friend who'll look after this. Used to be a medic."

He was there beside her. Jumbo Jack, still standing after she'd shot him, taking the phone from her, picking up the gun while she, wide-eyed, watched the dark patch on the shoulder of his sport coat grow like the time-lapse blooming of a blood-red rose.

"I shot you, Jack. I'm sorry." She looked up. Why wasn't he angry? "We have to do something. You're bleeding."

"It smarts, too. But I don't think you hit anything but fat. It went clear through, see?" He turned to show her the matching flower in back. "If you had to shoot me, this was the way to do it."

"I didn't. I wanted to—"

"You got the documents you wanted?"

"The ID, yes. Thank you." She stared, befuddled. "Where's Joey?"

"They're gone. We've had a changing of the guard here. New nanny, new rules." He turned toward the bar, his movement faltering slightly. "Shit, look at that mess. We gotta find that bullet and pick up the—"

"What can I do, Jack? We need towels, we need…I think you should let me drive you to a hospital."

"I don't do hospitals, little girl." But he allowed her to tuck herself under his arm on the uninjured side and help him to a chair. He wouldn't sit, but he braced himself on the high back. "I'll bleed to death first."

"No, you won't. Tell me what to do, Jack. This wasn't meant for you."

"Since your mark is outta town, no murder will be done tonight. So what I'm gonna do is, I'm gonna take you with me. We'll get me fixed up, and we'll get you—"

"I want to see my baby. Please, Jack."

"I'll arrange for that. I promise. But can we take care of this first?" He waved his hand toward the bar. "I'll let you pick up the glass. We don't want him to see somebody's been here."

She brought ice and towels, cleaned up the debris and found the bullet lodged in the dark oak cabinetry. By the time she finished, Jack had taken a seat and was looking slightly peaked.

"Do you want me to drive? We can't afford to get stopped."

"I almost forgot to get what I came for." He hauled himself to his feet and took some papers from a desk drawer. "Okay, I'm gonna let you drive, but don't let me pass out, okay?" He chuckled. "It's not that bad. It's just the blood. Makes me light-headed."

"The sight of blood?"

"Only when it's mine. Crazy, huh?"

★ ★ ★

Lauren had her doubts about Jack making the climb to his friend's apartment. What he'd claimed were "a few steps up" turned out to be three dimly lit flights. The apartment smelled of Pine-Sol and burnt toast, and the square-faced woman who lived there seemed more disgusted with than concerned for Jack's condition.

"Jack Reed, you never come here but you're draggin' ass and spilling blood all over my floor."

"I brought supper and a movie over just last Tuesday."

"Like I said, barbecued pork butt sandwiches and *Rocky*. Get in here before somebody sees you." The woman offered him a hand, but Jack took the offer as an invitation to brace his hand on her shoulder and use her as a crutch after he'd refused Lauren's repeated offers. "Who's the girl, and why should I let her in?"

"Harrie, this is…what name are you goin' by now?"

"Joey," Lauren said, following the pair to a kitchen table that reminded her of the one in Nick's trailer. "Harry?" Lauren smiled. "Joey and Harry."

"It's Harriet." She peeled Jack's jacket off before settling him into one of the two chairs flanking the table. "What's he done now?"

"It's what I've done. It was an accident. Mistaken identity."

"Interesting." Harriet padded into the kitchen, sliding pink scuffs across the laminate floor, adjusting the tie belt on her flannel robe. "Hard to mistake Jack for a quail, so it must be moose season."

"I thought he was a—" Lauren winced at the sight of the hole in Jack's shirt, the blood, the damage she'd done "—prowler."

Harriet peeked around the cabinet door she'd just opened. "I know who you are, missy."

"Harrie, don't," Jack warned.

"I've known Jack a long time. Since Vietnam."

"He said you were a medic." And somehow she'd been expecting a man. Harriet's face didn't scream *female*, but the mass of gray-and-black hair that hung past her waist must have been glorious in its day.

"Jack's word for nurse. I've patched him up more than a few times." Harriet was filling a stainless-steel kettle with water. "I saw the story about you on the news. Jack said you got away okay and didn't want to be found."

"She came back for Little Joe," Jack said. "I was afraid she would."

"Where is he, Jack?" Lauren perched at the edge of the sofa. "You said I could see him."

"I said I'd arrange it. It might take me some time." He'd plunked his shoulder holster on the table and set about unbuttoning his shirt. He and Harriet had clearly gone through this routine before. "What was it you wanted me to do about that horse you've been talking about?"

"Raymond loves owning the winning horse that comes out of nowhere. I thought I had one for him. I thought if I rode him, staged Lauren Davis's public resurrection, then we'd all have something on

each other, so nobody could afford to cross anyone else. Plus he'd get the horse, I'd get my life and my baby back." She sighed. "Joey's nothing to him, Jack. An ego trip."

"Why didn't you go to the police?" Jack wondered, sucking air through his teeth as Harriet started the process of cleaning the back side of his wound.

"And tell them what? You left me on the highway? I know how Raymond operates. He would have come away smelling like a rose."

"Is that a wedding ring?" he asked.

Her right hand flew to cover the gold band. Protect it, keep it safe from doubts of any kind. If she had nothing else to her name, there was still the ring and the sweet memory of the man who had thought to buy it.

"Part of the act?"

"I took his name," she said quietly. "I took…"

"His gun?" Jack's chuckle turned into a *youch!* He jerked away from Harriet's prodding, but then he was back to reprimanding Lauren. "That was stupid. Slim chance you would have plugged your real mark."

"I plugged you, didn't I?"

"Yeah, but *he* woulda plugged you right back. I picked up some information. Haven't had a chance to look it over, but I'm thinking there's a chance…"

"A chance of what?" He was thinking about helping her. While his friend tended the wounds Lauren had inflicted on him, Raymond's personal enforcer was toying with a notion. "Jack?"

"You're gonna have to stay here for a while with Harrie," he told her finally.

"You're not going anywhere for a few days, either," Harriet warned.

"I'll keep my promise, little girl, but I need one from you. No more of this." He brandished the shoulder holster he'd laid on the table. "Can you keep her away from the windows and doors?" he asked Harriet.

"What are you going to do?" she asked.

"I'm going to see a man about a horse."

"You're not talking about Nick, are you?" Lauren panicked. "Because he's totally out of the picture now. He gave me a place to stay, and I came up with this racehorse scheme. He almost went for it, but I think he realized… Well, he got cold feet."

"Usually they get cold feet *before* the wedding." Harriet slid a pointed glance in Jack's direction.

"Nick decided gaining a wife and losing a horse might not be such a great deal. I decided my chances would be better with Jack." She hastened to add, "For getting my baby back. You'll help me, won't you, Jack?"

"I said I'd arrange for you to see him. I don't know what it's gonna take yet, but you're staying with Harrie until I say otherwise. You're not equipped to kill anybody, little girl. Get that out of your head. *Fuck!*" Another assault on his torn flesh had the big man turning on his nurse. "What have you got to drink around here, woman?"

With stitching to be done, the patching up of Jack

Reed turned ugly. Lauren cried. Jack got a little teary himself, but mostly he got drunk and finally passed out. Harriet, the battlefield nurse, drank a little, cursed a lot and did her job with a steady hand. Jack was removed to the sofa, and Harriet finally accepted Lauren's offer to help out.

"You can clean up the operating room while I make us a nice cup of chamomile tea."

"I'm sorry to impose. Story of my life, I guess." Lauren rolled Jack's ruined clothes in a towel. "You and Jack must be very close."

"What makes you think that?" Harriet deposited a rag and a bottle of Pine-Sol on the table.

"He trusts you. A man in Jack's position can't afford to trust just anyone. In all the time that I was with Raymond—and Jack was always around, you know, Raymond's right-hand man—I never heard anything about Jack's personal life. He never mentioned friends or family. Of course, I never asked. I knew better. I didn't even know he'd been in Vietnam," she said as she mopped blood off the chair. "It was all about me. My experiences, my acquaintances, who could and couldn't talk to me, never going to the track unless he was along. For my own protection, he would say. And when I got pregnant, when I had Joey, oh! Don't get me started. Jack was like this hulking shadow, always there."

"You resented it?"

Lauren glanced at the big man sleeping—passed out—on the sofa. "I'm sure it seemed that way, but the truth is, for a while I enjoyed being treated like a queen. But I got pregnant, and I was dethroned."

"The only reason he told me as much as he did about that night—about you getting away and calling him and all that—was because the whole thing tore him up pretty bad." Harriet emerged from the kitchen with steaming mugs hung with tea bag strings. She, too, glanced at the man on the sofa.

She lowered her voice. "He doesn't have any family. No friends to speak of. But he had a daughter. Jack tried to get her and her mother out of Vietnam, but they were both killed."

"Oh, no," Lauren whispered in his direction. "Poor guy. No wonder he wasn't too keen on the baby-sitting job."

"Men like Jack live by their reputation," Harriet said quietly. "They're efficient, obedient and loyal, much like the best soldiers. Any deviation, word gets out. When that happens, they're expendable." She lifted a shoulder, sipped her tea, met Lauren's gaze. "Like soldiers."

"But soldiers are allowed friends and family."

"I said *much* like. Jack never allowed himself any attachments until you came along. You were part of his job. Couldn't be avoided." She sat in the chair Lauren had just cleaned. Too late to warn that it might still be wet. Too late and too trivial.

Harriet set her tea aside. "I know all about how he beat you up and left you. I know it was raining. I know it was cold. I've heard." She pulled her sheaf of hair to one side and began braiding it. "He should've gotten rid of that cell phone, but he couldn't bring himself to cut you off."

"Do you think he'll help me get Joey back?"

"Yeah." She gave a tight smile. "He'll try. He hasn't said, but I have a feeling he's not working for Vargas anymore. Whether Vargas knows it or not." She pulled a rubber band from the pocket of her robe and popped it over the end of her braid. "You ask me, Jack's got some kind of mission in mind. And if you pull any more stunts, you're liable to fuck him up big-time. So you're staying with me until he gets your ducks in a row."

When the call came, Nick snatched the phone off the hook. He'd been expecting to hear from Dacotah for hours. Days, it seemed like. He had been ready to hit the road ever since Dacotah had made the suggestion. The only question was, where were they going?

"Is this Red Shield?"

Wrong voice.

"Who's asking?

"A friend of your wife's. Are you missing a pretty little semiautomatic Ruger .22?"

Shit. "What happened to her?"

"Your wife or the pistol?"

"Is Joey okay? Where is she?"

"She's all right, but you oughta be pistol-whipped

for letting her take that gun with her. She didn't know what she was doing."

"She could've taken *me* for protection. She chose the gun."

"She thinks you're safely out of the picture. Safety first. Safe for you, that is." Pause. "Well, are you?"

"Who's asking?"

"The guy who took a bullet meant for Raymond Vargas."

"Jesus." Guns, bullets and Vargas. "What's going on? Where is she?"

"She's in a safe place, but I don't know how long I can keep her there. She's trying to get her kid back. Listen, Red Shield, I don't know what kind of a man would let her come back here after—"

"You listen to me," Nick growled. "I *do* know what kind of a man it takes to beat her up and leave her to die."

"She wasn't left to die. She was left alive. Look, I have her safe now, and I might be able to get the baby. Anything beyond that is out of my hands. If Vargas isn't neutralized, everybody involved is in deep shit."

"Are you a cop?"

The caller laughed.

"Can I talk to her?"

"She doesn't know I'm calling. The two lives she cares about are Little Joe's and yours. Look, she says you've got some kind of a flashy, dashy horse that might interest Vargas. He's pretty sensible about everything but horses. Put the right kind of bug in his ear about some up-and-comer, he'll get him a jones on, and he'll go for it. We can work this from two sides."

"Me and who else, and what two sides are we talkin'?"

"The name's Jack, and I'll be workin' the dark side."

"Everybody claims the dark side lately." Nick smiled. It didn't much matter—light or dark, fire or ice—he was ready for whatever waited for him wherever Joey was. "All right, Jack, my horse has run and won exactly two races, so I don't know if that qualifies him as dashy. I'll go for *flashy*, though. His looks, and the way Joey rode him was definitely flashy."

"Then all you have to do is sign him up and get him down to Oklahoma. You bring the dash, and I'll meet you there with the flash. Don't worry about Vargas getting the line on the horse. I'll set that up. And the jockey is Joey Red Shield."

"Will she know?"

"All she'll know is she gets to see the kid."

Dacotah was going to love this no matter what, but Nick had to ask. "Why Oklahoma?"

"Lots of horse racing, lots of betting. Vargas went down there to set up some business. It's got nothing to do with the size of the track. It's the simulcasting, offtrack betting, the race book." He chuckled. "I'm not into this stuff myself. I'm just a hired gun. You know more than I do about Indian casinos and those rebate shops."

Yeah, right, Nick thought. The Indian's latest "government handout." Casinos and rebate shops.

He wondered whether Jack was Italian.

19

Nick was skeptical, but Michael Dacotah was all over Jack Reed's plan, or what there was of it. Reed would get Joey to the track if Nick would bring the horse. The part that interested Dacotah was that Vargas was already there and he was "doing business." But Nick wasn't letting Dacotah in on part B—hooking Joey up with her kid—mainly because Reed hadn't gone into specifics, and Nick didn't want anyone screwing up that part of the deal. Reed had promised Joey that she would see her baby. "And she'll have him back for good, long as you work with me on this without asking too many questions. Trust me."

Trust me. Damn, but he hated those words.

Dillon all but outfitted himself in cloak and dagger,

and Joey's silks were packed in a duffel bag, along with the jeans and boots she'd left behind. Nick admitted that he didn't know much about Reed except that he claimed to be Joey's friend. Nobody was making book on his reliability. But he was all they had. And he had Joey.

Blue Belle Downs in eastern Oklahoma was the biggest racetrack Nick had ever seen up close and personal. Large grandstand, glass-enclosed clubhouse overlooking the track and the paddocks, restaurant, racino for televised action, poker parlor—all the amenities for a day at the races. The barn was huge, and it was almost as clean as Nick's. True Colors occupied a pricey box stall in a prominent location, thanks to some influential friends.

It was prominent enough to attract the attention of a man who stood out in the Oklahoma crowd. His upscale dress with a touch of gold jewelry, shiny shoes, slick hair and slicker demeanor drew attention to his party of four. He was touring the barn in the company of a quiet man, a stylish woman and a baby in a stroller.

Sitting six inches from the floor in his low-rider with nothing to commune with but big people's knees, the little guy looked lost and lonesome. Nick caught his attention with a look and a smile. He waggled his eyebrows, then tossed and caught the shiny apple he was just about to share with True Colors. A wide-eyed stare morphed into a friendly baby grin.

"What's the story on this Paint?"

Every muscle in Nick's body tensed at the sound of the pretty man's voice. No question, this was the enemy. A vision of cold-cocking the bastard made his hand itch. He tucked his right thumb in the pocket of his jeans and waited for a remark worthy of response.

"I'm looking over some of the claimers. Pretty hefty claiming price on this one," the man said.

"I don't really want to sell him. Had to put the price on him to get him into the race."

True Colors stuck his head over the stall door and sniffed Nick's arm, shoulder to elbow. He knew there was an apple around here somewhere.

Talk of this prick claiming his horse brought a bitter taste up from Nick's gullet. But he glanced down at the baby, who had him, the apple and the horse in his sights. Nick winked at the boy.

I'll get you to your mama, little man.

"I figure nobody's gonna claim him at that price," Nick continued. "Hasn't shown in enough races."

"He's a beauty." The man was shuffling through a handful of literature he must have picked up in the track office. "Is this the right pedigree?"

"That's it. Solid top and bottom sides. I'm the owner, Nick Red Shield."

"Ray Vargas. Pleasure." He had the good sense not to offer his hand. "Who's the jockey? A relative, obviously."

"Yeah. We're new at this, so we're using home-grown. But we think we've got something special here."

KATHLEEN EAGLE

"So I've heard. He's about the prettiest Paint I've seen. They're really coming into their own on the track." Vargas reached, but True Colors went high-headed to avoid the hand.

Vargas turned to Nick. "I'm here with a friend who has a horse running against the big fella, here. Pretty stiff competition. There's a lot of interest in this race."

"I didn't know."

Maybe someone else would claim his horse. As Nick understood it, if multiple claims were made, the management would draw lots to determine the new owner. Anybody but Vargas. Unless the deal came down to True Colors for the little boy who was pulling against the stroller restraints, quietly working to free himself.

"Oh, yeah, you put this boy up against some movers," Vargas said. "Should be an interesting race. Marla, get the kid out of there before he gets loose in here."

Nick rammed his thumbs into the stem end of the apple and snapped it in half. Little Joey took pains to watch, leaning away from the woman who threatened to get in his way. As she lifted him, Nick showed him half the apple before offering it to True Colors. Joey laughed as the horse crunched it up.

"This horse loves apples," Nick told the boy with a smile.

"Ap-ple."

"Can he have this?" Nick asked the woman. "It's from the restaurant's buffet. I just—"

"He has his own food." The woman turned to Vargas. "I'll take him outside. Now he's going to want an apple."

"I'm finished here," Vargas said, and to Nick, "Good luck with your claimer."

Over the woman's slender shoulder, the baby's big blue eyes held Nick's gaze until the group turned the corner at the end of the aisle.

"Was that him?" Dillon asked.

Nick turned, surprised to find Dillon and Dacotah coming up behind him. Nodding, he took a bite of the apple. He loved the smell of a juicy apple. Comfort food. Sweet and soothing. He swallowed his consolation and gave the rest to True Colors.

"Why can't I just kill him and get it over with?"

"He's goin' down, Nick," Dacotah said quietly.

No consolation there. Nick imagined having the man's blood on his hands, marking his own face with it. Now, *that* would be cause for a victory dance.

"Have you heard anything about Joey?" Dillon asked.

"I don't know what good this thing is." Nick plunged his hand into his pocket and came up with the mobile phone Dacotah had provided. "It doesn't ring."

"Sure you've got it on?"

Nick handed it to the expert for another equipment check. "I've gotta get out of here. I feel like this place is crawling with unseen eyes and ears." He turned to Dillon. "You mind staying with True? With Pretty Man and his kind skulkin' around…"

Dillon gave a subtle thumbs-up. "Keep your powder dry and your phone on."

Dacotah wasn't letting Nick out of his sight or the cell phone out of earshot. But once they'd safely closed the pickup door, he didn't seem to mind clueing Nick into what he'd learned earlier in the day through his local contacts, as though Nick were part of the team.

"Vargas has been down here for more than a week now," Dacotah said. "Supposedly on vacation with his family."

"His family?"

"Oh, yeah, he looks like a real family man, taking the baby and the nanny all over—casino, horse farm, zoo—totally average guy. Last week's nanny apparently became this week's girlfriend. That's the public stuff. But he's had several meetings at the tribal casino I told you about. We think their race book might be vulnerable. They're a small band, and they have a new management company."

"Does Vargas bet on these races?"

"Not at the track, but he does plenty of offtrack business. And he buys and sells horses all over the place. He picked up a claimer last year and won big with him later on in the season. There were rumors of doping, but no solid evidence. *Yet.* These guys are pros, and they do it all, from petty to grand. You pay for their lunch while they're stealing your soul. That's the way they operate."

The cell phone vibrated against Nick's hip. He flipped it open. "They're here."

★ ★ ★

Another flight, a rented car, another hotel room. Lauren was reduced to tagging along with the man who had done her a favor by putting her out on the highway with nothing but the clothes on her back. Following, trusting, hoping that the flight to a small-town Arkansas airport and the crossing of another state line really would get her closer to her baby. She wouldn't have to deal with Raymond, Jack had promised. He would take care of that. It was necessary that they act quickly, and all Lauren had to do was cooperate.

She was trusting the henchman.

Another racetrack, a room at the Blue Belle Motor Inn. Lauren tried to remember a time in her life when she'd felt like she actually belonged somewhere. Vargas's house had actually been *home* for a time, especially when she'd prepared the nursery, and when her baby had come and filled the space in the house and in her life. And Nick's house. Her time there had been too short. Her time with a good man had taught her heart to hold out for nothing less. If she got through whatever action was to be taken, if she came out on the other side with her baby in her arms, she would find a way to get back to Nicholas Red Shield. Once their gangster-loaded, landlocked coast was clear. And this time, she would tell him everything from day one, right up front. *This is who I am, and this is how I feel about you.*

She checked the room service menu while Jack

took a phone call. He left the room, and Lauren knew something was coming. She could feel it, from the phone call to the way he'd told her to wait to the key in the lock a few minutes later. She jumped off the bed, praying he had Joey with him and not, *please, God, not Raymond Vargas.*

But it was the antithesis of Vargas who walked through the door.

"Nick?" Lauren's pulse raced. She wanted to run to him like some pathetic lost lamb, but she managed to hold her whole coming-apart-at-the-seams self in check. "What's going on?"

"Jack called me."

"Why?" She searched the two faces—the beloved brown one under the cowboy hat, the familiar bassett hound one under the receding hairline. "What are you doing, Jack? You said Raymond would be here with Joey."

"He is," Nick said. "I saw him at the track not too long ago. He came into the barn, checkin' out the horses."

"You saw *Raymond Vargas?*"

"I saw your baby, too." He took one step closer, the softness in his eyes giving his heart away. "Cute little guy. Looks like you—big blue eyes, light-colored hair. Not much of it, but it's coming. He saw True Colors, and he was ready to—"

She closed the distance between them, and he was ready for her. She buried her face in the open vee of his shirt and inhaled the tangy scent of his skin. The sting of tears engorged her eyes, but she held. And she held.

"It's gonna be okay, Joey," he whispered.

She nodded against his chest. "You can't be here, Nick. I should have left you alone with your ranch and your horses and your—" she looked up, searched his loving eyes "—your life. Nick, what are you doing here?"

"We're getting your baby back. That's all I know."

She backed away, loving him more and trusting him less. He didn't know what he was doing any more than she did. She turned to the man who damn sure better have a plan.

"Why did you do this, Jack?"

"Because you're gonna need him, little girl. He's your friend, lover, husband, whatever. He's the man."

"No, he's...I *left* him."

"So what?" Jack tossed off as he slumped into a chair. "You tried to kill me."

"I was trying to kill—" She turned back to Nick. "I went to the house to get Joey back. It's true that I had every intention of killing Raymond."

"I figured you were going back with him." Nick gave his hat a needless adjustment. "You put me to shame, Joey. I had the same urge myself today. Wanted to break the bastard's chicken neck so bad I could..." He shook his head, smiling. "But you actually took a shot."

"You can't be involved with this, Nick. You didn't sign on for this."

"I signed on for you. For us, for whatever chance we have."

"You didn't know what you were getting into," she insisted.

"Who does?"

"This is different. Please let me handle this. I'll come back to you as soon as I get Joey back. It's all I've thought about since I left. You and me and Joey *together*."

"Which would explain why the part about getting past Raymond Vargas wasn't very well thought out," Jack put in from his sideline chair. "I told her I'd arrange for her to see the baby. She thinks she's just gonna take off with him." He hauled himself to his feet again. "That's how you got into this mess, little girl. I don't know anybody who crossed Ray Vargas and lived to tell about it."

"I brought a couple of guys with me," Nick said. "How many do we need?"

Jack laughed as he sauntered across the room. "First off…" He unzipped the bag he'd left on the desk, stuck his hand under some clothes and pulled out Nick's pistol. "Don't give it to her," he warned as he laid it in Nick's hand. "She's lucky she got me in the left wing instead of the right. So Ray came lookin' for your horse? Who else was with him?"

"A woman, mostly lookin' after the baby, and some guy. Vargas said his friend's horse was entered in the same race as mine."

"He doesn't have as many friends down here as he

does at home, so that's something. The day they left, he told me I wouldn't be going with them, that I was due some time off. I don't know how stupid he thinks I am." Jack rubbed his grizzled chin. "The guy who was with him is probably my replacement. Either him or the guy who took a shot at me the day after they left." He waved off any coming protest. "Not you, little girl. The one the forensics specialists haven't identified yet." He turned back to Nick. "Tell me about the woman."

"Tall and skinny, long dark hair, talks with a Texas accent."

"New girlfriend?" Lauren asked.

"New nanny. He had the hots for her from the day she was hired. Guess I'm not the only one who just got replaced."

"I brought the horse, and he's entered to run in the seventh race," Nick said.

"Am I riding him? Of course I am. If you want to win, I'm riding him."

Nick laughed. "What difference does it make if he comes in dead last? He's set up to be claimed." He turned to Jack. "That's what it's gonna take, right? You told me to get down here with my horse and you'd see to it that Vargas would come after him. I don't know what we're in for tomorrow, but I'm thinkin' I should hire a jockey off the track."

"No, she rides the horse." Absently Jack flexed his left hand and rubbed his sore shoulder. "Her name is

Joey Red Shield. She can even pass for a boy. Nobody's gonna recognize her."

Nick hadn't told Jack Reed that he was working with federal agents, nor did he plan to give Jack up to Dacotah. As far as Nick was concerned, the agreement was all about getting Mama Joey and Baby Joey safely out of Vargas's hands. Dacotah was hoping to get an indictment against Vargas out of the deal. The possibilities made him fairly salivate as they stood behind the backstretch fence and watched Dillon work True Colors early on race day.

Whatever happened with Vargas, Nick still risked losing his dream horse. But he couldn't think about that. Not now.

"If Vargas plays this true to form, one of these horses is in for a milkshake after his morning workout." Dacotah squinted, used his hand to block the rising sun. "Sounds like a treat, doesn't it?"

"It sounds like doping." And Nick didn't like the idea of his horse and jockey sharing the track with an animal all hopped up on any of the host of drugs that were banned at all racetracks. But horse racing was no different from every other high-stakes sport. Bans were made to be broken. Joey could handle her own horse, but it was always the other driver who caused the accident. Leaving Nick to wonder, "What are you gonna do about it?"

"We're going to take some pictures. My agency

wouldn't be interested except for the connection with the casino. But if we can catch him and his associates in the act, we could be launching the case against Vargas from here, this track, this day. Every big bust starts with one seemingly insignificant—"

"Wait, now, this sounds like some dragged-out affair. I'm banking on you putting the sonuvabitch behind bars *from here*. This track, this day."

"With any luck," Dacotah mused, ostensibly watching the workout field.

"So who's taking pictures? I'm getting ready to put my wife up on a horse in the middle of all this." Nick sighed. He was keeping her off the track as long as he could. He had relayed her workout instructions to Dillon, who, just as she'd predicted, was struggling with a frisky horse invigorated by the morning chill and the company of the "morning glories," the workout show-offs who wouldn't do squat when the time came. He shook his head. "I don't like it."

"If this goes down the way it's supposed to, Vargas won't get close to your wife. We'll have the police take custody of the baby, and she'll have him back where he belongs immediately."

"And if it doesn't go down that way?"

"With any luck he won't get away, and if he does—"

"That's the second time you've mentioned luck," Nick pointed out. Dacotah stayed silent, apparently out of predictions. No answer for *if he does*. It was all a big gamble.

And Jack Reed was Nick's ace in the hole.

Lauren had done everything she could think of to conceal her identity. Joey probably wouldn't even recognize her when she finally got to see him. No sunworshipper, she had gotten herself a tan in a can and was pleased with the results. She might not look like a Red Shield in Nick's eyes, but she would pass in some circles. With time on her hands the morning of the race, she'd gone shorter and darker with her hair. The generous cut of her silks and unisex breeches gave her a nondescript body. She looked small and boyish, like most jockeys, male or female.

Nick seemed impressed and maybe even relieved when he picked her up. "Quite a transformation," he said.

Every step in the routine leading up to post time seemed like one more hurdle she'd put behind her. She presented herself and her equipment to the clerk of scales. Making weight was not a problem, but she was mindful of every person who came around her at the scales, avoided speaking any more than necessary, remained utterly calm and supremely vigilant. Jack had promised that she would have her baby after the race. *Where?* she'd asked. *Should I look for you? Meet you?*

He'd pointed to a radio speaker built into the hotel

room wall. "Listen for an announcement. When the roll is called up yonder, little girl, you be there."

She hadn't seen him since he'd left the hotel, but she knew he was there at the track. Somewhere. The henchman would not let her down.

Nick and Dillon met her in the saddling paddock, where the less-than-expert groom and trainer—it was hard to tell which was supposed to be which— prepared her mount. She was there to speak with True Colors, to assure him that they were in this together, that her eyes and ears, hands and mind, would be looking after him, and all he had to do was run with her. She could feel him collect himself at the sound of her voice and the touch of her hand. It was her best advantage. Horses liked her.

"He's going to do fine," she told the two men.

"You ride safe," Nick insisted. "Take no chances."

"I can scratch him, Nick. If the jock says there's something wrong—"

"There's nothing wrong, is there, big guy?" Nick adjusted the saddle cloth. They were number four. "We're running clean and safe."

"And we're the only ones with Yum on our side," she said as she touched his hand. Their gold bands glinted in the sun.

Jockeys from the earlier races had passed through the jock room grumbling about a heavy track, but Lauren determined during the post parade and her warm-up gallop that it wasn't really heavy, though

there was some moisture. She would call it slow, and
True Colors would call it good.

It was a full starting gate. They were up against
some high-strung horses. Lots of blinkers and shadow
rolls to keep them from seeing scary things like their
own shadows. Every jock in the gate carried a stick
except Lauren. She was a hand rider. When the horse
in the stall next to her tried to crawl the gate and True
Colors ignored the show, she half wished she could
scratch right then. He should never have been a
claimer. He was the horse her father had spouted
poetry about, straight off the cuff. True Colors was
one in a million.

He was on the bit from the minute the gate
opened. Every muscle, every sinew, every bone, pro-
pelled him forward. Lauren steadied her mount as the
pack closed around her, then found a hole and broke
free. It was then that the number six horse streaked
past and took the race by eight impossible lengths.
True Colors was a solid second.

Rocket's Blue Streak was still running flat out as
the announcer declared him the winner. The animal
had streaked, all right, wild eyes nearly popping out
of his blinkers as he'd passed True Colors. If they were
going to dope the horse, they should have warned the
jockey, Lauren thought. The man had probably
broken a finger trying to pull him up.

The results of the race were disputed immediately.

"I've been beaten like that before," Lauren told Nick

as they walked True Colors through the restricted paddock area. "That horse was feeling no pain."

"Won't they test him?" Dillon asked. He'd assumed the duty of leading True Colors.

"If he had a milkshake for breakfast, it won't show up in any testing," Lauren said. "Of course, if they injected him with testosterone, that's sometimes detectable."

"Let's hope the pictures turn out," Dillon said.

"What pictures?" She glanced from pillar to post, looking for familiar faces as she unsnapped her chin strap and pulled off her helmet.

Nick gave her flattened hair an affectionate tousle. "You two were beautiful together. I wish I had pictures."

"The stewards must have something, or there wouldn't be a dispute. Have you seen Jack?"

"We've been busy watching you win another race," Nick told her as he pulled the saddle for her second weigh-in. "In my mind, you won."

"*You* won. Wolf Trail Ranch is the owner. And if they disqualify the doper, you'll get first-place money."

"They allow up to ten minutes before the race to drop a claim in this state," Nick said. "I guess I'll find out about that little detail soon enough."

"I'll take care of True," Dillon said. "It's time to see which comes first, the cheater or the cheated. Let's hope our friend didn't lay an egg."

"What friend? Jack?" Lauren tucked her arms under the saddle. "Never mind. I can't have this conversation now. Jack knows where to find me. After I weigh in—"

An announcement came over the public address speakers.

"Would Mrs. Nick Red Shield please report to Security? *Mrs.* Nick Red Shield."

When the roll is called up yonder…

"You go with her," Dillon said to Nick. "If they took Rocket's Blue Balls to the test barn, that's probably where all the action is and where I wanna be. Along with the lights, cameras and guys in white coats with horse-size specimen cups."

"I'll catch up," Nick promised. But first he had to catch up to his wife.

She made quick work of her weigh-in and asked for directions to Security. The uniformed guard's escort made her nervous, as did his urgent pace. She glanced over her shoulder more than once to be sure Nick was still with her. The tall young guard ushered them down a narrow hall and through a door, where three more were gathered around a fourth, who was holding…

Joey.

"Ma-maaa!"

Yes, yes, *yes!* Her baby knew who she was. No haircut or fake tan could fool her son. His little arms clung so tightly around her neck that she could hardly breathe. His skin smelled like sunshine, his wispy hair like rainwater. Yes! She was awake and breathing, and her arms were full of Joey. She brushed a tear away from her cheek and another from his. He wore the blue bib overalls she'd bought half a size too big. They fit him now. Oh, she'd missed days and days and days.

"Where'd you find him?" Nick asked.

"The guy who brought him in—big fella, said his name was…"

"Reed," another guard supplied.

Lauren lifted her chin, opened her eyes and ears to the room beyond her and her baby.

"Jack Reed," the guard with Murphy written on his name tag supplied. "Said his babysitter walked off the job during the seventh race. Was that your race, Mrs. Red Shield?"

"There's a diaper bag here," said the portly guard on the far side of the desk where they'd been gathered. He pointed to a manila envelope. "He left some pictures of you and the baby, passport—must be in your maiden name—birth certificate. You carry this stuff with you all the time?"

"Homeland Security," Nick said. "I'm her husband. Did Jack say where—"

The office door flew open, and the tall escort leaned in. "There's been a shooting! We've got gunmen in the horsemen's bookkeeper's office."

There was a flurry of guards finding their legs and their guns. Lost and found, they were used to dealing with. Shooters on the premises, not so much.

"Stay here," Murphy told Lauren.

"That guy who left the baby was one of them," the tall one said.

"Oh, God." Lauren hugged Joey close and looked for Nick. *He's here. We're safe.*

"Stay with them," Murphy told the big slow guard behind the desk. And then, to Nick, "Don't go anywhere."

They were left with the big man, who had found his gun but not his legs and looked as stunned as Lauren felt.

"What's going on, Nick? Was this…you and Jack…?"

"No, not me and Jack. I'm here, and Jack's in the bookkeeper's office. And you've got Joey back. That's what I know." He glanced toward the open door. "But I don't know where Dillon is."

"And Raymond?"

Nick started toward the door.

"Murphy said—"

"Shit. I left the damn gun in the pickup." He snapped his fingers. "Maybe I'll get to break his neck after all." He turned to Lauren.

Michael Dacotah appeared in the hallway. "You hear the sirens? We've got casualties."

"Where's Dillon?" Nick demanded.

"I don't know. But Vargas is dead. His associate took a bullet, but he might pull through. Jack Reed…" Dacotah glanced past Nick. His question was for Lauren. "Is he a friend?"

"Yes," she said, following Nick into the hallway. "He's our friend."

"You'd better come now."

The commotion had turned the business end of the racetrack facility into a transit station, with guards directing the traffic of race-walkers, joggers, foot-draggers and rubber-neckers.

"Everything's under control. Nothing to see."

"Move to the west end of the building, please."

"Stay on this side. Nothing you want to look at here."

Dacotah flashed his security pass as he shouldered past incoming policemen and outgoing spectators, leading the way to the "money rooms." Vargas. Reed. Had Lauren not been summoned, Nick would have made his way to the horsemen's bookkeeper sooner to see whether a claim had been dropped on his horse. He would have been there when the shooting went down, too.

"We had him," Dacotah told Nick as they approached the door marked *Horsemen's Bookkeeper*. "Three other guys actually tubed the horse, but Vargas was present. He calls in his bets, like, seconds before post time, and we had that, too. We could've nailed…"

Beyond the door lay a grisly scene. Four men were moving Jumbo Jack from a pool of blood to a lowered gurney. Another man lay on a desk in a spread of more blood, and a third person was sprawled on the floor, the head covered with a bloody towel. Lauren pulled Joey's face to her shoulder as though they'd been assaulted by a cold wind. She turned away, loath to see more, but she couldn't help noticing a shoe, a shiny shoe that no real horse lover would wear to the track.

Jack opened his eyes as Lauren called out his name.

He lifted one bloody hand from the hole in his stomach, grabbed the bottom of Nick's jacket and labored over the words, "Make her go."

"I can't make her do anything. You know that." Nick leaned closer and said, "They covered him."

"Little Joe." Jack's attempt to smile nearly broke Lauren. Paramedics were barking orders. The gurney was moving, and Jack was trying so hard. "Good Dakota…cowboy…name."

"We'll see to it," Nick promised. He'd grabbed Jack's hand and was holding on, squeezing. "They're both going home with me."

"My…little girl." Lauren nodded. He motioned for her to lean closer. "Don't…look…back."

She nodded, blinking against tears. *Say something. Anything.*

"Thank you, Jack," she croaked.

"Thank you," Joey echoed his mother. "Big Jack, big Jack. Go bye-bye."

"We'll follow the ambulance," Lauren called after the retreating gurney. "We'll be there with you, Jack. It's just another…"

But he was gone.

She looked up at Nick. "It was you and Jack. You got Joey back."

"It was him," Nick said. "He made the trade. His life for Vargas's."

20

On the first anniversary of Jack Reed's death, Lauren Red Shield prepared a meal to honor him. Thanks to his wife, Nick had gotten into the habit of celebrating every milestone she could come up with, but this one was different. This one was a mixed bag.

The others had been wonderful, often wacky, always joyous. They had celebrated his adoption of Joey with a traditional Lakota ceremony. The groundbreaking for the new house had called for handprints in cement. Birthdays were celebrated with cakes that generally looked better than they tasted, because making them pretty was her strong suit. And the big birthday—the birth of their daughter, Nicole—had been a day for prayers and promises when his tiny wife

had refused to consider anything but natural child-birth. She had done it once, she'd said, and by all that was holy, she would do it again. And Nick, who hadn't set foot in a hospital since the last of his burn surgeries, had silently, desperately, taken a vow of chastity with the unholy upsurge of every contraction.

Days ago, on their first wedding anniversary, his wife had released him from his vow. But he'd meant it when he made it. As beautiful as their children were, he'd told her that if she wanted any more, she'd have to figure out a way to get him pregnant. She dedicated their anniversary celebration to exploring that possibility, theorizing that it was a question of position, muscle control and visualization. And she proceeded to drive him wild.

But now it was time to remember Jack Reed. In the backyard of the work in progress that was their new house, Nick hosted a Wiping of Tears ceremony. He announced to his family—now his wife's family—that it was time to let their friend go.

"This man had no family that we know of, but he treated my wife and my son as his family. Whatever else he did, this man gave his life so that Little Joe could return to his mother and me. He was a warrior and a protector. He spared my wife's life when he was under orders to kill her. For these actions, we honor him, and we sing him across the Wolf Trail."

Dillon gave the equivalent of an amen—*"Hau, hau"*—as he struck a traditional drum four times before lifting his voice in an honor song. Then the guests formed a line to receive the ceremony. A holy man brushed everyone present head to foot with an eagle feather and gave them all water to drink.

Louise and Bernadette had helped Lauren prepare the meal. She had made small gifts, which she and Nick presented to their guests. Before they performed their final duty to Jack, Lauren slipped into the bedroom to nurse the baby. With everyone fed, the cleanup complete, and the children chasing one another around the house, Nick looked in on his girls. He could not get enough of the sight of his daughter's tiny mouth tugging on the nipple he loved so well.

"I'll be with you in a minute," Lauren promised.

"No hurry, as long as we get started while there's still enough light."

"I thought we were looking for stars."

He smiled, thoroughly enchanted. "Got a little surprise for you first."

They left the children in Auntie Louise's charge and met True Colors in the corral. His first racing season had come to an abrupt end when Lauren had discovered her pregnancy, but he'd been a consistent winner. Not only had he made a name for himself and his progeny, but he'd helped to furnish his jockey's new house.

They rode double the way they had done the night he'd proposed, and when they topped the first rise, Lauren gave a squeal of delight. On the first anniversary of Jack's death, a buckskin mare—possibly the many-great-granddaughter of Sitting Bull's favorite horse—had given birth to a black-and-white foal. True Colors whinnied, letting his mares know they could look forward to more of the same.

"Horse colt," Nick said. "Looks like his daddy. Lots of color and legs that don't quit. Thought we'd call him Jumbo Jack."

"You think? Sounds more like a moose." She chuckled. "Moose season. That's what his friend Harriet said after I shot him."

"Why did she give his ashes to you? You said you thought she was his woman."

"She said it would please him. He lived his life as a loner, but that isn't the way he died." She rested her head against Nick's shoulder. "Don't look back, he said. And I'm really not. But I have to believe that he chose us, and once he'd made the choice, he did the only thing he knew how to do. If he hadn't been killed, I suppose he would have gone to prison. Still, he chose us over...over his boss."

"Dacotah said the other bodyguard copped a plea as soon as he got out of the hospital. He testified in the case they were working on. But they were pissed about losing Vargas in a gunfight."

"Whatever happened to the nanny? The one Jack locked in the storage room at the track."

"I hear she's looking for a job," Nick deadpanned. "You need some help?"

She jabbed him with her elbow.

"Just a little Indian humor."

Slowly they made their way to the promontory Nick now called "Proposal Point," where they waited for the Wolf Trail to make its appearance. A sudden breeze rustled the grass, and grass-dwellers answered with night music. And finally, unfurled like a white ribbon, the river of stars flowed across the black-velvet sky.

Never one for singing, Nick found himself making a song for the ashes his wife spilled into the wind.

The grass would claim the dust of a life, but the warrior's soul would find the Wolf Trail.

★ ★ ★ ★ ★

Turn the page for an early look at
MYSTIC HORSEMAN,
the next novel from
New York Times *bestselling author*
Kathleen Eagle,
available in
March 2008
only from
MIRA Books

Monica stood looking out at the pool standing empty in the backyard. She would have it filled and tended, though after Emily left for the summer, it would get little use. Monica's television show was called *It Only Looks Expensive*, and she had spared no expense in creating a showplace where she and her children could, in theory, spend quality time making Kodak moments and entertaining their friends. The pool had gone in just in time for Emily's high school graduation party. Two more years and Monica would have the place all to herself, at least when she wasn't broadcasting her show from her own kitchen or workroom. If she hung on to the house for two more years.

If she *had* two more years.

But of course she would. Why wouldn't she? Things had a way of working out, because Monica wouldn't have it any other way.

She'd built the show herself, growing it from weekly ten-minute spots on a local morning show to half-hour syndication for cable. She'd built a lot of things from the ground up—contacts into networks, opportunities into accomplishments, children into young adults. Monica was a go-getter, and given more time, she would go get a good deal more.

Two was the magic number. In six months she would be two years beyond her surgery. Not that she was marking off the days or anything. That kind of behavior would be counterproductive, and Monica was nothing if not productive. There would be no sidelining Monica Wilson-Black. She was a major player.

She thought back to her last phone conversation with Emily.

"You just don't want me to spend another summer with Dad," Emily had claimed. "It has nothing to do with what's going on with you or with D.J. or any internship you want to arrange for me, and you know it. You want me to be like you, and I'm not. It's as simple as that." She paused long enough for dramatic effect, then lowered her voice to a tender timbre. "I love my father. I know you don't, but I do."

"You *should* love your father. I have no problem with that, Emily. It's just that you have so many opportunities right here, and this might be the last—"

"It's not going to be the last *anything*, Mother." Emily sounded almost disgusted, as though Monica had been piling on the guilt, which she definitely hadn't been.

"The last summer you spend at home," Monica said firmly, finishing the sentence exactly as she'd intended to "But yes, I have a problem with you choosing his home instead of mine. *Again.*"

"It's not about you or him. It's about the horses. It's about—"

"It's about your father." Monica took time for her own dramatic pause. "I know him."

"You know him? What's that supposed to mean?"

"I know all about his pie-in-the-sky schemes and how seductive they can be."

"The Mystic Warrior Horse Camp is a good idea, Mom. We proved it last summer."

"All right, then here's an idea." Monica smiled, enjoying the notion that she was about to stun her daughter. "Remember how you said renovating your dad's ranch for the camp would be perfect for Ella Champion's makeover show?" Monica allowed herself a moment of silent self-congratulation for landing a spot as a guest decorator on the Big-5 network reality show *Who's Our Neighbor?,* which focused on small communities and common people in need of an *un*common infusion of television fairy dust.

"And how you laughed and said *get real?* Like you thought I was serious."

"You sounded serious."

"Yeah, right. Like I don't know what Dad would think of having a TV crew come in and mess with his property."

"His property? A trailer house and an old church?" Monica almost laughed, but she caught herself and changed her tune. "No, really, honey, I think you hit on something. Your father and I get along well now and, frankly, pie-in-the-sky schemes make for good TV. Plus he's got the Indian mystique going for him. And can you imagine what I could do with that place? I can. You planted the seed in my head, and it won't stop growing. This could be—"

"Now *you* sound serious."

"I'm *always* serious about work, Emily, you know that. This is going to be quite a project."

74 Seaside Avenue

New York Times **Bestselling Author**

DEBBIE MACOMBER

Dear Reader:

I'm living a life I couldn't even have dreamed of a few years ago. I'm married to Bobby Polgar now, and we've got this beautiful house with a view of Puget Sound.

Lately something's been worrying Bobby, though. When I asked, he said he was "protecting his queen"—and I got the oddest feeling he wasn't talking about chess but about me. He wouldn't say anything else.

Do you remember Get Nailed, the beauty salon in Cedar Cove? I still work there. I'll tell you about my friend Rachel, and I'll let you in on what I've heard about Linnette McAfee. Come in soon for a manicure and a chat, okay?

Teri (Miller) Polgar

"Those who enjoy good-spirited,
gossipy writing will be hooked."
—*Publishers Weekly* on *6 Rainier Drive*

*Available the first week of September 2007,
wherever paperbacks are sold!*

MIRA®

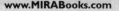

REQUEST YOUR FREE BOOKS!

2 FREE NOVELS FROM THE ROMANCE/SUSPENSE COLLECTION PLUS 2 FREE GIFTS!

YES! Please send me 2 FREE novels from the Romance/Suspense Collection and my 2 FREE gifts. After receiving them, if I don't wish to receive any more books, I can return the shipping statement marked "cancel." If I don't cancel, I will receive 4 brand-new novels every month and be billed just $5.49 per book in the U.S., or $5.99 per book in Canada, plus 25¢ shipping and handling per book plus applicable taxes, if any*. That's a savings of at least 20% off the cover price! I understand that accepting the 2 free books and gifts places me under no obligation to buy anything. I can always return a shipment and cancel at any time. Even if I never buy another book from the Reader Service, the two free books and gifts are mine to keep forever.

185 MDN EF5Y   385 MDN EF6C

Name	(PLEASE PRINT)	
Address		Apt. #
City	State/Prov.	Zip/Postal Code

Signature (if under 18, a parent or guardian must sign)

Mail to **The Reader Service:**
IN U.S.A.: P.O. Box 1867, Buffalo, NY 14240-1867
IN CANADA: P.O. Box 609, Fort Erie, Ontario L2A 5X3

Not valid to current subscribers to the Romance Collection,
the Suspense Collection or the Romance/Suspense Collection.

Want to try two free books from another line?
Call 1-800-873-8635 or visit www.morefreebooks.com.

* Terms and prices subject to change without notice. NY residents add applicable sales tax. Canadian residents will be charged applicable provincial taxes and GST. This offer is limited to one order per household. All orders subject to approval. Credit or debit balances in a customer's account(s) may be offset by any other outstanding balance owed by or to the customer. Please allow 4 to 6 weeks for delivery.

BOB07